HELLFIRE

HELLFIRE

METAL LEGION™ BOOK THREE

CH GIDEON   CALEB WACHTER   CRAIG MARTELLE

Hellfire (this book) is a work of fiction.

All of the characters, organizations, and events portrayed in this novel are either products of the author's imagination or are used fictitiously. Sometimes both.

Copyright © 2019 by Caleb Wachter & Craig Martelle writing as CH Gideon
Cover artwork by Luca Oleastri, Typography & Logo by Jeff Brown

LMBPN Publishing supports the right to free expression and the value of copyright. The purpose of copyright is to encourage writers and artists to produce the creative works that enrich our culture.

The distribution of this book without permission is a theft of the author's intellectual property. If you would like permission to use material from the book (other than for review purposes), please contact support@lmbpn.com. Thank you for your support of the author's rights.

LMBPN Publishing
PMB 196, 2540 South Maryland Pkwy
Las Vegas, NV 89109

Print ISBN: 978-1-64202-438-8
First US edition, January 2019

DEDICATION

We can't write without those who support us
On the home front, we thank you for being there for us

We wouldn't be able to do this for a living if it weren't for our readers
We thank you for reading our books

HELLFIRE TEAM

Thanks to our Beta Readers

Micky Cocker, James Caplan, Kelly O'Donnell, and John Ashmore

Thanks to the JIT Readers

John Ashmore
Crystal Wren
James Caplan
Misty Roa
Kelly O'Donnell
Peter Manis
Micky Cocker
Jeff Eaton
Paul Westman

If I've missed anyone, please let me know!

Editing services provided by LKJ Bookmakers www.lkjbooks.com

1

OPERATION BRICK TOP

With the opening riff of Judas Priest's *Painkiller* filling *Elvira*'s cabin, Xi keyed up the battalion-wide channel.

It was time.

"Dragon Brigade, this is Captain Xi," she announced. "Engage target."

Operation Red Rock, her subconscious replayed the mission briefing. *The Vorr had disclosed there was material evidence of the Jemmin conspiracy buried more than thirty kilometers below the surface of a planet affectionately known as "the Brick." Even with its dry, lifeless surface, there was a thriving human colony who were expected to fight the so-called invaders. The rebels, the enemy, the locals...whatever they were called, they were lightly armed and would present little resistance while the battalion supported a TBM, a tunnel boring machine, to access the deep underground. Easy mission.*

Captain Xi Bao had never believed the resistance would be light or the mission would be easy. They'd heard the same thing before landing on Durgan's Folly. Her experience led her to believe the opposite.

Elvira's SRM tubes cleared, sending a flight of armor-piercing ordnance soaring toward the target facility. Built into a half-kilometer-tall plateau, the rebel fortress had walls of natural stone estimated to be seven meters thick. Given its dozens of heavy weapon fixtures and scores of automated defensive drones, the installation would be hard to bring down.

But certainly not impossible, as Xi and her people aimed to prove.

A dozen other mechs cleared their launch tubes, sending nearly two hundred bunker-busting projectiles tearing away from the semicircular formation of Xi's mechs.

The first of the missiles stabbed into the rocky plateau, ripping multi-ton boulders from the red-brown rock that covered nearly every surface of the dead, blasted planet. Most of the penetrative ordnance slammed into the plateau with simple kinetic force, while some of the higher-end platforms delivered secondary and tertiary payloads which detonated dozens of meters behind the plateau's rocky exterior.

Counter-missiles flew out from the enemy fortress as soon as the first of Xi's warheads hit their targets. Hidden behind cleverly-concealed panels of rock and metal, the launch platforms were only exposed for an average of two seconds each before their protective doors slammed shut. But in that brief interval, during which the embedded launchers spewed eighty-six missiles in a coordinated wave of counter-fire, Xi's people scrubbed three of the placements with expertly-placed strikes that snuck in before the doors could close.

Her people had trained for this assault for weeks, and she watched with satisfaction as the Legion loosed its intercepting counter-rockets against the enemy salvo. The first flight lost sixty-three of eighty-six missiles to the wave of counter-rockets, and the remaining twenty-three missiles were shorn from the planet's exceptionally thin air by Dragon Brigade's railguns. Not a single enemy missile broke the shield, filling Xi with pride at her comrades' collective display of skill and focus.

The accuracy of the Metal Legion's arsenal was once again put on display when every artillery cannon in the battalion thundered in near-perfect unison. *Elvira*'s dual fifteen-kilo guns roared, sending high-explosive shells downrange at a particularly exposed patch of the fortress' superstructure. Twenty-two other cannons, most of them fifteens like *Elvira*'s, added their voices to the second barrage.

The fortress' walls erupted in a satisfying shower of debris and shrapnel as the Legion's rounds dug deep into the exposed frame. Xi felt a surge of endorphins flood her nerves as the neural linkage connecting her body and *Elvira* gave the distinctly pleasant feedback she had come to expect when they successfully delivered weapons on-target.

Even before the cloud of red dust settled, a dozen enemy vehicles scurried from the plateau and sent micro-rockets slicing toward her battalion's mechs. The micro-ordnance was too small to be intercepted by counter-rockets, which left Xi's people with computer-slaved anti-personnel chain guns and coil guns to address the incoming barrage.

Pivoting *Elvira* slightly to the left, Xi put her chain guns on-target and spat depleted uranium slugs into the sky. She sniped a pair of micro-rockets from the air and her fellow mechs had similar success, so together they scrubbed half the inbound fire before the enemy got their first hits.

A trio of rockets slammed into *Elvira's* forward hull, one even striking her cockpit's transparent alloy viewing windows. The micro-rockets were designed to take down small unarmored vehicles and did little more than dig fist-sized gouges in *Elvira's* armor. The rest of the battalion suffered similarly inconsequential impacts until a pair of mechs' missile launchers were taken off-line.

With the latest counter-wave spent, it was time for the battalion to get serious. The combined missile and artillery strikes against the plateau had been primarily designed to expose the structure to the biggest guns in the Metal Legion's arsenal.

The *Sam Kolt*, with its roughly humanoid frame supporting a comically large cannon capable of engaging warships in low orbit, lowered down to all fours and engaged its charge cycle. Its massive capital-grade railgun's capacitors thrummed to life.

Meanwhile, *Cave Troll*'s dual plasma cannons charged up on the opposite side of the plateau from the *Sam Kolt*. In a surprisingly poetic display of asymmetry, *Cave Troll*'s capacitors began charging after *Sam Kolt*'s, but *Cave Troll*'s guns managed to clear first by a half-second.

In spite of firing later, the *Sam Kolt* put a bolt of hyper-velocity tungsten on target before *Cave Troll*'s slower blue-white infernos poured into a gap in the fortress' defenses.

The conflagration that ensued was every bit as glorious as Xi had hoped it would be.

The *Sam Kolt*'s capital-grade railgun tore a ten-meter-wide gash in the plateau's southeastern face, sending a geyser of rocky debris skyward. The weapon's tremendously destructive tungsten bolt carved a miniature canyon more than halfway across the two-hundred-meter-diameter chunk of rock, exposing a dozen tunnels and conduits that had formerly connected the fortress' disparate nests.

On the other side of the rockface, *Cave Troll*'s sluggish bolts of plasma surged inside the structure. Five distinct eruptions rippled along the rockface as munitions cooked off within, destroying launch tubes, gun nests, and gutting the fortress' interior.

Elvira's SRMs had reloaded with explosive warheads several seconds earlier, and Xi sent those warheads into a pair of exposed missile boxes just as they fired in defiance of the Legion's devastating assault.

But this second wave of fire had less than half the potency of its predecessor, and Xi's people easily sniped the inbound missiles with nothing but railgun fire. Demonstrating their tactical superiority, the Legion's second missile wave utterly devastated what remained of the fortress' exposed nests.

Rubble was thrown in vast arcs as explosions rippled across the rockface. Amid the facility's death throes, the fortress' fusion plants lost containment, as demonstrated by a pair of thoroughly satisfying earthshaking tremors deep within the plateau. The entire plateau erupted, a million tons of rock flung skyward like water from a geyser.

"Recover," Xi ordered, intently watching the blips of the mechs that had been closest to the fortress, *Cave Troll* and *Sam Kolt*. The two mechs moved slowly away from the rocky conflagration. Bao let out a breath and conducted a quick tally.

Nothing could have survived the fortress' violent destruction, but Xi had no reason to believe that a single human life had been lost during the assault.

Even with the facility itself neutralized, there were still over a dozen agile, fast-moving drones zigzagging across the rust-red ground surrounding the former plateau. Ducking into and out of shallow artificial gullies, the drones would be nearly impossible to target with artillery and were too quick to hit with missiles reliably. They needed to be hunted down and engaged at close range.

This was where her newest recruits would show their mettle.

"*Starfox* and *Grasshopper*," Xi called over the battalion-wide while simultaneously issuing virtual order packets via the command link, "move to engage target package Bravo. *Gecko* and *Cleaver*, you take package Charlie. *Forktail* and *Blackbeard*, you're on Delta. *Blink Dog*, you're on Alpha with me. Everyone else, maintain a defensive posture in place until we've taken out the trash."

The mech teams acknowledged their orders as Xi maneuvered *Elvira* toward the nearest trio of enemy land-drones. Xi's drone hunters were comprised exclusively of walker-type mechs since the ground surrounding the plateau was dotted with landmines. Walkers not only limited the potential exposure to the explosives, but they also kept their crews safer due to the elevated cockpits.

"*Blink Dog*," Xi called over First Squad's channel, "flush 'em out."

"Copy that, *Elvira*," Corporal Miles "Blinky" Staubach acknowledged with his usual enthusiasm as his four-legged mech loped off toward the group of drones designated as "Alpha package." Blinky had been Xi's Monkey and her Wrench prior to being assigned to the newly-deployed *Blink Dog*, and this was his chance to prove the merit of one of Xi's first roster decisions after receiving command of the brigade-slash-battalion.

Blink Dog was exceptionally fast, capable of reaching speeds in excess of a hundred and twenty kilometers per hour on flat ground. Proving his gift for the pilot's seat, Blinky was pushing the recon mech to its limits.

As Blinky's mech approached the trio of drones, they scattered and opened fire on the relatively lightly-armored *Blink Dog*. Micro-rockets zipped through the nearly-nonexistent atmosphere, nine of them targeting the fast-approaching mech.

Xi loaded a pair of air-burst shells into *Elvira*'s fifteen-kilo guns, calibrated them to explode on the micro-rockets' plane, and fired in hopes of intercepting at least a couple of the rockets.

One of the air-burst shells took two micro-rockets down, but the other shell failed to explode before striking the ground.

Seven inbound rockets streaked toward *Blink Dog*, aiming

to end the vehicle. Just before they impacted against the canine mech's hull, Blinky fired a chaff cloud while pivoting hard left and dropping to the deck. Two of the micro-rockets exploded in the diversion, another two whistled past *Blink Dog*'s previous position, and the other three struck the right flank of the juking mech.

Even the lightly-armored *Blink Dog* was able to shrug off the micro-rocket impacts, but Blinky's mech was delicate in comparison to *Elvira*. A lucky hit against *Blink Dog* might cripple it, whereas the worst *Elvira* would suffer was a weapons system failure or damage to a leg mechanism.

Blinky deftly resumed his nimble mech's charge, bearing steadily closer to the zigzagging drones and looking every bit the hungry dog chasing down a fresh meal. He sent a hail of chain gun fire at the nearest target and managed a trio of impacts before the drone ducked back into the cover provided by the trenches.

Digging out surface vehicles would normally be simple, the standard procedure being to use aerial drones, but the atmosphere was so thin on this blasted rock that the only way to get airborne and stay there was via rocketry, making standard aerial support unavailable during this deployment. That didn't mean Xi and her people were completely without eyes in the sky, though.

The *Dietrich Bonhoeffer* had assumed geostationary overwatch of their position after deploying Dragon Brigade to the world's surface. Live sensor feeds streamed from the *Bonhoeffer* to Xi's people, showing them precisely where the enemy units were at all times with less than a tenth of a light-second delay.

"Come on," Xi muttered irritably, "show yourselves..."

Eight seconds later, she got her wish.

Her sensor board lit up, Christmas-treed with indicators of artillery fired from seemingly random points on the ground.

The enemy had buried dozens of weapon platforms, turning an otherwise empty field into a potential death trap. The pop-up mortars and eight-kilo artillery embankments sent a cloud of fire at Xi's unit, with the majority concentrated on the lighter mechs actively engaged in flushing out the drones.

The enemy weapons' reports were immediately answered by the Legion's railguns and artillery.

Xi bracketed a trio of mortar banks with SRMs and fired just as *Blink Dog* took two indirect hits from high explosive shells. The loping canine mech's stride nearly faltered, but Blinky proved his chops by keeping it upright and continuing to pursue the fleeing drones.

An eight-kilo shell struck *Elvira*'s topside, causing a subdued warning klaxon to sound in the rear of the compartment.

"I need that hydraulic leak plugged, Gordon," Xi snapped, deactivating the alarm and focusing on the shower of artillery that pulverized the enemy's scattered emplacements.

"On it, Captain," acknowledged her new Wrench, Chief Warrant Officer 4th Class Gordon, who served as *Elvira*'s current mechanic and troubleshooter. As on Durgan's Folly, personnel were stretched thin across the battalion, so Xi had opted to take one of the more experienced recruits as her Wrench while foregoing the addition of a Monkey, the third crewman normally assigned to a mech team.

While *Elvira's* Wrench did his work, Blinky managed to pour twenty consecutive chain gun rounds into a fleeing drone, blowing its capacitor and cratering the nimble vehicle.

"Good shooting, Blinky," Xi muttered, uncertain if she could have done any better given the myriad variables the younger Jock was contending with. A quick check of the tactical overlay showed that the other hunt teams had already scrubbed five more of the surface drones. *Six down, six to go*, she thought.

"New contact, Captain," came Styles' voice over the command channel.

"What have you got?" she asked.

"I'm showing two rocket-powered launch platforms emerging from cover two hundred kilometers east of your position," Styles replied. "They're hugging the deck and moving fast. Estimate they'll reach firing range in twenty-five seconds."

"Paint it for *Preacher*," Xi commanded before switching to *Preacher*'s direct line. "*Preacher*, *Elvira*. Engage inbound bogeys with Blue Boys. I say again: engage inbound bogeys with Blue Boys."

"Roger, *Elvira*," *Preacher* acknowledged, sparking a quartet of fresh icons to appear on the tactical overlay. "Interception in eighteen seconds."

The Blue Boy missiles tore skyward, climbing aggressively for several kilometers before leveling off and aiming at their quarry. Precisely on *Preacher*'s eighteen-second mark, the sky was split by a fusion-powered burst of blue that, for an instant, surpassed the illumination of the system's red dwarf primary.

Blue Boys were mobile laser platforms powered by single-use micro-fusion cores that funneled much of the released energy through a beam generator. While terribly inefficient and costly to produce, this beam generation system was one of the best anti-aircraft weapons in the Terran arsenal. The devices cost several times more than a tactical nuke, but their accuracy was unrivaled, and they were essentially impossible to counter on a terrestrial scale since the laser beams they generated were direct-fire speed-of-light systems.

The inbound bogeys disappeared from the board, but Xi held her breath as she awaited confirmation from the *Bonhoeffer* that none of their birds had cut loose before the platforms had been scrubbed.

"Bogeys down, Captain," Styles reported professionally

while her hunt teams continued scouring the field for the enemy's surface drones. "No weapons fire detected. The skies are clear."

"Copy that, Chief," Xi acknowledged before switching to the battalion-wide as the last of the drones were scrubbed. "*Thrasher*, clear a path to the Gash. Second Company, escort Trapper's forces as they secure the plateau. Third Company, establish Aegis Three missile shield formation. First Company, on me," she commanded. "Let's prep the LZ." The flood of virtual acknowledgments streamed across her board as she switched to *Blink Dog*'s private channel. "Blinky, what's your status?"

"I'm nursing a paw, but this dog can still hunt," Blinky replied with his usual infectious energy.

"Good to hear," she acknowledged. "Pull back to Third Company and make whatever repairs you can under their shield. Downtime's going to be hard to come by, and I need *Blink Dog* able to sprint."

"Wilco, Captain," Blinky replied, clearly disappointed but just as interested as she was in putting his mech back in good order before they received the pending mission-critical delivery from *Bonhoeffer*.

"*Bonhoeffer* Control, this is Dragon Actual," Xi called up to the orbiting assault carrier. "We are T-minus twenty minutes to a drop-ready LZ. Requesting status update on Project Red Rock, over."

"Roger, Dragon Actual," acknowledged Chief Rimmer aboard the *Bonhoeffer*. "Project Red Rock is green across the board, awaiting confirmation of drop-ready LZ."

Xi bit her lip irritably, knowing that Rimmer was merely relaying Colonel Li's by-the-numbers approach to deployment schedules. Xi had hoped to shorten the deployment window, thereby cutting their potential exposure to enemy SAM strikes on the package during transit, but it seemed that Li's orders were clear: he would not authorize Operation Red Rock's final prep until after she had cleared the LZ.

"Understood, *Bonhoeffer* Control," she acknowledged measuredly. "We'll make the bed nice and fluffy for you."

After severing the line, she directed a particularly choice string of curses and epithets at her fellow Terra Han native, Colonel Li.

"What was that, Captain?" Chief Gordon asked.

"Nothing, Gordon." She refocused on the task at hand. "Let's go clear that LZ of any remaining IEDs. Can't have our mail and chow getting blown up."

As far as opening maneuvers went, it was hard to argue against any facet of Dragon Brigade's first operation on the blasted, lifeless surface of the Brick.

2

HAT IN HAND

Colonel Lee Jenkins' aircar dropped below the puffy white clouds that wreathed Terra Han toward the sprawling megalopolis of Chengdou. In spite of having seen images of the Terran Republic's most populous city, he was unable to disguise his awe at the sheer scope and modern beauty of it.

Home to three hundred million Terrans, the megacity was arranged in a series of concentric interlinked communities, which optimized logistics for the vast population by creating self-sufficient rings. Habitat high-rises filled the rings, with most of the living structures towering hundreds of meters above the ground. The gaps between the larger rings were filled with smaller communities or, less frequently, packed with industrial equipment and commercial spaces such as the mass-transit nexuses that facilitated travel throughout the beautifully arranged ring-shaped communities.

Some of the smaller rings housed tens of thousands of people and held everything they would need for self-sufficiency, including office buildings, industrial parks, recreational facilities, fusion plants, food factories, and educational centers. The larger rings held as many as two million humans apiece, with these more densely-packed spaces designated higher-value than the lower-rent smaller rings. The larger rings primarily housed information specialists or artists whose professions were best plied from the comfort of their private lodgings.

At the center of it all stood a collection of spires, which seemed to caress the clouds like the fingers of Terran humanity's outstretched hand.

Among those towers was the Bronze Phoenix, from which Sarah Samuels had broadcast her special report during the inaugural Durgan Investigative Network upload. In stark contrast to its fellows, Bronze Phoenix Tower was wedge-shaped and did not taper to a point.

Much as he might like to thank Ms. Samuels for her work, Jenkins' aircar was not bound for the Bronze Phoenix. As his aircar made its approach to the central collection of structures, Jenkins fixed his eyes on the tower that was his destination: Ivory Spire One.

Part of a symmetrical pair of curved tusk-like towers, the tips of which met to create a delicate-looking arch that was the shortest of the structures at Chengdou's center, Ivory Spire One housed many of Terra Han's most influential corporate headquarters.

"Showtime," he muttered as the aircar slowed its approach, gently slewing onto a parking balcony affixed to the structure's exterior. The door opened, and its blue-and-black-clad driver wordlessly gestured for Jenkins to disembark.

Stepping from the aircar, Jenkins was immediately met by a woman wearing a traditional Chinese cheongsam featuring a stellar-phenomenon-themed motif rather than the more usual floral designs.

"Colonel Jenkins," she gestured to the entry, "Director Kong is expecting you."

During the Terran-Solar disjunction that resulted from the

Illumination League's decision to remove humanity's access to the Nexus and its interconnected jump gates, Terra Han had made the radical decision to adopt English as its primary language rather than Chinese. Their descendants had been rewarded for their foresight with a near-continuous series of technological innovations that easily overshadowed those made by the rest of the Terran Republic's various colonies. What Terra Han had embraced had worked.

And Durgan Industrial Enterprises had been in the mix of many of those innovations, which suggested some of these forward steps might have come from the Vorr instead of from human ingenuity.

With that thought in his mind, Colonel Jenkins followed the woman into the building, where they soon came to a lift. He examined some of the patterns on her dress and noticed several identifiable structures, such as black holes, neutron stars, and famous nebulae from Earth's perspective.

They even dress *smartly here*, Jenkins thought appreciatively as the lift came to a stop and the doors parted.

His guide led the way through a series of hallways, all of which proudly displayed the regalia of that particular floor's sole occupying entity: Falcon Interworks.

Director Durgan had previously arranged two dozen meetings between Jenkins and various captains of industry located across the Terran Republic. Normally Jenkins would have pushed such meetings back, but Durgan's urgency during their last meeting had spurred him to follow the business mogul's lead.

For now.

"Here we are, sir," the cleverly-dressed woman declared, gesturing to a silver-and-gold door at the end of a particularly long hall. "The Chairman is expecting you," she said, opening the door with a wave of her hand.

"Thank you," Jenkins said before stepping through the door to find a long, narrow table.

At the far end was seated a surprisingly youthful man, apparently no older than his mid-thirties. "Colonel Jenkins," the Chairman of Falcon Interworks greeted him, gesturing to a chair pulled out suggestively beside his own. "Please, sit."

"Thank you, Chairman Kong," he replied as he moved down the table to the proffered chair.

"I trust your journey from orbit was uneventful?" Kong asked perfunctorily.

"I've never ridden a skyhook platform before," Jenkins said truthfully. "Most of the time my planet-side trips are made via military shuttle, so doing it the civilian way was a breath of fresh air."

"And eye-opening?"

"You could say that," Jenkins agreed, knowing that this man was likely to be the most difficult of all those on Durgan's potential donor list.

Kong nodded agreeably. "Good. Then let's get down to business."

Jenkins produced a polymer sheet and slid it across the table. "To start, I'm offering your organization a robust package of tax incentives and regulatory relaxations in exchange for the first tier of items previously identified as being of interest to my organization. If we can agree to that exchange, I'm authorized to offer, on behalf of Durgan Industrial Enterprises, a handful of contracts for which Falcon Interworks and DIE have competed but which your organization failed to secure." Jenkins slid a second polymer sheet beside the first one.

Kong looked down with scant interest at the first sheet, barely glancing at it before plucking the second from the table. His eyes scanned it faster than Jenkins could have done, even if he was already familiar with the document's layout, and the FI

Chairman snorted derisively. "I trust you realize that he won those contracts through bribery?"

"I don't claim to know the intricacies of the high-level corporate game, Chairman Kong," Jenkins said matter-of-factly, following Durgan's limited advice about dealing with Kong, "although it seems likely to me that Falcon and Durgan play it with few peers, and that in every competition there is only one winner."

Kong laughed, although it was hardly a jovial sound. "You have courage, Colonel. Yes, he is in fact better at that particular facet of our 'game,' as you call it. These contracts have significant value," he said, placing the polymer sheet precisely beside its companion with machine-like symmetry. "Any one of them would revolutionize the economy of any Terran colony save New America or Terra Han."

"I'm aware of their economic value and what it represents," Jenkins said, although in truth he knew he didn't understand these contracts' broad impacts anywhere near as well as people like Durgan or Kong. "Which is why I would urge you to consider accepting them."

"Slow down, Colonel Jenkins," Kong said with a plastic smile that never reached his eyes. "Deals of this magnitude are rarely agreed to even in principle on the first date. There are details to be examined, alternatives to be presented, and counter-proposals to be fashioned."

"To be blunt, Chairman Kong," Jenkins said respectfully, "my people are presently deployed and under fire. I know that Falcon Interworks is the third-richest corporation in the Terran Republic and that your firm fulfills more military contracts than any organization outside of the Durgan umbrella." He gestured to the second sheet. "Director Durgan was generous enough to share that inventory with me in hopes of expediting this meeting."

"Yes, 'generous' is indeed the word I would use to describe Durgan's conduct of late." Kong rhythmically drummed his fingers on the table before waving those fingers toward the second itemized list. "The value of the items in this proposed exchange is nowhere near equal, Colonel Jenkins. In fact, it would not be inaccurate to say I have never seen such a 'generous' offer in my entire life. My surprise at the offer's terms is surpassed only by its source. Which makes me ask a simple question, to which I expect the answer is anything but simple: why? Why would my chief rival and, although it pains me to admit it, the most successful businessman in the Terran Republic, hand over fifteen percent of his company's wealth to me in exchange for a few showpieces and derelicts that aren't worth a tenth that much?"

"Perhaps he thinks you'll find some way to reciprocate the gesture in the future?" Jenkins asked.

Kong's eyes flashed dangerously. "Careful, Colonel. My patience does not extend to those who fail to respect my intellect."

"It was not my intention to insult you. I don't move in your circles, and in mine, a handshake represents an acceptable agreement," Jenkins allowed. "Yet, I apologize for my offense. A man of your station, privy to as many of the inner workings of the Terran Republic as you are, must know that whatever might spur him to extend such a generous offer would almost certainly involve the security of the Terran Republic."

"Better," Kong said coolly. "But you're not done yet. Go on. Pique my interest, and you just might walk away from here with more than you thought possible."

Jenkins set his jaw for a moment. Kong was playing with him, but the truth was, he had no choice about indulging the businessman. He grudgingly continued. "Director Durgan is more concerned with the stability of the Terran Republic than he is in his organization's profit margins or quarterly reports at this point in time."

"His conduct over the last sixty years would suggest otherwise," Kong observed mildly. "Which means something has changed."

"If something has changed," Jenkins said, careful not to give away anything unnecessarily, "then the magnitude of this gesture should be sufficient to demonstrate how serious the repercussions of that change might be for *all* humanity."

Kong quirked a brow in surprise. "Was that a slip of the tongue or did the colonel just subtly suggest that it is not merely *Terran* interests which Director Durgan ostensibly seeks to address with this exchange?"

"I can assure the Chairman," Jenkins said, meeting the other man's gaze steadily, "that every word I've spoken since sitting at this table has been carefully considered."

"Interesting..." Kong mused, steepling his fingers and leaning back contemplatively in his chair for a long, silent moment. "I applaud you for your forthrightness," Kong eventually said. "So, in an uncharacteristic turn, I will reciprocate." He leaned forward, his forearms gently resting on the table as he fixed Jenkins with a piercing look. "I think that while you were on Shiva's Wrath, you made contact with the Vorr and they told you something that they had only previously shared with Director Durgan, with whom they have enjoyed a clandestine line of communication for quite some time.

"I think they convinced you that Terran humanity, and perhaps *all* of humanity, is under severe threat from the Jemmin and its puppet the Illumination League. I think they scared you and Durgan so badly with their tale that he sent you here with this offer, at the same time your people are being shot at in Finjou space, to secure my support in whatever action the Vorr convinced you is worth taking." Kong leaned back in his chair, a victorious smirk on his lips. "A commander abandons his men as readily as a businessman abandons his capital, and yet here you are, making both gestures in equal measure as far as their contributors are concerned. Which means you not only believe the Vorr, but also you have *reason* to believe them; reason that is worth abandoning your troops in the middle of a battle, and that said reason is based on *evidence*."

The more the Chairman spoke, the more anxious Jenkins felt. How could Kong know so much about the situation and yet get some of the crucial details (like the absence of the Zeen from his theoretical version of events) so wrong?

"If there was such a motive, Chairman Kong, and if that motive was indeed based on *evidence*," Jenkins said carefully, "you could hardly expect me to endanger the integrity of whatever operation I might or might not be a party to by sharing its details with someone who has yet to adequately demonstrate his support for that operation."

"And therein lies the crux of the matter." Kong nodded approvingly. "For *you* won't get what *you* want until *I* get what *I* want."

Jenkins nodded sharply. "I'm sorry to have wasted your time."

"No time was wasted, Colonel," Kong said with a light, hollow chuckle. "As I said, deals of this magnitude are rarely agreed to in principle on the first date. But let me reiterate something else," he continued, his eyes hardening. "If you give me what I want, I will send you from here with more than you could have ever hoped to gain. You know my price, and as a gesture of good faith, I've arranged for you to make a personal inspection of the assets I'm willing to part with...should you agree to my price. I know you've already secured twenty-five vehicles in various states of disrepair during your recent tours of New America, New Australia, and New Britain. And I also know that what I'm offering exceeds that amount combined with everything you might be able to secure after leaving Terra Han. To facilitate your inspection, I've arranged for you to stay in Ivory Spire One. Please allow my people to see to your every need while you're here."

Jenkins stood from the table. "I appreciate your time, Chairman Kong."

"It has been my pleasure, Colonel Jenkins." Kong stood as well, offering a hand. Jenkins accepted it before leaving the offices with one question blazing at the fore of his mind.

How the hell did Kong get his intel?

3

DRILL, BABY, DRILL

"*Bonhoeffer* Control, this is Dragon Actual," came Xi Bao's voice over the control room's speakers. "LZ is clear and ready to receive the package."

"Roger, Dragon Actual," Chief Rimmer said, giving 2nd Lieutenant Andy "Podsy" Podsednik the thumbs-up to commence deployment of the package.

Podsy raised the CAC as soon as Rimmer gave the go-ahead. "CAC, this is Drop Control," Podsy said urgently. "LZ is clear, and we are requesting fighter escort for Operation Red Rock."

"Copy that, Drop Control," came the reply from Lieutenant Colonel Moon, the *Dietrich Bonhoeffer*'s Commander of the Interceptor Group, or CIG. The IG was comprised of both void fighters and aerospace fighters attached to the Terran Armor Corps Assault Carrier, giving the *Bonhoeffer* another versatile layer of defense. "Escort launch in six minutes."

"Acknowledged," Podsy said as a sudden flurry of activity arose at the other end of the drop-deck's control room. "Six minutes," he confirmed before muting his mic and moving toward the anxious crews at the heart of the commotion.

"Report," Chief Rimmer demanded before Podsy felt compelled to do likewise.

"The *Zero*'s drop-wing is having trouble with the new load profile, Chief," replied one of the petty officers in frustration.

"I thought we flash-loaded the profile directly into the flight control system," Rimmer growled as he pulled up the relevant data streams on a nearby workstation.

Looking over Rimmer's shoulder, Podsy quickly realized what had gone wrong. "You need to deactivate the diagnostics," he explained, leaning forward to point out a small cluster of numbers. "Those are the wing's presets, which haven't been changed since the *Zero* underwent its most recent refit eighteen years ago."

"He's right," Rimmer said through clenched teeth. "Ever since they bulked up the *Zero*'s forward armor, the wing's been set to the modified front-heavy profile. The only way these figures could have gotten in there is if an auto-reset process started returning profile variables to the hard-coded defaults. Here..." Rimmer grunted, tapping out a series of commands on the virtual interface before declaring, "It should be good to go now. Re-flash the new profile and we won't miss our drop window. Do *not* make me look like an asshole right now," he barked.

"Yes, Chief," acknowledged the petty officer.

Podsy made his way back to his original station, where he double-checked the drop-wing's flight profiles. The wing was designed to be plugged directly into the *Bahamut Zero*'s systems, which would control it during deployment. But the only way to deploy their sensitive, mission-critical package to the surface was to use the *Zero*'s deployment wing as a modified descent-control system.

Podsy had helped Styles and Rimmer develop the new

program, but as the moment of truth drew closer, his confidence in their preparations began to wane.

"Approach trajectory achieved," reported Chief Rimmer in a raised voice. "We drop in two minutes."

The seconds ticked down as the steady stream of status reports came back green, until the *Bonhoeffer* was in position to deploy the package.

"Red Rock drop in five...four..." Chief Rimmer called, "...one...*drop!*"

Podsy watched as the *Bahamut Zero*'s purpose-built deployment wing detached from its bay. Instead of the *Zero* nestling between its collapsed wings, the deployment platform carried a custom drop-pod kludged together from parts of six damaged drop-cans deemed unfit for combat duty.

It had taken teams of fifteen fabricators twelve days of round-the-clock effort to prep this special drop-can with the equipment necessary to protect its precious cargo during transit. The entire mission hinged on this drop going by the numbers, and for the first fifteen seconds of the wing's flight, that was exactly how the op went.

With ten of the *Bonhoeffer*'s aerospace fighters moving into a diamond formation and racing ahead of the drop-wing just as they had done during the *Bahamut Zero*'s deployment back on Shiva's Wrath, the package was finally in the pocket and en route to the surface.

Suddenly an alarm began to sound. "Attitude is creeping out of alignment," declared the same PO who had discovered the drop-profile error. "Our drop trajectory was zero-point-zero-four degrees out of alignment."

"Compensate with the wing's auxiliaries," Rimmer ordered, his voice taut as he worked his own remote console. "Light engines five through eight and burn until we're back in the bullseye."

"Firing engines five through eight," acknowledged the PO, and the drop-wing's attitude stabilized as it descended toward the LZ. It took several seconds of continuous burn before—thankfully—the correct approach vector was reestablished, and the package was back on course for a clear landing.

"I've got a pressure drop in the main cabin," reported a second PO.

"How fast?" Rimmer demanded, his eyes fixed to his own display.

"Half a millibar per second," replied the PO.

"We blew a few welds," Rimmer said dismissively. "We were planning to vent that pressure on approach anyway. Adjust the primary burn profile to compensate."

"Compensating," the flight control PO acknowledged, while Podsy surreptitiously shadowed his efforts and double-checked his work, albeit far slower than he would have liked due to the computer access restrictions he was still saddled with.

True to his word after Shiva's Wrath, Colonel Li had restricted Podsy's computer core access to the sub-net DI systems only, which made most virtual tasks borderline impossible to complete in a timely manner. But Podsy had made peace with the punishment, especially after Colonel Jenkins' ingenious ploy to trick the *Bonhoeffer*'s CO into pinning lieutenant's bars onto Podsy's collar.

"Approach is green," Rimmer called as the package fell through the nearly-nonexistent atmosphere toward the reddish planet.

Deploying the collapsible wings in the thin atmosphere would barely slow the can's descent, but every last micro-gee of deceleration had been accounted for. Precisely on schedule, the wings unfurled and the package's descent fractionally slowed.

"Prepare to fire primaries on my mark," Rimmer commanded, waiting several seconds before declaring, "Mark!"

The drop-vehicle's braking engines burned with enough force to kill any human inside the vehicle. There was no gentle way to deliver this cumbersome package, so only machinery had been loaded.

The main engines burned for so long their manifolds turned bright orange and warning alarms began to flicker across the various control monitors.

"Steady on," Rimmer intoned as beads of sweat ran down the face of virtually every person present, including Podsy. "Six more seconds," Rimmer declared. "Four...three...two...one. Cut it!"

The primary engines ceased firing, and the package cleared the yellow zone. At this point during a *Zero* drop, the wing would level off and give the battle mech a constant altitude from which to fall the rest of the way to the surface. This drop package was considerably less maneuverable than the *Bahamut Zero*, though, which meant they needed to bring the wing as close to the ground as possible before detaching.

The package fell steadily through the yellow zone at a speed of just over two hundred kph, and when it kissed the red zone, Chief Rimmer declared, "Detaching package!"

The custom drop-can detached from the wing, which burned its drive rockets at maximum. The expansive wing missed a brush with the surface by less than three hundred meters before it pulled up and began to climb back to its retrieval altitude.

Meanwhile, the drop-can's braking motors erupted in a hellish blaze, sending billowing clouds of vapor and exhaust skyward as it finally touched down less than a hundred meters from the bullseye. The touchdown's deceleration was rated at eighty-three gees, which was well below the 120-gee limit for the most sensitive equipment aboard the can.

"Touchdown!" Rimmer declared, igniting a chorus of

whoops and cheers from the control room. Podsy wiped the sweat from his brow and even managed to join in the jubilation for a moment before raising the CAC.

"CAC, this is Drop Control," Podsy declared. "The package has arrived, and deployment platform is on rendezvous course."

"Copy that, Drop Control," acknowledged the CAC comm officer. "Good work."

"All right," Xi called over the battalion-wide, "let's unpack this can and get moving. All Red Rock team members, proceed to the drop-can. How's my highway coming, *Thrasher?*"

"The road's clear for thirty-two kilometers, Captain," replied the battalion's dedicated minesweeper. "I think I see a few palm trees in the distance," he added jokingly.

"You're not getting a psych exemption that easily, *Thresher*," Xi chided with a grin.

"It was worth a try, *Elvira.*" *Thrasher* chuckled.

"Wise man once said 'do or do not, there is no try,'" Xi scolded.

"What is that, some fortune cookie wisdom?" Lieutenant Winters wondered.

"Oh, for fuck's sake!" Ford groaned. "Does *nobody* know the classics anymore?"

"Just you and me, *Forktail.*" Xi snickered.

"You know you give me nightmares when you talk like that, Cap," Ford said with mock fear as Trapper's infantry moved to secure the drop-can.

"That makes two of us, Lieutenant," she replied half-seriously.

"Wait, wait," Winters said as though receiving an epiphany. "I remember. Little green puppet guy, yeah? Kind of a weird voice?" he ventured while the first of the industrial-scale vehicles disembarked the drop-can.

"Thank God," Ford said in relief. "I was afraid you were beyond hope."

"Part of the Disney empire. Name was Kermit, right?" Winters deadpanned, causing a riot of laughter to erupt across the channel.

"Jesus Christ!" Ford exclaimed. "I can't believe I fell for that."

"Chin up, Lieutenant," Xi said in a tone of patently false conciliation. "One of these days we're bound to find someone to replace you as the butt of every joke."

"Don't count on it." Winters snickered. "He's the gift that keeps on giving."

"Glad I can be the entertainment center for the battalion," Ford grumbled.

"All right, enough chatter," Xi said after the last of the three industrial haulers had emerged from the drop-can. "Red Rock One, are you in position?"

"In position, *Elvira*," acknowledged the first team of excavation specialists.

"Red Rock Two, sound off," Xi continued.

"Red Rock Two is ready to roll," replied the second team's leader.

"Red Rock Three, acknowledge."

"Team Three ready to go," said the third team leader after several seconds' delay.

Xi rolled her eyes, muting the mic as she annoyedly muttered, "Civvies..." Unmuting the mic, she said, "All right, people, let's roll out. 1st Company, we take point. 2nd Company, double-column escort formation centered on the package. Last Company, bring up the rear...as always."

The battalion began to move out in a column, with the trio

of heavy equipment movers at the center of the elongated formation. On the backs of those three transport vehicles were the various components needed to assemble one of the most powerful tunnel-boring-machines ever designed by humanity. It could cut an inclined four-meter-diameter tunnel through a kilometer of soft stone in two hours and had all the necessary equipment to excavate that much waste to a depth of twenty kilometers before the pace would slow significantly.

Now that the TBM was on the ground, Xi's first job was to escort it to the dig site a full day's ride from the LZ.

But she still had a rogue Terran colony to address, and she doubted they would be happy about her destroying one of their fortresses earlier in the day.

4

COUNTERATTACK

"There it is, ladies," Xi declared when the most notable feature on the Brick came into view. "The Gash."

Stretching in a nearly straight line five hundred kilometers long, the Gash was a canyon formed by an asteroid strike tens of millions of years ago. The crust of the Brick was so brittle and dry that the impact's shockwave, centered nearly four thousand kilometers away, had caused such a violent upheaval of the world's crust that it had torn this twenty-kilometer-deep, hundred-kilometer-wide wound in the planet's surface.

The north rim of the Gash was as sheer as any rockface on Earth, while the southern rim was rubble-strewn and pitched between twenty and fifty degrees. Climbing down that grade, even at its least treacherous points, would take balls of steel.

Fortunately, the Terran Armor Corps was all metal.

"We'll reach the South Channel in six hours," Xi declared. "Keep your eyes peeled for any upstart colonists. The first habitats they set up on this rock eighty years ago were high in the Gash's south side. While those facilities looked abandoned on the latest aerials, I don't want to take any chances."

The Brick's atmosphere was so incredibly thin that many of

the Legion's support vehicles were incapable of navigating it. Combined with gravity that was eighty-five percent of Earth-norm, it was impossible to deploy most aerial support vehicles from the ground. Missiles functioned perfectly well, and artillery was even more potent here than in environments with thicker atmospheres due to diminished drag on the shells in flight, but drones of any stripe were completely useless. That left the *Bonhoeffer*'s eighty-four mixed fighter craft as the only potential aerial support available to the Legion during its deployment on this particularly desolate world.

Xi hoped she would not have to call on those fighters, and had painstakingly crafted her battalion's battle plans in order to minimize their reliance on air support. But in her brief career, she had learned that while battle plans were nice, they tended to disintegrate shortly after the first shots were exchanged.

"Captain," Chief Gordon called, "the ambient radiation is causing some trouble with the onboard data relays."

"What kind of trouble?" Xi asked in alarm.

"Primarily, we're getting brief delays in targeting solution plots due to interrupts in the cross-talk between parallel systems," Gordon explained. "Recommend we request two cans of isolating gel for each mech, and when we receive them, we coat every unhardened vehicle-critical data system in the battalion."

"I thought the extra anti-rad coating we applied to the hulls pre-drop was supposed to counteract the Brick's ambient radiation?" Xi scowled.

"Theoretically, it should have," Gordon agreed, "but I'm still getting enough leakage to cause our systems trouble. Have everyone run radiation sweeps in their cabins, but *Elvira*'s looks tight enough for us to stay locked down for months before we accumulate enough to give our bodies trouble. It's the targeting systems that have me concerned."

"I've just added the requisition to the latest form," Xi assured him, having done so via her neural link with a few seconds' thought. "Good work, Gordon."

"Thank you, Captain."

Another hour passed, during which time the convoy rolled steadily nearer to the Gash. *Thrasher* led the way, sweeping a path clear of any potential IEDs and thankfully encountering none, while the rest of the column moved at a relative snail's pace. In another hour, Xi would take First Company to secure the South Channel, their best approach to the Gash's floor, where the TBM would be deployed.

Then the enemy announced their defiance.

"Incoming!" Xi snapped, her board lighting up with mixed missiles and artillery. "All mechs, Intercept Package Gray. I say again: Intercept Package Gray."

Acknowledgments streamed in, and the battalion never missed a beat as railguns and anti-missile rockets launched a stream of countermeasures at the inbound ordnance. Explosive shells burst hundreds of meters in the air, intercepted by precision railgun fire. Missiles were expertly torn down by the battalion's rockets, and for a moment it seemed like the enemy had just foolishly revealed the locations of over two dozen heavy weapon emplacements.

Then the salvo's purpose became clear.

"Multiple contacts at knife range!" Styles called over the battalion-wide as a hundred different vehicle signatures sprang to life—some less than ninety meters from the column.

"Engage targets," Xi barked, spraying her chain guns at anything that moved out to five hundred meters. Two rebel surface drones were torn apart in the opening seconds, while the rest of the column spewed out a terrifying display of close-in firepower. In four seconds, thirty thousand rounds were spat by the battalion's anti-personnel weaponry, and a hundred SRMs were loosed from their moorings. Fifty surface drones were reduced to scrap metal in those seconds, while the rest unleashed their relatively meager arsenals against the column.

Fortunately, the enemy failed to prioritize the TBM haulers. Unfortunately, a hundred micro-rockets could pierce even the most robust armor fielded by the Terran Republic.

"*Blackjack* is down," reported Lieutenant Ford grimly as the light humanoid recon mech was scrapped by a hail of surprisingly effective micro-rockets. Unlike those Xi's people had received at the plateau fortress, these tiny missiles carried warheads capable of penetrating all but the heaviest armor. *Blackjack* fell, but the battalion's guns shredded the remaining drones in knife range before they could add to the butcher's bill.

Then the second enemy salvo took flight.

"Incoming," Styles reported, thankfully taking control of battalion communications from his temporary post aboard *Cyclops*, one of the recent additions to the battalion.

"Intercept Package Gray," Xi called, but this time the amount of inbound ordnance was triple that of the first flight. Some of this new ordnance originated from points nearly two hundred kilometers from the column's current spot. "Clear the board," she snarled, loosing *Elvira*'s full complement of anti-missile rockets while the battalion's railguns spat tungsten bolts at the incoming artillery shells. After unloading her rockets, Xi assigned two dozen targets within range of the column's SRMs. "All crews, engage targets. Fire! Fire! Fire!" she barked as the first inbound enemy ordnance struck the Legion.

Elvira's guns thundered, sending extended-range shells onto an artillery placement thirty-one kilometers to the north. A few seconds after clearing her guns, Xi's mech rocked from a direct hit. The impact threw the crew against their restraints, strobed the lights, and shook the old girl like a rag doll.

An explosion on the mech's right flank caused a shower of

sparks to erupt inside the cabin. Warning alarms screamed in protest, and alert indicators strobed urgently on her virtual HUD.

"Leg Five is down," Gordon reported in a rising voice, "and the starboard power coupler is off-line. I'm rerouting everything through the port coupler."

Xi slowly pivoted her mech toward the source of the shot which had hit them. She was so focused on returning the favor to her would-be killers that she barely registered that her last two ER shells had scrubbed their targets. "Bracketing," she declared, using the sensor link with the *Bonhoeffer* to isolate the artillery shell's point of origin. It was fifty-three kilometers downrange, which put it near the limit of her ER HE shells. "Fuck it!" She grunted, silently issuing the loading command via her neural link. "ER HE up. On the way!"

Elvira bucked with the dual recoils, tilting slightly to the right due to the offline Leg Five failing to evenly distribute the shock as her guns sent their massive loads downrange. Rocket-assisted extended-range shells screamed through the air toward the enemy artillery bunker. Xi had personally inspected each and every shell in her mech's magazine, and part of her inspection was the individual marking of the shells with distinct phrases.

The first of the shells was marked "Terran Diplomacy," which perhaps unsurprisingly missed the mark by about thirty meters. The second shell, marked "Bend Over and Say 'Ah'" struck true, collapsing the rebel artillery's ten-meter-deep pit and spiking the gun within.

Throughout the battalion, every mech expended ordnance at the cyclic rate as enemy missiles and artillery tore into the Metal Legion's vehicles. Six Terran mechs were downed, three destroyed outright, as missile after missile exploded against the best armor produced by the Republic.

Rebel shell after rebel shell fell through the interception shield, overwhelming the relatively slow-firing railguns that were the only systems capable of reliably sniping them from the sky.

Throughout it all, Xi wanted to scream in frustration—to give voice to her anger at the men and women dying beside her under enemy fire—but she knew that wasn't what they needed from her.

What they needed was focus and a plan to hit the enemy back.

Xi knew what she had to do.

"*Bonhoeffer* CIG, this is Dragon Actual," Xi called over the priority P2P line while transmitting the priority targets up the same channel. "Requesting aerial support against indicated targets."

"Dragon Actual, *Bonhoeffer* CIG," replied the CIG. "Confirm targets package, over."

"Targets confirmed," she acknowledged, double-checking the pips on her HUD and affirming her previous transmission with a digital signature.

"Viper Squadron inbound," the CIG declared. "Time to target eighteen seconds."

"Eighteen seconds, copy," Xi acknowledged as another of her mechs died. *Please don't be too long.*

Legion artillery and missiles destroyed thirty-one embankments in all, removing over half of the rebel platforms as they methodically expanded their field of fire to include the increasingly distant enemy targets. All the surface drones had been eliminated, but the longest-range artillery was still wreaking havoc on the column.

One of Sergeant Major Trapper's APCs was hit by inbound artillery, fragging the vehicle and killing all forty-three of the grunts it carried. Xi's people dealt fiery retribution for their losses, but the ambush had already cost them half a company of mechs and one of their six APCs.

Then the air support arrived.

"Cease fire on aerial targets. Clear the skies, people. The cavalry has arrived," Xi ordered.

Stabbing down from the sky in the span of four seconds, sixteen bolts of hyper-velocity tungsten tore into the ground concealing the last of the enemy embankments. After the initial strike, the fighters of Viper Squadron broke formation, each peeling off toward its own target as the Terran interceptors swept from one side of the engagement zone to the other. As the pilots dealt swift destruction to the automated placements, the phrase "death from above" took on a personal, profound meaning to Xi and, she suspected, to the rest of the brigade.

A bolt of yellow light stabbed upward from a previously-concealed platform next, slicing through Viper Three and transforming the death-dealing fighter craft into a fiery inferno which consumed its pilot before she could eject.

The three remaining Viper pilots broke evasively, two climbing high into the pale blue sky and the third zeroing in on the source of the anti-aircraft fire. Without so much as a word, the pilot sent a pair of railgun bolts into the offending emplacement, annihilating everything within it.

"Dragon Actual, this is Viper One," came the voice of the squadron's commander. "The board is clear."

"Copy that, Viper One," Xi acknowledged, her voice as tight as her nerves. "Thanks for the assist."

"Any time, *Elvira*," the pilot replied in a tone that sounded so detached from the loss of a fellow pilot that, for a moment, Xi was consumed by a single thought:

I hope I never sound like that after losing people.

She gathered her wits, knowing that the warriors under her command needed her to coordinate their efforts. "Lieutenant

Koch, deploy your R&R teams," she commanded. "Sergeant Major Trapper, support with search and rescue of all downed vehicles. Dr. Fellows, prepare to receive wounded."

Acknowledgments came across her screen, and after thirty minutes all survivors had been rescued, and the three salvageable mechs were aboard the recovery vehicles as the column resumed its march toward the Gash.

After sorting through the details of the engagement, two things became abundantly clear to Captain Xi Bao: the rebels were dug in a lot deeper than they had suspected, and they were much better armed than they should have been. That meant the operation was going to be a lot more complicated than anyone had thought.

And that was if they managed to avoid Jemmin entanglements.

5

TEMPTING BAIT OR UNIQUE OPPORTUNITY?

"Colonel Jenkins," the same docent who had met him at Falcon Interworks' headquarters the previous day greeted him.

"Ma'am." Jenkins nodded, having spent the last twelve hours poring over every scrap of information he could find on the remaining stops on his scheduled trip throughout the Terran colonies. He was prepared to meet with Chairman Kong's contacts, but he had little hope that he would get anything meaningful done.

"The Chairman has directed me to escort you to our offices in Jingzhou District, Sector Nine," she explained, gesturing to the hallway that led to one of Ivory Spire One's many lifts.

Jenkins followed her down the hallway, boarding the lift which took them down several floors to a transit station. They made their way to an aircar platform several times the size of the one he had landed on the day before, and when they reached it, there was a vehicle with the Falcon Interworks logo awaiting them.

In spite of having already seen it, Jenkins was still captivated by the seemingly endless sprawl of Chengdou's myriad ring-shaped sub-sectors. Three hundred million humans, living in what he considered miserably cramped conditions, formed the beating heart of Terra Han.

And some had convincingly argued that Terra Han was the beating heart of the Republic.

Jenkins put those thoughts from his mind as he entered the aircar and quickly made eye contact with its pilot: a woman whose features were identical to those of the docent who had greeted him.

He looked back and forth between them with a wan smile. "I thought cloning was forbidden under Terran law?"

"We are not clones," the pilot replied while the docent smiled mischievously. "And neither are our fourteen sisters."

"Early embryonic division." Jenkins nodded knowingly as he sat down in the aircar's seat.

"Technically not cloning," the docent agreed, taking the seat across from him.

"And therefore not illegal," the pilot added as the aircar lifted off from the platform and began its journey toward one of the outermost rings of Chengdou.

Jenkins knew about the various loopholes and legal trickery Terra Han had employed since its founding. Ever since the wormholes had gone offline, cutting the colonies off from Sol, the far-flung human settlements needed to expand far faster than the human norm. Even the more aggressively-reproductive families produced only five or six children, which was nowhere near enough to establish fully self-sufficient societies on the disparate Terran-colonized worlds.

New America and New Australia had adopted particularly clever reimbursement schemes which rewarded the parents of productive children with a relatively small portion of their offspring's earnings. Such reimbursements were exceptionally clever in that they were only collected if the children thought their parents deserved them.

The social fabric had been strengthened to unprecedented levels as a result, with each generation taking an active interest in every facet of all others, and families began rightfully viewing the role of full-time parent as one of the most productive careers they could pursue. New Australia and New America had revolutionized the redistribution of wealth from one population to another, and the government was no longer concerned with cross-distributing effort from one geographically-defined community to another, but rather from one *generationally-defined community* to another. It was an overhaul of epic proportions and had transformed the way many Terrans viewed their roles in society.

Terra Han approached the situation from a different angle.

Built on the most Earth-like planet in the entire Republic, Terra Han had enjoyed major advantages in its early establishment and advances. Technology developed on Earth needed little modification to function here and, as a result, the early inhabitants were able to hit the ground running. Industrial-scale fusion plants were up in weeks, not years, and biotech corporations anchored their interests on Terra Han to take advantage of the early infrastructure edge. This gave Terra Han's residents access to the best medicine and food in all non-Solar human-controlled space.

One of the key developments of Terra Han's early society was safe, cheap access to artificial wombs. No longer were men and women required to pair up in order to procreate. On Terra Han, for the cost of an average year's salary, anyone could purchase an artificial womb and install it in their home. Some of the more expensive models were the size of a backpack and could even be carried around without fear of harming the developing child within.

Taking advantage of these reproductive amplifiers, Terra Han's government spun its propaganda machine into overdrive.

Everyone was encouraged to participate in the act of procreation, with the government going so far as to subsidize womb purchases or leases for those deemed likely to be high-quality parents. For those not so fortunate, artificial wombs were still readily accessible and relatively cheap, with financing available at reasonable interest rates.

The early days of this wide-open reproductive marketplace featured "genetic material" exchanges where anyone could submit his or her genes for inspection, grading, and rank order. Limitations were imposed on the number of offspring any individual person could author through the system, but the marketplace made the process of acquiring genetically-compatible donor material far easier—and less cryptic—than anything humanity had previously known.

In just a few decades, nearly all genetic diseases had been wiped out—not by forced eugenics, but by the revelation of the cold, hard reality of what every person's genes contained. Some called it inhuman, others a necessary step that neatly avoided the issues of direct genetic modification, a crime on par with cloning. Darwin would have considered it a warped process of natural selection, probably condemning it as unnatural.

Careful selection and pairing of donors eventually saw the incidence of predisposition to hereditary diseases plummet to near-zero. Things like diabetes, heart disease, cancer, and even many of the worst kinds of mental illness all but vanished in Terra Han's earliest "home-grown" children or, as they are less flatteringly referred to, "can kids" (an epithet often hurled at Terra Han's citizens by certain antisocial sub-communities in the Solarian Republic). Life spans increased, health care needs declined, and productivity skyrocketed for all of Terra Han's citizens. The system was so successful that eventually all Terran colonies had genetic databases and exchanges, although none permitted the freedom and aggressive trading that Terra Han encouraged.

The result? In less than two centuries, Terra Han's initial population of four hundred thousand had exploded to over a billion.

In truth, in his early life, Jenkins had considered moving from New America to Terra Han so he could independently raise a child under the system, but that had been before he met the woman who became his wife.

Jenkins shook the thought from his mind as the aircar merged with a lane of flying traffic several hundred meters above the tallest buildings in the central-most rings of Chengdou. His eyes scanned the sharp cheekbones of the car's pilot and the woman wearing the astronomical cheongsam. He had no way of knowing if they were in fact sisters cultivated from a common fertilized egg or if they were clones whose life had been granted through an outlawed process.

For that matter, he had no idea if either of them was the same woman he had met the day before. And it was that thought which he came to suspect was the Chairman's purpose in having them escort him to his destination.

Nothing here is what it appears, he thought, understanding Kong's message. It was far from a comforting notion, but it was at least mildly reassuring that the Chairman was taking sufficient interest in their negotiations to pass him such a subtle note.

The aircar dipped, merging into an even more heavily-trafficked lane of flying vehicles. Traveling at speeds in excess of two hundred kph and completely unobstructed by traffic, it did not take long to reach Sector Nine of the Jingzhou District.

Located in one of the industrial parks squeezed between a quartet of ring communities, Jingzhou district featured towering exhaust stacks that served to purify the power plants' emissions and cool them before they were released back into the atmosphere. For all the human activity in and around Chengdou, the air was immaculate, cleaner than even that of Jenkins' native New America. For all their potentially objectionable social programs, Terra Han's inhabitants took pristine care of their planet and had no reservations in reminding the rest of the Republic's colonies that none of them surpassed Terra Han's dedication to preserving the environment.

As the aircar gently lowered to the ground, Jenkins sighted a trio of men wearing the uniforms of Terra Han's Colonial Guard, a supporting branch of the Terra Han PDF. One was a major, the others lieutenants. As Jenkins stepped out of the car, the major stepped forward.

The square-jawed, blue-eyed man greeted him with a salute. "Lieutenant Colonel Jenkins, I'm Major John Brighton, Terra Han Colonial Guard."

"Major Brighton." Jenkins returned the salute.

"These men," Major Brighton turned, "are with the Guard's Special Projects team. Lieutenant Chin," he gestured to the shorter of the two before addressing the taller, thinner man, "and Lieutenant Matsuzaka."

"Lieutenants," Jenkins acknowledged with a nod. "I don't mean to be curt, Major, but I'd prefer we get down to business."

"Of course, Colonel." Brighton gestured to a nearby building. "This way, sir."

He followed the trio while the Falcon Interworks escort remained on the landing pad. The building before them was a standard low-rent concrete structure like those which housed thousands of mid-sized factories throughout the Terran Republic. The door was already open as they approached, and the building's interior was revealed to be a vast nearly-empty warehouse, a pair of vehicles at the far end the only feature.

"Follow me, Colonel," Brighton urged as he led them the length of the building to where the vehicles waited.

One was a track-based light-duty vehicle not unlike some of the mechs Jenkins had deployed on Durgan's Folly. Twin anti-personnel chain guns, a nine-kilo main cannon, and a pair of bolt-on SRM tubes were fixed to the stern. All in all, a fairly meager piece of machinery compared to the gear Jenkins had fielded on Shiva's Wrath and what Captain Xi presently commanded on the Brick.

The other was more promising, but not by much. A versatile humanoid mech designed in the early days of Terra Han, it was a hybrid capable of urban pacification or battlefield support work. Its official design name was "Jackrabbit" due to the long reverse-kneed legs and the pair of versatile weapon mounts situated above its head, which to some apparently resembled backward-sweeping rabbit ears. But without modern protective armor, neither of these mechs would be much use to the Metal Legion as anything but support vehicles, and overhauling their armor would be expensive and time-consuming.

"These have seen better days," Jenkins remarked as Brighton led him past the pair of outdated weapon systems.

"Yes, sir," Major Brighton agreed before arriving at a patch of nondescript concrete floor behind the vehicles. He keyed in a command to his wrist-link and the seemingly ordinary floor parted at a nearly invisible seam to reveal a dimly-illuminated vehicle-grade lift platform measuring nearly thirty meters across.

Jenkins took one last look at the two poorly-maintained mechs, realizing they were camouflage for the real assets he was there to inspect. As he did so, the major proceeded down the short set of stairs and came to stand before the lift's control panel.

Jenkins followed him onto the platform with the lieutenants

close behind. Once the four were aboard, the major lowered the platform down the shaft as the lift's motors filled the area with the thrum of their effort.

The warehouse above had smelled faintly of grease and dust, but the air in the shaft seemed to crackle with electricity. The unmistakable scent of ozone grew steadily the deeper they went, and Jenkins hazarded a look above in time to see the panels slide shut twenty meters above their heads.

The platform continued to descend, and judging by the spacing of the various girders and conduits lining the walls, Jenkins guessed they descended over five hundred meters before the platform finally came to a stop.

Major Brighton made his way to a small, vault-like door built into a larger metal door (one large enough for vehicles to pass through). Brighton submitted to a retinal scan, a palm scan, and even tissue extraction before entering an alphanumeric passkey. The inputs were acknowledged by a pale-blue light that wreathed the hatch as it popped loose, permitting Brighton to swing it fully open and gesture for Jenkins to proceed. "Colonel, if you will."

Jenkins stepped through into a cavernous chamber beyond. It was lit by hundreds of giant droplights, casting their illumination from the dome-like roof of the cavern. He was unable to determine its precise dimensions, but the chamber was similar in diameter to the junction where Jenkins and his people had attacked the Arh'Kel on Durgan's Folly.

Several kilometers across and at least a hundred meters high, it was easily one of the most breathtaking natural caverns he had ever seen. His current vantage point was at least twenty meters above the cavern floor, which gave him a perfect view of the cavern's precisely-arranged contents.

Set in perfectly straight rows were two full battalions of mechs. And unlike those in the warehouse above, these vehicles were state-of-the-art and of the same Razorback design as Jenkins' command mech, *Roy*.

"Attention on deck!" Major Brighton boomed, his voice echoing through the cavern and causing trios of smartly-dressed black-clad mech crews to step out from behind each of the vehicles and snap to attention.

With precision and unity that would have made any serviceman proud, each of the crews was perfectly positioned beside their vehicle. He only needed one word to describe what he saw—professional.

"All crews, prepare for inspection," the major ordered, his command echoing across the chamber. The crews moved in unison, discipline and training reflected in their choreographed actions.

Each Jock moved to pop the access of the mech's cockpit, each Wrench began opening external hatches and panels on his or her assigned mech, and each Monkey clambered up to the vehicle's roof to visually inspect the weapons systems. It was textbook, right down to the near-perfect coordination of the crews' efforts.

Major Brighton turned to Jenkins, beaming with pride. "I've been authorized to assist your inspection of Lotus and Orchid Battalions, Colonel Jenkins," he declared officiously. "Lieutenants Chin and Matsuzaka are here to answer any technical questions you might have pertaining to our system specifications. My orders are to answer any and all questions you might have regarding the assets in this cavern. Are you prepared to conduct your inspection, sir?"

Jenkins took the man's meaning clearly enough. By limiting his ability to answer questions specifically to "the assets in this cavern," he was making it clear that there were numerous questions to which he had the answers but was under orders not to provide.

But looking out at the seventy-two perfectly-arranged mechs, Jenkins knew that the fighting power arranged before him was more than double what he currently had in the Terran Armor Corps' complete inventory.

Which, among other things, meant they weren't going to come cheap.

"Well done, Major. Most impressive," Jenkins complimented the officer. "After you."

"Colonel Jenkins," Chairman Kong greeted him later that day after Jenkins had satisfied his curiosity regarding Lotus and Orchid battalions. "Please, sit." The head of Falcon Interworks gestured to the chair opposite the one he had occupied the previous day.

Jenkins made his way to the chair and assumed it without delay. "An impressive demonstration, Chairman," he said sincerely.

"I'm glad you think so." Kong nodded approvingly. "Can I expect you to reciprocate in a meaningful capacity, or am I to endure a string of vapid attempts to peddle tax credits and the social cachet your unit recently received from Ms. Samuels' glowing report?"

Jenkins straightened in his chair. "I'll be blunt, Chairman Kong: I'm not authorized to give you what you asked for."

"Honesty is a reasonable starting point." Kong sighed in mild disappointment. "But I dislike the direction you seem to be going."

"I'd ask you to hear me out," Jenkins replied. "If Armor Corps has in its possession information of the type you previously alluded to, the only man who could release it is General Akinouye."

"Sadly, the general and I have never seen eye-to-eye," Kong said neutrally.

"Which I assume is why he sent *me*," Jenkins replied pointedly.

Kong's interest seemed piqued, but even if Jenkins had gotten his attention, he knew it would take more to wrangle the magnate's cooperation. "Go on, Colonel," the Chairman urged.

"Does the general know about Orchid and Lotus Battalions?" Jenkins asked.

"Probably," Kong shrugged. "Terran Armed Forces' brass dislike individual colonies maintaining 'militias' beyond a minimal capability. In this regard, General Akinouye is no different from his colleagues at the other branches of the Terran Armed Forces. But everyone in the Republic knows that Terra Han is first among equals in Terran society. We built our world by revolutionizing human interaction and society at the most fundamental levels. Why would we kowtow to the dictates of a possibly outdated militaristic hierarchy?"

"Thankfully for both of us, and for my people currently on the ground," Jenkins said neutrally, "the high-level politics of colonial-TAF relations don't concern me."

"I think they concern you more than you'd like," Kong observed.

"Let me make something clear, Chairman." Jenkins leaned forward intently. "I'm not interested in fighting some politician's battles. I'm not even that interested in fighting my own branch's political battles. I've got men and women wheels-down on a blasted rock three gates from here," he said with genuine feeling. "My primary objective is to support them in their mission, and my secondary objective is to strengthen my unit for future operations. Maybe I'm naïve, and maybe I'm shortsighted, but right now I'm not concerned with the fallout of cutting deals that address both those objectives."

"I'm not sure I understand you, Colonel," Kong said with fractionally narrowed eyes. "Are you suggesting that you do, in fact, have access to the information I seek?"

Jenkins held his breath, knowing this was a defining moment that he would look back on for the rest of his life. He could deny having the knowledge that interested the Chairman, thereby cutting the negotiations short and slamming the door on the opportunity to triple the strength of the Terran Armor Corps.

Alternatively, he could agree to clue Chairman Kong in on the reality of the Jemmin-Sol situation, which included the shocking revelation that humanity had been technologically uplifted to FTL capability for some as-yet-unknown purpose. However, doing so was a betrayal of the guarantees he'd personally given to Chairman Durgan.

Should Kong leak the information to Republic officials involved in the so-called "Jemmin Conspiracy," the swiftest and most certain way to remove the threat to that conspiracy would be the mass slaughter of everyone with first- or second-hand knowledge of the events on Shiva's Wrath. All it would take was a single dreadnought to destroy the *Bonhoeffer*, and there would be nothing the Armor Corps could do to defend itself.

Which left Jenkins a choice between the frying pan and the fire, with the only intelligent option to decline either option. That was precisely what he did.

"Chairman," Jenkins said with grim determination, "I can neither confirm nor deny anything at this time, but what I *can* say is that I'm prepared to consider your offer and, in doing so, I'm ready to postpone the rest of my acquisition drive indefinitely."

Kong's fingers drummed rhythmically on the tabletop for several tense, silent minutes. His eyes were unreadable, and his breathing was steady as a beating drum at twelve breaths per minute. His carotid artery throbbed between fifty-five and sixty times per minute during the interlude, suggesting he was far from stressed by the outcome of the exchange—unlike Lee Jenkins, who knew that the future of his brigade likely rested on the outcome of this meeting and, hopefully, those which followed.

"Very well, Colonel Jenkins," Chairman Kong agreed. "You may return to your apartments. I have other business I can conduct for the next two days. When I return, I trust you will have validated my decision to extend this negotiation window."

"Thank you, Chairman," Jenkins replied, standing from the chair and making for the door.

"Oh, and Colonel," the Chairman called just before he reached the door. Jenkins turned and saw the eyes of a merciless predator peering at him as the Chairman said, "I do not appreciate having my plans interrupted or, more importantly, my time wasted."

Jenkins took the other man's meaning clearly enough. A threat was a threat, no matter how it was packaged, but the truth was that Jenkins did not yet know if he was prepared to endanger his people—and potentially the entire fate of humanity—for a couple battalions of ready-to-roll mechs. Had Captain Murdoch been right about him? Was this all about Lee Jenkins' ego? It seemed that by accepting the Chairman's offer, he would be validating that particular vein of criticism.

Unfortunately for Jenkins, and for the first time since hearing that surprising accusation come from his former XO's mouth, he began to wonder if there was something to it.

6

INTO THE DEPTHS

"Watch that scrabble, *Forktail*," Xi snapped as a trickle of stones broke loose beneath Ford's mech. That trickle quickly became a rockslide that would have taken out any mech beneath it, had any been positioned in its path. "If I'd thought Second Company was this jittery, I'd have put Last Company on escort and let you lot take point to minimize the damage. We've already lost two mechs to rockslides on this jaunt, and I'm not about to let you add to that number."

"Sorry, Captain," Ford replied tersely. "This stuff's looser than my first crush."

"Did you just make an off-color joke, *Forktail*?" Xi asked in genuine surprise, more frustrated than she expected to be at standing overwatch at the Gash's rim while Second and Third Companies escorted the TBM gear to the gorge's floor. "Did anyone else hear that, or have you people finally driven me beyond the point of no return?"

"I didn't hear nothin', Captain," Winters replied with his usual stoicism.

"Sargon, Blinky?" Xi continued as the column carefully made its way down the twenty-degree pitch of the Gash's southern slope. "Is *Generally*'s hearing gone along with my sanity, or did something even more improbable happen to *Forktail*'s sense of humor?"

"You mean he might have grown one?" deadpanned Sargon, *Eclipse*'s Jock.

"Jesus!" Ford groaned. "I play it straight and get accused of being humorless. I crack a joke, and everyone's up my ass like a gerbil on stims. I can't win with you people."

"Hang on," Sargon quipped. "What do you mean 'you people?' I'm offended by whatever implication you may or may not have intended by that and demand an immediate apology!"

"Hear, hear," Winters agreed. "Being judged guilty by association with you lot is one thing, but having someone like *Forktail* do it when he's just a few weeks out from his surgical transition crosses too many lines to count."

"Will someone please answer my original question?" Xi asked, fighting to keep the amusement from her voice as 3rd Company finally reached the point where the twenty-degree slope flattened out to about half that.

"Sorry, Captain," Sargon said with mock sincerity. "I'm too triggered by *Forktail*'s slur to remember anything before he made such an insensitive comment. Can I get a hug from someone? Oh, and congratulations on the transition, *Forktail*," Sargon continued dryly. "2nd Company in this battalion has always been run by a woman, and I happen to think that maintaining tradition is important. Good on you for such a meaningful sacrifice, my man. You're an inspiration to us all."

Xi was no longer able to control her laughter, which meant it was time to cut this particular round. "And Sargon is the winner. *Again*. I suggest we pay the man and bring our 'A' game next time, ladies. And yes, *Forktail*, that was for you."

"It's not exactly a democratic judging system," Ford protested meekly.

"Military life features many interdependent systems, *Forktail*," Xi chided. "By the grace of God, may democracy never be among them."

The next twenty minutes were spent in relative silence as 2nd and 3rd Companies navigated the treacherous slope. Thankfully no more mechs were damaged by rockslides, but Xi was riding the edge after thirty-two consecutive hours in the chair. She had resisted the urge to take stims, but her willpower was weakening with every passing minute. She was tired, she was getting jumpy, and the dig team would need her people to maintain a defensive shield over their position for at least ten hours while they assembled their equipment and began the dig.

Their target was located twelve kilometers beneath the surface. If the Legion's intel was right, they would need to dig through at least thirty kilometers of synthetic stone before reaching an open passage roughly five times that long. Whatever was buried on this rock must have been important for its previous owner to bury it behind a thirty-kilometer-thick wall of molecularly-assembled stone designed to look exactly like the natural stone it adjoined.

Such an undertaking seemed extraordinary, but Xi knew it was a relatively minor thing compared to mining the core of a gas giant for rare minerals, which the Jemmin and Vorr appeared capable of doing on at least some level. Still, she found her curiosity rising the more she thought about what they might find buried so deep beneath the Brick's surface.

The Vorr had sent Armor Corps on this merry chase, and even at its commencement, Xi had been more than a little skeptical about their motives. Colonel Jenkins seemed more convinced than she was that the Vorr were trying to help, but why leave something of such importance buried on a desert world like this, even for just a few decades?

The minutes ticked by, stretching into hours before finally she received word from the Gash's floor.

"This is Styles, calling *Elvira*."

"*Elvira* here, go Styles," she acknowledged.

"We're ready to deploy the package," he replied. "Awaiting your orders to commence."

"Mr. Styles," Xi said urgently, "the order is given. Operation Red Rock is 'go.' I say again: Operation Red Rock is 'go.'"

"Copy that," Styles said, and her mech's visual pickups showed exo-suited workers disembark the various vehicles which had conveyed them to the dig site. Those workers began unfastening components of the complex machine from their moorings on the heavy haulers, and within minutes the first laser drills were carving into the hard stone of the Gash's northern face.

"Unbelievable," Styles said in amazement as he analyzed the stone they were cutting away from the rock-face. It had taken nearly an hour for the rock to cool down enough for his instruments to process it, but the data coming back was fascinating.

"What is it?" asked Glenda Baldwin, the dig crew's boss, as she came to look over his shoulder at the handful of dust he had scanned.

"The radiation," he lied, knowing he could not reveal any sensitive information to the civilians. Or his own people, for that matter. Of the men and women on the Brick at that moment, just Xi, Ford, Winters, and Styles were aware of the dig's details. "It's remarkable that it can be so much lower down here."

"Yeah, right." Baldwin grunted. "Look, my people and I are getting four years' salary for a two-week dig. We understand that whatever we're looking for here is important and that you can't tell us what it is, but don't treat me like I'm stupid." She snorted, turning and clomping off toward the drill vehicle as it tore chunks of stone off the cliffside. "Radiation, my ass!"

Styles couldn't blame the woman for being uncomfortable, but she was right: he couldn't afford to tell her anything.

He refocused on the basketful of debris he had gathered from the rock-face and compared it to some of the loose material from farther up the slope. Chemically it was a perfect match, which made sense given that whoever had made the tunnel in the first place would have wanted to use the same material when sealing the thing back up.

But the molecular rearrangement necessary to make the rock-layer appear identical to the rest of the cliff face boggled Styles' mind. It would have taken a computer core as powerful as the *Bonhoeffer*'s a full year of continuous runtime to match the level of precision they were seeing at this end of the tunnel.

It was possible, even likely, that the farther in they went, the less detailed the arrangement would become. But the early indications were that this was either a fool's quest and they were digging into a previously-unmolested wall of rock on a desolate, worthless planet...or that whoever buried this chamber didn't want anyone finding it without knowing precisely where to look.

The fate of the Metal Legion—and possibly even humanity itself—rested on which it was. Colonel Jenkins and General Akinouye had placed their bets, and Styles was inclined to agree with them.

But as he looked up at the nearly-vertical fifteen-kilometer-high cliff-face above him, he was unable to completely shake the feeling that this was all part of some elaborate ruse.

"*Elvira*, this is Trapper," came the unexpected hail from the grizzled sergeant major.

"Trapper, *Elvira*," she acknowledged.

"We've dug out our nests on the southern face," Trapper explained. "We're ready to arm up."

"Roger," Xi replied approvingly. Trapper's people had dug out two dozen nests using explosives and plasma torches, and they had done so nearly a full hour ahead of schedule. "I'll call the *Bonhoeffer* and get the first supply cans delivered ASAP. I'm also bringing up the heavy haulers so they can retrieve the cans for your people to use as barracks. They'll be exposed for now, but after we arm your nests, my people will be able to carve out some more breathing room."

"Much obliged," Trapper replied, and for a moment he sounded precisely like his son.

Xi initiated a P2P with the Assault Carrier and transmitted the coordinates for the next drop. "*Bonhoeffer* Control, this is Dragon Actual. We're ready for room service."

The voice that greeted her was a pleasant surprise. "Copy that, Dragon Actual," Podsy replied. "Relay target coordinates, and we'll make sure it's still steaming when you get it."

"Do my ears deceive me?" Xi asked, unable to keep from grinning like an idiot at hearing Podsy's voice. "*Bonhoeffer* Actual authorized you to use a mic?" she pressed while sending a confirmation of the drop-zone's coordinates, which were just two klicks to the south.

The terrain there was too broken for the TBM to have come down since the heavy lifters required a relatively flat surface, which was why they had brought it down considerably farther out. But the APCs were more than capable of running across the rocky, shattered landscape to retrieve these much-needed supplies.

"Consider my comm privileges early parole for good behavior." Podsy chuckled.

Xi snickered. "Your butt-snorkeling skills are legendary."

"Not all of us are built like brick shithouses, Captain," Podsednik retorted. "Each according to his means."

"Better dead than well-fed, eh, Lieutenant?" she quipped.

"We'll hit our drop window in three minutes," Podsy said, cutting short the banter. "Keep an eye on the sky. *Bonhoeffer* Control, out."

The line cut before Xi said, "It's good to..." Her voice trailed off, realizing the connection was dead as she meekly finished, "...hear your voice, Podsy." For some reason, she felt legitimately bad that she had failed to open the conversation with her former Wrench on those terms. They had been deployed on the Brick for nearly a week now, and this was the first communication she had received from the newly minted lieutenant. She felt like such an ass for reasons not entirely clear to her.

Xi shook her head to clear it of the distractions. She keyed up the channel to 3rd Platoon. "*Cave Troll*, we've got a delivery inbound. I'm forwarding the coordinates and itinerary. Escort Sergeant Major Trapper's team out there, recover the supplies, and return here on the double. We should be able to pull it all back here in two trips."

"Roger, *Elvira*," *Cave Troll* acknowledged. "3rd Platoon en route."

Six hours later, supplies collected, Sergeant Major Trapper's people began installing a missile defense system that would be even more robust than that provided by Xi's mechs.

They would finally be dug in.

7

WALKING AWAY

Two days had passed, and Lee Jenkins was ready to meet the Chairman. He had considered the offer from every possible angle, and he was ready to accept the consequences of his choice.

An offer of seventy-two fully-crewed, top-of-the-line assault-grade mechs came once in a lifetime. It would infuse the Terran Armor Corps with an overwhelming amount of fighting power. With a full brigade of three battalions under his command, Colonel Jenkins could conduct planet-wide offensives on a scale not undertaken by the Metal Legion in half a century.

It was the chance to raise the visibility of the Legion and everyone in it. This would increase the Legion's political protection from the types of maneuvers that had already tried to sink Armor Corps.

Counterbalanced against that choice was the safety of his people on the Brick, and possibly even the operational integrity of their ultra-secret mission to uncover the truth of the Jemmin conspiracy. The Vorr had already provided Director Durgan with material assistance, and as far as he could tell, they were genuinely concerned with humanity's well-being. Their dispute with the Jemmin would undoubtedly come to a head, and they had offered the Metal Legion a chance to protect humanity from the fallout of that inevitable conflict.

The knock at his apartment's door snapped him back to the moment. Standing to his full height, Jenkins moved to the door and saw a quartet of perfectly identical women wearing the same astronomical cheongsam as their predecessor (or, more likely given the number of women present, their *predecessors*).

"Chairman Kong is expecting you," they said in near-perfect unison, parting and gesturing down the hall toward the lift.

Jenkins had thought the Chairman's unspoken message regarding the identical women had been "nothing here is as it seems," but if that had indeed been the extent of his subtle missive, why send *four* of them to his door as a follow-up? Was Kong suggesting he thought Jenkins was too dense to understand him the first time around? *Had* Jenkins misunderstood the message, or was the Chairman saying something new?

Knowing he was not cut out for a game of such high-level subtlety, Jenkins made his way through the four women who assumed their places at his side and escorted him to the lift. They moved with grace, but also with purpose rarely displayed by simple docents and facilitators. Their musculature was superior to most human women's, but then again, the residents of Terra Han were generally superior in physique to the rest of the Terran Republic's citizenry.

They led him to the same aircar platform as he had previously used, where an identical aircar awaited them. Sure enough, the car was crewed by another quartet of the identical women, except this batch wore identical bronze-on-white bodygloves with Falcon Interworks heraldry.

The first four women accompanied Jenkins to the car and entered, while their counterparts gestured for Jenkins to board the vehicle. He did so, and the car sped off toward Ivory Spire

One. He took the opportunity to more closely examine the faces of the women in the car.

They each had unique identifying features, like moles and subtle variations in the structures of their ears, but these women were identical in every meaningful respect. Two had barely-visible scars on their cheeks, suggesting at least some martial arts training.

The car pulled to a stop on the platform, and two of the women disembarked before gesturing for Jenkins to do likewise. He stepped off and followed the women to Chairman Kong's boardroom, where the youthful Chairman awaited in his seat at the end of the table.

Except this time, instead of a suggestively angled chair awaiting Jenkins, not a single chair lined the table aside from the one the Chairman occupied.

The women closed the door behind Jenkins, and the Chairman got straight to the point. "You have enjoyed my hospitality, inspected my offer, and tested my patience, Colonel Jenkins. I hope, for all our sakes, you did not waste our time."

"I appreciate your hospitality, Chairman," Jenkins said seriously. "And your offer is one I would be a fool not to accept. It would turn my ragtag fighting force into one which could compete with any ground force fielded in the history of humanity, let alone the Terran Republic."

"And here comes the inevitable 'but.'" Kong's lips parted in a thin sneer.

"But," Jenkins said with a grave nod, "I have a responsibility to something more than Armor Corps, more than myself, more than the Terran Republic...and even more than humanity."

"Are you truly that self-interested?" Kong asked, his sneer turning to a condescending smirk. "Would you place your pride above the opportunity to rebuild your beleaguered branch from the ground up using the best material resources available to Terran humanity?"

"No, Chairman." Jenkins shook his head firmly. "Not to myself, but to the men and women under my command."

Kong's eyes narrowed. "Go on, Colonel. The least you can do is explain to me why this effort was somehow more than a colossal waste of my time and energy."

"We both know those mechs were built using Terra Han's resources," Jenkins said stiffly. "They represent a trove of blood and treasure that your government could not be expected to release without certain assurances. Even if I had the information you seek," he continued, measuring both his tone and his body language as he spoke, "and even if I was inclined to provide it to you, I could not permit that information to be disseminated until my current objectives have been achieved. Terra Han has every right to be proud of Lotus and Orchid Battalions, and it would be unreasonable to expect them to release those assets without a certain degree of…call it 'oversight' into how they were deployed."

"Is a little oversight truly too high a price?" Kong asked, his expression disdainful but his eyes intent.

"Frankly?" Jenkins drew a short breath. "Yes. My Legion is walking a tightrope. We spend every waking minute staring into a political abyss which would consume us for the slightest misstep. We're surrounded and outgunned, Chairman Kong; that much is true. The smart money would be against us, but if we're going down, we'd rather do it unified than to be torn apart by internal strife."

"Are you certain your people would agree?" Kong asked as an unrecognizable expression flashed across his visage.

"More than anything, Mr. Chairman," Jenkins said with conviction. "Armor Corps would be more than happy to accept whatever material and human assets Terra Han can provide.

God knows we can use them," he said gravely. "But I can't, in good conscience, agree to something I know I'll have to renegotiate later. That's not how the Metal Legion rolls," he finished, more confident than before that he had made the right choice.

Kong hesitated. He had more to say, but what was equally clear was that he had little hope for his desired outcome.

"Very well, Colonel Jenkins," the Chairman allowed. "I understand your position, and on some level, I admire you for holding it. But I am certain of one thing above all else," he said, waving a hand languidly over a panel built into the conference table, causing the door at Jenkins' back to slide open. "You will come to regret this decision."

"Thank you for your time, Chairman Kong," Jenkins said with a nod, turning and leaving Ivory Spire One before making for the nearest spaceport. The courier ship Director Durgan had provided was still on standby, and every second Jenkins spent on Terra Han was time he and his people no longer had.

"Colonel Jenkins," Thomas Oxblood, the captain and pilot of the Durgan courier ship, greeted him as soon as Jenkins boarded the sleek vessel. "We're ready to break orbit when you are."

With a twenty-year service record in the New Britain/Terra Britannia PDF, Oxblood was one of a growing number of servicemen who had gone from a highly-respected military career into private security. Jenkins could understand much of the appeal, given the relative lack of political pressure and maneuvering in the mercenary world.

"Let's go to New Africa," Jenkins told him. "I've done all I can here."

"Very good, Colonel," Oxblood agreed, and three minutes later the ship received clearance to break orbit and proceed to

Terra Han's jump gate. The courier vessel, simply designated DC04 for "Durgan Courier Zero Four," was among the fastest in the Republic. With acceleration couches capable of protecting their occupants from the tremendous gee forces of high-speed interplanetary travel, ships like DC04 were prized possessions since they cut the trips from planet to jump-gate to a fraction of what a standard liner could manage.

Even the *Bonhoeffer* and other Terran warships were incapable of matching a courier's speed, but what a courier like DC04 featured in speed it sacrificed in style.

Stripping to his underwear, Jenkins prepared for his ride in the couch. The pressure-suit he donned with Oxblood's assistance was similar to those employed by fighter pilots, providing external pressure on the softer, fleshier parts of human anatomy into which blood would naturally pool during high-gee acceleration. The suits were anything but comfortable, and were custom-fit to each passenger. Jenkins knew the cost of such a suit and its many attachments was nearly as high as one of his mechs.

"Just relax, Colonel," Oxblood urged as he prepared an injection which would activate the devices previously installed throughout Jenkins' body. Some of those devices were essentially stents, designed to keep certain blood vessels from collapsing, while others regulated blood pressure throughout his most sensitive organs (chief among them his brain) to prevent damage during the sustained acceleration.

Other tubes, hoses, and apparatuses were attached to his body through the flight suit's myriad ports. And in fifteen minutes, he was seated in the couch with a specially-designed mouthpiece clenched between his teeth that would provide him with the oxygen he needed during flight.

"Are you ready?" Oxblood asked, pointedly waving a syringe.

Jenkins wordlessly nodded, knowing that there was no way he could survive the flight without going under a general anesthetic that would reduce his bio-functions sufficiently that he would suffer little physical harm. Oxblood and other courier pilots underwent extensive cybernetic augmentation specifically so they could maintain consciousness for extended periods during flight, but even a courier pilot was unable to withstand the stresses indefinitely.

Human beings simply weren't designed for high-speed interstellar flight, and until someone finally cracked artificial gravity, it was unlikely that the experience would be any more pleasant than what Lee Jenkins was about to experience.

"As always," Oxblood explained before injecting the cocktail into a purpose-built port in Jenkins' suit, "this will take a few minutes to kick in, and when it does, the ship's life support system will cut the engines out if your vital signs become unstable. We'll be pushing fifteen gees on this flight, which should last about nineteen hours before we reach the first gate. The second flight to the Nexus will take just four hours. Nod twice if you're ready."

Jenkins nodded twice in reply and immediately felt the wave of lethargy wash over him. Everything tingled from his nose to his toes, but in spite of the bizarre feeling, he felt as completely at peace with it as he had the previous three times the doctor-turned-pilot had administered the drugs.

As his consciousness slowly faded, Jenkins was haunted by lingering doubt that he had in fact made the right choice on Terra Han.

8

NEGOTIATIONS

Elvira's comm board lit up with an incoming transmission, waking Xi from her hard-earned shuteye. The signal was in the open on standard Terran hailing frequencies, and Xi rubbed her tired, itchy eyes before focusing more intently on the signal's characteristics.

The battalion was on comm blackout save for misinformation broadcasts and P2P linkage, which meant either someone was breaking protocol...

Or someone else on the planet was trying to contact her.

She switched to the inbound channel and hesitated before opting to forward the exchange to the rest of the battalion via the P2P. "This is Captain Xi Bao, commander of the Terran Armor Corps currently deployed on this world. Who is this?"

"My name is Jean-Philippe DuPont the Fourth," came the reply in a decidedly French accent. "You have invaded our home world and attacked our defensive installations without provocation. Why do you come here? We've done nothing to the Terran people. We simply wish to be left alone."

"Your presence here is a violation of multiple interstellar treaties, Mr. DuPont," Xi retorted, fighting down the urge to mention the sixty-one Terran men and women who had already died on the Brick, most of them because of his people. "The Terran government has treated with this world's human inhabitants on no fewer than thirty-two occasions to facilitate your withdrawal, but those efforts have not produced the emigration of a single member of your community."

"This is our *home*, Captain Xi Bao," DuPont said fiercely. "You are invaders who destroyed one of our most important defensive installations without receiving so much as an active sensor-sweep in your direction."

"You failed to respond to our official hails," Xi shot back, "and Terran Armed Forces protocol for situations like this are clear, Mr. DuPont: while outside Terran territory, the failure of Terran citizens to respond to an official communique from duly-recognized representatives of the Terran Republic must be viewed as an act of rebellion. Your people have covered half this planet with installations like the one we were forced to deal with, and we were unable to establish a secure position without neutralizing that facility."

"You bureaucrats are all alike," DuPont snarled. "You think that with writs and waivers you can coerce compliance from people who want nothing more than to be left alone. And when your paper-waving fails to convince people who disagree with your authority, you abandon any pretense of civility and open fire. What you cannot take by intimidation, you take by bloody force."

"The Terran Republic has authorized Armor Corps to secure this planet and facilitate the evacuation of its inhabitants, Mr. DuPont. And talking of force, you had an excessive amount of firepower available to you, the purchase of which violated a number of interstellar laws," Xi said, her face flush with anger at the man's absurd suggestion that she of all people was a pen-wielding pencil-neck bureaucrat who sought to curtail the freedoms of others. "As the ranking Armor Corps officer on the ground, my orders in this matter are clear. I suggest you cooperate so we can find a peaceful resolution to this situation. No one else needs to die."

A lengthy pause ensued. "I am disinclined to oblige your demand, especially since it comes at gunpoint, but my people insist that I meet with you and listen to what you have to say. They would have never believed that fellow Terrans would come here to destroy what we have worked so hard to build, but your hostilities have had some fraction of the desired effect upon them. I am transmitting coordinates for a meeting place where we may discuss this matter in person. But I warn you," DuPont's voice rose sharply, "if you are determined to fight, I will demonstrate my willingness to oblige *that* particular impulse. Be there in fourteen hours. Alone."

The channel went dead, and she heard Gordon chuckle from the Wrench's station. "How are you going to play this, Captain?"

Xi smirked. "With every bit as much sincerity as Mr. DuPont. But we're here to safeguard the dig-site. If that means hanging a little ass in the wind to buy some time, that's precisely what we'll do."

"You're not seriously going to march down there alone?" Gordon scoffed.

"I said 'a little ass,' Chief," she chided as she prepared an official missive to the *Bonhoeffer's* CIG. "Not the whole thing."

After a thirteen-hour slog across the Brick's broken terrain, the Scorpion-class mech arrived at the meeting site with less than ten minutes to spare. The site was a crater four kilometers in diameter, likely made sometime in the last half-million years. It was the perfect spot for an ambush, but the *Bonhoeffer's* sensors showed no recent activity anywhere near the crater.

Still, the pop-up artillery embankments and missile launchers had also eluded the *Bonhoeffer's* scans, so it was possible the crater had been turned into a kill-box by the renegade colonists. As Xi guided the mech to the center of the depression, she saw no sign of the other party through the vehicle's various sensors.

"Come on," Xi muttered, biting her lip as a peculiar bit of feedback in her neural link sent an unwelcome buzz up and down her body. "Come out, come out, wherever you are..."

"Negative contacts, Captain," reported Gordon as the timer counted down to three minutes to go before the fourteen hours expired. "They're not going to show."

"A bottle of Koch's worst says they arrive on schedule," Xi challenged.

Gordon scoffed. "Koch's *best* is barely fit for human consumption. No way I'd agree to down a whole bottle of the worst. For a gearhead, he's not very good at brewing moonshine."

"I understand," Xi quipped. "Your mouth's bigger than your stomach. I'll be sure to bear that in mind."

"Fine, fine." Gordon sighed. "You've got two minutes and eight seconds before *you* have to down the damned thing."

"Done," Xi agreed, and they waited while the countdown neared zero. As it did, the mech sat motionless to spare Xi the discomfort of the neural link's bizarre feedback sensation. Doing so left the vehicle exposed and unresponsive, but if she was right about Mr. DuPont's intentions, it wouldn't matter whether the mech was combat-ready or completely shut down.

When the clock hit zero, Xi reactivated the linkage. "This is Captain Xi of the Terran Armor Corps' Dragon Brigade. By my watch, the fourteen hours are up, so unless you keep time differently down here—"

"I'm reading something—" Gordon reported urgently before the Scorpion-class mech was enveloped in a blinding flash of light. Radiological alarms went off, indicating the crater had just been hit by a low-yield nuclear explosion of about sixty kilotons. When the dust settled, nothing was left of the Armor Corps vehicle which had occupied the crater's center but a field of half-molten shrapnel.

Xi ran a series of confirmation checks on the sensor feeds, and the initial findings were validated. A nuclear device had indeed destroyed the mech, although it had been the damaged *Devil Crab 2* and not *Elvira*.

"*Bonhoeffer* Control, this is Dragon Actual," Xi called over the secure P2P. "Execute Operation Ares Descendant. Confirm."

"Dragon Actual, this is *Bonhoeffer* Actual," came the stern voice of Colonel Li. "We are green for Ares Descendant and awaiting your mark."

She flashed secure instructions to the rest of the battalion, with every vehicle promptly acknowledging readiness to proceed. "This is Dragon Actual," she declared with relish as she prepared to send the fire order to her people. "Ares Descendant on my mark: three...two...one...*mark*."

The *Dietrich Bonhoeffer*, having dipped to the lowest permitted altitude above the red surface of the Brick, reoriented itself until its primary weapons arrays were trained on a pair of hidden fortresses like the one the battalion had destroyed a few days earlier.

When the Assault Carrier's weapons were on-target, they unleashed their pent-up fury on the world below.

Capital-grade railguns tore into the hillocks and mountains that housed a pair of mutually-supportive fortifications even more robust than those Xi's people had already neutralized. The thin atmosphere was torched by the bolts of hyper-velocity tungsten that left billowing trails of brownish smoke in their wake before they slammed into the surface of the planet with kiloton upon kiloton of raw destructive force. Like chain gun rounds slowly but surely drilling through a half-meter of solid steel, each railgun strike dug deeper than the last into the thick layer of rock.

Explosions rippled across the ground surrounding the pair of heavily-fortified installations, indirectly confirming the presence of a vast subterranean power grid that suffered catastrophic failure under the *Bonhoeffer*'s guns. Hundreds of kilotons of explosive force were released when fusion reactors failed spectacularly, sending geysers of stone and dust several kilometers into the pale-blue sky.

Precisely three seconds after the first railgun strikes kissed the Brick's ruddy crust, Dragon Brigade unleashed a hail of extended-range artillery, MRMs, and LRMs on secondary targets surrounding the main fortresses.

In reply, twenty-nine rebel anti-orbital missiles surged upward from concealed silos, soaring with murderous intent toward the *Bonhoeffer*, which continued to bombard the fortresses with hypervelocity spears of death.

The Metal Legion's mech-based railguns tore into the volley of missiles, rending eleven of them from the sky before they reached three kilometers' altitude. Xi would have sent interceptor missiles after the rest, but the *Bonhoeffer*'s CIG had denied her the chance.

His people were going to show the rebels what they were capable of. And frankly, Xi was excited to see how they acquitted themselves.

All sixty of the *Bonhoeffer*'s void fighters were on sortie in preparation for Ares Descendant and the rebels' predictable counterattack. Roving in squadrons of four, the void fighters buzzed around the *Bonhoeffer's* position like hornets patrolling their nest as the missiles surged upward. Each rebel missile was capable of carrying a warhead powerful enough to destroy the assault carrier outright.

Without breaking formation or even seeming to acknowledge the approaching engines of death, the void fighters unleashed interceptor rockets that raced down to meet the upcoming missiles.

The rockets were laughably small in comparison to the intercontinental-range missiles, measuring just under a tenth the length and less than one percent the mass of the larger would-be ship-killers. A single interceptor rocket slotted in against each of the eighteen remaining missiles, showing either careless disregard for the dangerous missiles or absolute confidence in the rockets' efficacy.

As Xi's ground-based ordnance began to tear into the silos and other hidden weapon placements, the void fighters' rockets validated the latter.

The interceptors collided with their targets in devastating if anticlimactic fashion. No nuclear flares swept across the sky, and only a pair of fiery explosions registered on *Elvira's* visual feeds. One by one, and with ruthless precision, the rebel missiles were scrubbed from the board until it was as though the enemy counterattack never happened.

Then, just as the last of Dragon Brigade's ordnance fell upon its targets, the *Dietrich Bonhoeffer* provided the period to the end of the sentence.

And it did so in truly terrifying fashion.

A lone missile was launched from the orbiting assault carrier, and it fell toward the Brick with a seemingly peculiar target: the same crater where *Devil Crab* 2 had been scrapped.

The missile's primary motors engaged, igniting a trail of

plasma several times as long as the missile. The nose of the weapon turned red, then orange, then white as it drove through the Brick's thin atmosphere. Like the spear of the Archangel Michael, made to deliver God's wrath, the weapon plunged toward the ruined crater.

In the final seconds of the missile's flight, Xi winced in spite of herself at what was to come. One hundred and four meters above the ground, the weapon exploded in a miniature nova that made the rebels' sixty kiloton device look like a firecracker.

Even the thin atmosphere collapsed against itself, forming layer after layer of compressed gas as a faint but distinct mushroom cloud roared skyward, and the blast wave swept the ground clean for kilometers in all directions. Fifty megatons of fusion-powered fury permanently transformed the bowl-shaped crater that had previously featured so prominently on the Brick's chaotic solar-wind-blasted landscape. It was overkill, and anyone with functioning eyeballs knew it.

That was the point.

The rebels had thought they would break Armor Corps' resolve by deploying a thermonuclear device, but that bomb had only been a tenth of a percent as destructive as the device delivered by the *Bonhoeffer*. In this latest display of resolve, neither side had backed down from its former position, and Armor Corps had significantly raised the stakes.

She keyed up the hailing frequencies and threaded her voice with iron. "I trust you'll believe me when I reiterate that the Terran Armor Corps is absolutely committed to this mission, Mr. DuPont. We're here to oversee the evacuation of every living Terran from this rock in accordance with interstellar law, and that's precisely what we'll do. You've got twelve hours to think about exactly how you want the rest of your time here to be spent and, if you're capable, to think about what everyone who looks up to you wants. Dragon Actual, out."

"I know I'm supposed to be stoic," Gordon said with an awestruck tremble in his voice, "but that sent chills down my spine...and I don't think it was for all the right reasons."

"Ditto," she replied, torn between satisfaction at a job well done and the fear of irrational people turning this situation into a mass slaughter.

She had discussed Ares Descendant with both General Akinouye and Colonel Li, and while they had initially advised a less severe immediate escalation, she had won them over. Her reasoning had been based on the psychosocial makeup of men like DuPont, who would rather martyr themselves than give up on the things they had worked so hard to build. By letting him live but destroying his world, the odds would skew back to their favor that he'd surrender. She felt for him, but the Terran presence on the Brick was one of many factors which could contribute to an interstellar war between the reclusive Finjou and the Terran Republic.

And right now, the Republic needed as few enemies as possible.

She cut the line and called up to the *Bonhoeffer* on P2P. "*Bonhoeffer* Control, Dragon Actual. Ares Descendant is complete. Remind me to buy Gunnery a fresh cow to cook up," she said, venturing outside the bounds of strict comm discipline since she decided it was important to express her appreciation for their expert and crucial support.

The pause that followed was agonizing, but after eight of the longest seconds in her life, the inflectionless reply finally came back. "Dragon Actual, *Bonhoeffer* Control. Standing down and resuming geostationary overwatch. Havoc says, 'Don't forget the Worcestershire.' *Bonhoeffer* Control, out."

The line went dark, and Xi laughed in genuine surprise at the reply. She suddenly felt as though half the weight on her shoulders had been lifted. It made no sense to the rational side of her mind that she should feel that way. Nothing had changed on the ground, but knowing that the men and women in the sky over her head were with her bolstered her spirits in an unexpected way.

The *Bonhoeffer's* P2P resumed, and when she accepted the connection, she was greeted by Podsy's voice. "Dragon Actual, have you got a minute?"

"Affirmative, Lieutenant," she replied warily. "What is it?"

"I found something in the sensor logs you need to see," Podsy said, and the grim tone of his voice was so uncharacteristic that all of Xi's previous elation vanished instantly. "I'm forwarding it now."

Her screen populated with a stream of data, which took her a few moments to digest before she understood what she was looking at.

The data featured flight profiles of the missiles that the *Bonhoeffer's* Combat Interceptor Patrol, or CIP, had destroyed with their impressively simple-but-effective counter-rockets. The acceleration numbers and apparent fuel consumption of the anti-orbital platforms' motors were highlighted, and those figures were connected to others found on a series of attached technical diagrams.

It took her nine seconds to understand Podsy's meaning, at which point her teeth clenched in a mixture of anger and surprise.

"Those motors..." she muttered over the secure line to Podsy. "They're not Terran tech. They're *Solarian!*"

"Affirmative, Captain," Podsy agreed darkly. "And I'm guessing they're not the only bits of equipment the rebels have that we'll trace back to Sol."

"Lock this information down immediately and go directly to the general," Xi ordered; technically she was permitted to issue direct orders to Podsy. His capacity aboard the *Bonhoeffer* was more of a liaison between Dragon Brigade and the ship than an official crewman, which meant that he fell into a decidedly gray area in terms of where his link went in the chain of command.

"Yes, Captain," he replied, and something in his voice told Xi that he would need to be brought into the loop on the Jemmin conspiracy sooner rather than later. That particular call was above her pay grade, though. Either the general or Colonel Jenkins would need to decide whether or not Podsy could be included. For now, all she could do was send him directly to the brass and let them decide.

After the line went dead, she raised Styles via a P2P relay established at Trapper's base camp on the Gash's southern slope. It took over half a minute before the Chief Warrant Officer finally replied, "Styles here, Captain."

"Lock this line down," she urged, closing the hatch behind her to keep Gordon from hearing the upcoming conversation.

"Stand by," Styles acknowledged, and a few seconds later his image appeared on her screen as he took a seat inside an APC's cab. "All right, Captain, this is as secure as I can make it down here."

"I'm forwarding a data packet for you to review," she explained, squirting the data to him. "Reply once you see the link."

Unsurprisingly, it took Styles less time than Xi to recognize the meaning of the data, but his eyes went as wide as hers had when he did. "Is this accurate?"

"Podsy cross-checked every available telemetry feed on their flight paths," she said grimly. "It's accurate."

The chief leaned back in the APC's co-pilot chair and contemplatively rubbed his forehead. "This complicates things...maybe a lot."

"I agree." She nodded, wondering if she would have

touched off the mega-nuke had she known the Solarians were somehow involved with the rebels on the Brick.

Much to her satisfaction, that particular doubt was short-lived and cast aside as soon as it arose.

"Ok, we're going to need to call down fresh supplies," Styles explained. "Solarian missile tech is decades ahead of ours, which means anti-Jemmin systems are the first order of business. And ever since Chairman Xing's 'One Star' speech back in the mid-twenty-first, Sol's government has had a nasty history of deploying bioweapons when things don't go their way. We'll need antivirals, quarantine gear, disinfection booths…"

Xi shuddered as he rattled off the list of supplies. She recalled shocking stories of Sol's government deploying targeted hemorrhagic viruses against its own citizens during some of the more contentious rebellions that came while the wormholes were down. The entire Europa colony had been wiped out by such an attack, and half of Mars' population of eight million had died from a similar "outbreak" that could have never occurred without the government's complicity or outright sponsorship.

"…and above all, we're going to have to lock down our people even tighter than we did back on Shiva's Wrath," Styles finished, his fear-filled voice hardening with each word until he was once again speaking like a calm, seasoned professional rather than an understandably terrified person contemplating death by hemorrhagic fever.

"No breathable atmosphere on the Brick," Xi quipped, "which means it shouldn't be too hard to keep the doors shut. Forward the new requisitions and I'll send them up to Chief Rimmer ASAP."

Styles nodded. "I'll have the rough outline in five minutes, and detailed forms in twenty."

"Good work, Chief," Xi acknowledged. "Sometimes it sucks to be the only ones who know things."

9

EVICTION NOTICE

After a meeting with the general which boiled down to orders along the lines of "Try to keep a lid on the Solarian angle as long as possible, kid," Podsy was hard at work packing the latest round of requisitions into the cans. As the crews went about their work, there was an air of tension throughout the compartment. The drop-deck was generally the last group on the *Bonhoeffer* to receive intel updates, but after receiving the latest revisions to their drop schedule, it didn't take a genius to figure out the possible reasons for the latest changes.

Cans One, Two and Three had all been packed with medical supplies generally reserved for combating the worst kinds of viruses ever encountered in human history. Topped off by magazines packed with the most effective (and expensive) anti-missile rockets in the Terran arsenal, it wasn't hard to figure out that things on the Brick were more dire than anyone had anticipated.

Scuttlebutt was running rampant, and the deck crews had correctly concluded that someone other than surprisingly well-armed border-jumpers was down there on that planet. There were only two nations which made these latest requisitions make sense: the Jemmin or, more chillingly, the Solarians.

Of course, Podsy had known all along, but it was still fascinating to see his fellow servicemen go through the process of discussing the reason for these order revisions. The older members of the *Bonhoeffer's* crew were decidedly less interested in working through the situation than the younger crew, but the same measure of grim determination filled the visages of every man and woman present.

As Podsy loaded a case of rockets with his forklift, his comm link went off.

"Podsednik here," he acknowledged.

"I need you in Control ASAP, Lieutenant," came Chief Rimmer's reply.

"Be there in twenty seconds," he remarked, pushing the case to its slot in the narrow support can before pulling back and letting the grease-monkeys secure the ordnance for shipment. He turned the forklift and sped off to the deck's control room, where Chief Rimmer sat alone before a workstation.

Podsy jumped down on his new awkward legs. His old legs had been amputated midway up the thigh by Doc Fellows, and during rehab, Podsy had been given a choice between conserving as much of his original tissue as possible or performing the most expeditious (and, in his mind, the most effective) replacement procedure.

He had opted to remove most of the rest of his soft tissue below the pelvis while also replacing his pelvic bones with an alloy frame. He had initially thought this would be a far more difficult procedure than simply grafting a prosthetic onto what was left of his body, but the truth was simple: Terran orthopedic surgeons were far better and more experienced at replacing entire limbs than they were at custom-fitting prosthetics to stumps of mostly-useless flesh and bone like his thighs had been.

The reason for this was simple: vat-growing limbs and grafting them onto the existing tissue was the preferred method for extremity repair.

The problem with that approach was that it would take a year to complete, during which time he would hobble around on mostly-useless legs and be a burden to everyone around him, so the choice to have most of his lower half replaced prosthetically had been a lot easier than he would have imagined. He had also put in for a full vat-grown replacement set of legs and pelvis. Though many of his fellow crew liked to rib him about whether or not his more sensitive parts were still all-original and fully functional, he thought that was getting too much into his business.

Podsy didn't have a problem, and that was probably the greatest relief of all, more so than losing his legs. He marveled at how shallow that seemed but accepted it as the male paradigm that no amount of evolution would change.

Looking down at his heavy metal legs, Podsy was comfortable that he had made the right call. They were still clunky and poorly-coordinated due to a combination of his inexperience at using them and, perhaps more importantly, because they were still dialed way down so that he didn't hurt anyone with their potentially outrageous power and speed.

"Lieutenant," acknowledged a passing corporal, who saluted with an all-metal right arm emblazoned with the Terran Armor Corps' heraldry. There was a certain fraternity between amputees, which Podsy found both comforting and distressing. Some of them seemed to center their identities on their injuries, which seemed like a pretty poor system of self-valuation. But others validated the legendary camaraderie which existed only between those wounded in the line of duty. It was one thing to take fire, another to take a hit, and still another to lose a part of yourself in combat. It was like a marksman award for the enemy.

And it took an exceptional person to not only refuse to slow down but also to pick up speed in the face of such opposition. Podsy was comforted to know that even if he was not made of such stern stuff, he was surrounded by people who made him aspire to be like them.

"Corporal." Podsy acknowledged the salute with a brief but meaningful look before making his way into Chief Rimmer's office. "What have we got, Chief?"

"Close the hatch," Rimmer said, and Podsy complied before making his way to the workstation. Once there, he saw an image of four seemingly frail and decidedly avian-looking warships. With the wormhole gate visible off their sterns, the quartet of warships looked every bit like predators who had just found a meal.

"The Finjou?" Podsy asked, although it wasn't a question. He had reviewed the files on the Brick's true owners and familiarized himself with their ship designs and capabilities.

"They came through the gate two hours ago." Rimmer nodded grimly. "Most of their arsenal centers on air superiority, so we have to assume they're going to antagonize the *Bonhoeffer* to push us off overwatch."

"What's the general's disposition?" Podsy asked, his mind already working through the myriad supplies the Brick-bound battalion would need if the *Bonhoeffer* was displaced.

"He's asking for your input, actually," Rimmer said, causing Podsy's eyebrows to rise in alarm. "He wanted you brought up to speed before you go up there, so consider yourself up to speed and get a move on."

Why would General Akinouye want my *input?* he wondered, the gears of his mind spinning out of control.

"Thank you, Chief," Podsy acknowledged after failing to answer his own unspoken question. He made his way to the drop-deck's interior blast doors and keyed in his access codes.

During active deployment, the exterior sections of the *Bonhoeffer* were isolated from the ship's primary hull, known to the crew as the "keel."

The reason for this isolation was simple physics. During battle, a warship like the *Bonhoeffer* could receive fire so powerful that it could sheer through a meter of the best armor used by the TAF. And while the venerable warship was built to withstand the physical shock-loads of those impacts, its human crew was considerably less hardy.

As a result, every section of the *Bonhoeffer* "floated" on independent shock-absorption systems, some of which Podsy passed by as he made his way through the ship's spine. Gears, hydraulic cylinders, mimetic gel-based damper pads, and even graphene sheets tensioned by high-powered magnets worked together to dampen the shock of kinetic impacts on the hull. But all of the ship's various outer sections were anchored to the keel, which made protecting it of paramount importance.

A hit to an outer section might overcome the shock-load systems, killing everyone in that area by throwing them with spine-breaking force, but a hit to the keel could do the same to *everyone* aboard the warship, no matter where they were stationed.

As a result, a condition-one call sent nearly every Terran aboard the *Bonhoeffer* to their crash-couches, where they would not only have protection from impacts, but they would also be provided several days' supply of air and water. During the deployment at Shiva's Wrath, the *Bonhoeffer's* drop-deck crews had been out of their couches in order to secure partially-prepped ordnance while the ship took fire.

Podsy disliked the idea of jumping into a crash-couch and riding a battle out, but he suspected he would soon be faced with that prospect if the Finjou decided to push the matter.

He finally arrived at the CAC and keyed in his credentials,

causing the trio of heavy blast doors to slide open one after another and permit him entry to the ship's nerve center.

Filled with three dozen expert technicians, their workstations were arranged in three levels around a bowl-shaped theater which featured a raised dais at the center. The imposing but purely functional captain's chair was situated there, occupied by Colonel Li as he conducted the ship's departments with the professionalism one would hope to see in a Terran warship commander.

General Akinouye had the privilege of occupying a similar chair built into the starboard edge of the bowl-shaped chamber, and he waved Podsy over with a faint flick of two fingers. The lieutenant skirted the upper rim of the CAC's theater and made his way to the general's simple but robust station. He offered a salute, which the general acknowledged before gesturing for him to stand at ease.

"Lieutenant Podsednik," Akinouye greeted him, and Podsy was reminded of his meeting just a few hours earlier when the general had summoned him to the same precise spot. "Colonel Li, if you have a moment," Akinouye called.

"Of course, General." Li nodded, moving down the short set of stairs which separated him from the rest of the theater. He then ascended a set of stairs that brought him to stand before the general.

"The Finjou are here, and I want options," Akinouye said, driving straight to the heart of the matter. "Colonel Li, your thoughts?"

Li shook his head firmly, seeming to ignore Podsy as he spoke. "Four Red Talon-class corvettes present a credible threat to the *Bonhoeffer*, General, but in a wide-open engagement, we'd mop the floor with them."

"I'm aware of our respective tactical ratings, Colonel," Akinouye said neutrally. "What are your recommendations?"

"The way I see it, we have two choices, General," Li replied. "We either move to intercept the Finjou and force an engagement that slows their approach, buying our people on the surface time to complete their mission. Or we permit the Finjou to make orbit and contend with them once they're here."

"I don't want to start a shooting war with the Finjou, Colonel," the general said with mild displeasure. "And by even the most charitable interpretation of the facts, we're *their* guests."

"Then we stand off," Li said matter-of-factly. "We'll be cutting off support to Dragon Brigade, but there's no way we can outmaneuver four ships intent on driving us off geo-synch without firing on them...or ramming them, I suppose. We can use that time to open a dialogue, but the odds of success on that front are questionable."

Akinouye nodded contemplatively. "Either way, Dragon Brigade is stranded unless or until the Finjou have been addressed, and the Finjou will make station in six hours."

Podsy took an unconscious step forward as the reason for his summons became apparent. "General, Colonel, if I may?"

Akinouye's gaze quickly pivoted to Podsy, and the colonel's grudgingly followed suit. "What is it, Lieutenant?" Akinouye asked pointedly.

"We're loading fourteen fresh drop-cans on Two Deck right now," Podsy explained. "If we keep them working on their current orders and transfer all available personnel over to Two Deck, we could load twenty-two more cans from there and drop them before the Finjou arrive. It's not ideal, but it addresses the supply issue. The entirety of our effort is to buy time for our people on the planet. Once the Finjou arrive, they are going to make things tough up here and down there. Better that we are each able to support ourselves independent of the other, and it gives the *Bonhoeffer* the room it needs to maneuver and avoid, or at least delay, a conflict with the Finjou."

"One Deck is already engaged loading those cans," Akinouye observed. "And the supplies being loaded into those cans are vital to the integrity of our ground-based forces. I don't want to pull anyone off that effort."

"First and Third Shifts can deal with One Deck if we transfer fifteen people from Engineering or Gunnery," Podsy explained. "Give Second Shift another thirty able hands and I'll pack Two Deck's cans with all the ordnance our people would need to secure their position against a continental-scale air-based invasion force."

The general nodded in thought before turning back to Colonel Li. "What do you think, Colonel?"

"I think half the cans on Two Deck are either down-checked or in the repair queue with urgent flags," Li replied with a grunt. "Any ordnance we sent down in those would get no better than a coin flip at surviving the drop."

"We spread out the drop-zone, Colonel," Podsy suggested. "Put half a klick between each can so that if one goes off on impact, it doesn't take the others out. And we load the highest-value ordnance into the cans we're most confident of."

"That breaks protocol in about nine ways, Lieutenant," Li retorted. "And it's a waste of perfectly good ordnance. Each of those cans is packed with assets with an economic value totaling the combined life's effort of between fifty and two hundred Terran citizens. You're talking about potentially blowing thousands of Terran lives by playing fast and loose with the rules. Considered preparation and precise execution are how you win battles."

"We've got 463 people down there, Colonel Li," Podsy replied unyieldingly. "And I know for a fact that each of them would gladly go work in a factory somewhere to pay off the debt incurred by a little wasted ordnance if it meant an improved chance to complete the mission and leave the Brick behind."

Li squared his shoulders to Podsednik and fixed him with a burning gaze. "You took a little fire on Durgan's Folly, narrowly avoided a court-martial after violating my ship's data core's integrity, and now you think you can lecture *me* on logistics? Are you some sort of unheralded expert on tactical analysis, *Lieutenant*?"

"No, sir." Podsy shook his head, letting the colonel win the short-lived contest of wills by briefly lowering his eyes to the deck. "But I was called up here to offer my input, and this is what I've got." He turned to General Akinouye, who had silently observed the exchange with a measure of bemused interest only now apparent to Podsednik. "We can do this, General. We can get those supplies planet-side before the Finjou arrive, and it will buy us the time we need to reach our objective without actively antagonizing the Finjou. To demonstrate our sincerity, we pull the *Bonhoeffer* off station-keeping as soon as we've delivered our cans, but we maintain a covering position which ensures we can effectively engage the Finjou if they become hostile to our people."

Akinouye's eyes flicked between the two of them before the wizened officer's lips parted in a toothy grin. "What do you think, Colonel?"

Li eyed Podsednik for a long moment, his face a professional mask as he eventually nodded. "He'll do, General. He's rough around the edges and has a cocky streak in him that might get him—and, more importantly, his *people*—into trouble, but he's right for the job. I do need to be absolutely clear on one thing before I sign off on this, though," he added frostily, fixing Podsy with a look that promised retribution. "If he ever fucks with my systems again without receiving prior authorization, I will treat it as mutiny under fire."

"Agreed." General Akinouye nodded, and Podsednik had never felt quite so small as he did at that moment with both Armor Corps veterans staring him down. "All right, Lieutenant Podsednik, we go with your plan. With one modification," Akinouye added, a twinkle entering his eye as he pointed across the theater to an empty workstation. "You conduct Second Shift's efforts from your new post at Ground Control."

Podsy had to mentally replay that last bit a few times before realizing what had just happened. He lifted a salute and nodded. "Thank you, General."

"Hop to it, son." Akinouye grunted, and Podsy moved across the CAC to the empty workstation labeled "Ground Control." Its former occupant was standing nearby, and after a few minutes she brought Podsy up to speed on the interface and helped coordinate the upgrade to his credentials.

He suddenly realized that Colonel Li had already ordered the exact personnel transfers Podsy had suggested.

And Li had sent those orders out while Podsy was still en route to the CAC. *We're already on the same page. I need to treat him like it.*

"Two Deck, this is Ground Control," Podsy declared, filling the distant battle-damaged deck with the sound of his voice. "Let's pack these cans."

"Roger, Ground Control," Xi acknowledged, surprised nearly to the point of shock to learn of Podsy's new post. "We'll arrange to pick up those cans, but we'll need aerial support while we do it. I'm forwarding our retrieval itineraries."

A few seconds passed before Podsy replied, "Your itinerary is acknowledged. Combat Interceptor Patrol will be active during all scheduled retrievals."

"Copy that, Ground Control," she said with a nod, knowing that she would need to get *Elvira* out there to help pick up some of the larger bits of gear. "We're glad to have you up there, Lieutenant."

"Stand by," Podsy said abruptly, leading to a lengthy pause before he resumed, "*Bonhoeffer* will be off overwatch in five hours and forty-six minutes. Be advised, CIG is dispatching Wasp and Stiletto Squadrons to your position."

Xi recoiled in surprise before realizing what he meant. "Roger, Wasp and Stiletto inbound. We'll clear the pad."

"We are receiving an inbound message from the Finjou," Podsy explained. "Forwarding now."

An auto-translated strangely-clacking voice came over the line. "This is Finjou Claw One-Nine-Six to all non-Finjou forces in this system. You are ordered to withdraw from our territory in thirty-one Earth standard hours, or we will facilitate your removal by any means necessary." As the creature spoke, it almost sounded like its teeth were chattering and striking each other, and Xi was not ashamed to admit that it was a decidedly unsettling sound. "Trespassers remaining in our sovereign territory after that time will be evicted with extreme prejudice."

Xi raised the battalion. "All right, people. Things just got a little more complicated. Let's go collect our supplies and hunker down. I think we're going to be here for a while, and it's probably going to get hot."

10

THE POWER OF PRINCIPLE

"Ready to break orbit, Colonel?" Thomas Oxblood asked after Jenkins boarded the sleek courier ship.

"I think we've gotten all we will from New Africa," Jenkins agreed, having just completed a particularly smooth set of negotiations with one of New Africa's provincial governors. The official had been kind enough to meet Jenkins near New Africa's terminus gate rather than make him come all the way to the system's interior. This was both courtesy and practical since New Africa's myriad settlements were more scattered than all Terran colonies except Terra Ukranya.

It was Jenkins' next stop, featured not a single habitable world but had such rich asteroid belts that every one of its citizens lived aboard a self-contained habitat module. He didn't expect to get much in the way of vehicles from the Ukrainians, but he did hope to secure micro-factories and missiles from the famously independent people who called Terra Ukranya their home. Still, Terra Ukranya was the end of the line, which meant he was close to rejoining his people in Finjou space.

They were close enough to the wormhole that Oxblood was

able to guide them through at non-hazardous speeds, meaning Jenkins didn't have to get into his couch. Yet.

Unlike transit aboard the *Bonhoeffer* or another fully-crewed military vessel, where pre-gate checklists were loudly conducted for all to hear, traveling with Oxblood on the DC04 was unnervingly quiet. Jenkins watched the expert pilot match his approach vector and rotation to the wormhole gate's settings, and everything looked right to Jenkins' eye. But that didn't make warping through a rip in the fabric of space-time itself easier to stomach.

They slipped toward the gate, and its blank event horizon was replaced by New Africa 2's dedicated anchor point, which was a fairly typical Jovian planet with few moons and a powerful EM field.

"Contact bearing one-one-three carom six-five. Range, two hundred thousand kilometers," Oxblood reported with surgical precision. "They're squawking Terra Han Colonial Guard idents and requesting a comm link with one Lieutenant Colonel Lee Jenkins."

Jenkins examined the DC04's sensor panel, quickly finding the Terra Han-flagged ship's profile and cocking his head in confusion.

"I'm not familiar with that design," he said, feeling a growing sense of urgency, but the ship's distance from the gate and foreknowledge that Jenkins would return through it suggested they were not hostile. And with Fourth Fleet standing guard at the wormhole situated on the other side of New Africa 2's anchor gas giant, it seemed unlikely that the Terra Han ship would open fire on a courier known to be carrying a TAF lieutenant colonel.

"I don't know it either," Oxblood concurred, "and I know *every* Terran ship on the books. This one's never been logged."

"It looks new," Jenkins mused as he examined the more

obvious features of the mysterious ship's profile. It was medium-sized for a warship, roughly a third the displacement of the *Bonhoeffer*, but it lacked external naval weaponry. It bore engines which were powerful but not exceptionally so, and Jenkins could see no fighter launch or retrieval systems, so it probably lacked a fighter escort. Its armor was exceptionally robust, however, and the strange warship likely featured a thicker hull than the *Dietrich Bonhoeffer*. But without armaments of its own, what was the point of a thick skin?

"All right," Jenkins agreed, "accept the link."

A few seconds later, a man's face appeared on the screen. He was clearly of Asiatic descent, with a peculiarly ruddy complexion and fierce-looking eyebrows that matched an equally impressive well-groomed beard that stretched below the video pickup. He wore a black uniform with gray trim, consistent with Terra Han's Colonial Guard. Proudly emblazoned over his left shoulder was the image of a bright red horse.

"Colonel Jenkins," the man began in a tone that suggested absolute disdain, but of the kind Jenkins had come to learn usually indicated supreme confidence rather than contempt. "I am Captain Guan Jia of the Terra Han Colonial Guard vessel *Red Hare*. I am sending over my credentials, along with a message from my superiors. I will await your acknowledgment of these documents' contents."

The man stood still as a statue before the pickup while Jenkins perused the encrypted documents. It was awkward having the feed live while he read, but he didn't dare cut the line and make the *Red Hare* contact him anew.

He scanned the man's credentials, which were so impressive he had no idea how it was possible that Captain Guan was unknown to him. A veteran of nine separate engagements with the Arh'Kel, including the battle between Sixth Fleet and the Arh'Kel at Durgan's Folly, he was young for a warship commander and came with the highest recommendations from the Terra Han military leadership.

"Have you ever heard of him?" Jenkins asked Oxblood while continuing to peruse the documents.

"I have," Oxblood replied with a rare wary note in his voice. "He's one of the best Terra Han has to offer. The only reason nobody knows about him is that that's how Terra Han wants to keep it."

Jenkins' eyes narrowed when he came to an attached recording, which he opened to reveal Chairman Kong's youthful, intense features.

"Colonel Jenkins," Kong's recording greeted him, "I trust my courier found you in good health. My government was impressed with your resolve, Colonel, and decided that in spite of your reluctance to agree to a more comprehensive arrangement, you are a man whose future nonetheless deserves a meaningful investment. Please join Captain Guan on his ship for further details."

The brief message ended, leading Jenkins to wonder what exactly was going on. He had spurned their offer, and now they were running after him with another one? Such conduct was far from usual for the shot-callers of Terra Han's society, which meant that in spite of the associated danger, he had no choice in the matter.

"Let's dock with them," Jenkins decided. "I want to see what they have to offer."

"Strap in for some hard gees," Oxblood replied. "We're about to find out how much you can take."

As it turned out, six and a half gees were about all Jenkins could manage without blacking out, but with the *Red Hare* moving to intercept, the rendezvous took place less than an hour later.

"Colonel Jenkins." Captain Guan Jia met him at the airlock, and Jenkins was impressed not only by the length of the man's beard, which stretched down past his waist but also that he would be permitted to wear it in that fashion aboard a military vessel. "Welcome aboard the *Red Hare*."

"Named for the mythical steed of Lu Bu and later Guan Yu." Jenkins nodded as he set foot aboard the dimly-lit ship. It was more cramped than the *Bonhoeffer* or any other Terran warship he had been aboard, but for some reason, it felt comfortable in spite of the relatively small interior dimensions.

"You know your literature." Captain Guan smiled, although the expression never quite reached his eyes as he gestured down the corridor and led Jenkins toward the ship's interior. "Names are powerful things, Colonel. They define us in meaningful ways. My family name has much history, and that history shaped parts of my childhood, which in turn molded who I am today."

As they walked, Jenkins took note of a particular female crewman who squeezed past him. Her face, physique, and the way she moved were all familiar to him, and it took him several seconds to realize just how badly he had misunderstood Chairman Kong's subtle message back on Terra Han.

"How many crew are under your command, Captain Guan?" Jenkins asked.

"An impertinent question," Guan chided, "but a relevant one which deserves an answer. The *Red Hare* has a crew of ninety-four, sixty-six of whom see to the ship's ongoing operations while the rest serve as support staff."

Jenkins suspected he knew what those twenty-eight crewmen supported, but he decided to let the tour play out on Guan's terms as they snaked through low-ceilinged sub-passages before finally arriving at a recognizable if unfamiliar chamber which opened up before them.

What Jenkins saw in that chamber was precisely what he had expected to see after recognizing the woman in the corridor.

"Colonel Jenkins, please." Captain Guan gestured with an outstretched hand at a drop-deck that currently housed a trio of mechs identical in every respect to those he had inspected with Major Brighton. The major was nowhere to be seen, though, and in his stead was a captain of diminutive stature whose eyes were as sharp as razors as they rose to meet Jenkins' gaze.

Jenkins immediately recognized the young man, whose name was Chao Yun. He had seen extensive deployment with the Terran Fleet a year earlier when the Arh'Kel had destroyed crucial military infrastructure in a surprise offensive. Chao's work in a gunship cockpit had saved thousands of lives before he had finally been shot down. Much to everyone's surprise, he had survived the ordeal and received an honorable discharge from Republican military service in reward for his efforts.

The discharge was in accordance with Chao's wishes, although it went very much against the wishes of Chao's estranged father—a man Lee Jenkins had recently encountered under less-than-congenial circumstances.

"Captain Chao," Jenkins greeted him, noticing the three-leafed clover emblem on Chao's shoulder in the same place Guan's uniform sported the *Red Hare*'s emblem.

"Colonel Jenkins," Chao replied. "It's an honor, sir."

Guan stepped forward. "Captain Chao is the CO of Clover Battalion, which unfortunately is not yet complete and features just two full companies of the Razorback Mark 2-V-class mechs."

"Apologies, Colonel." Chao bowed his head deeply.

"Razorback Mark 2-V?" Jenkins cocked his head uncertainly, recalling that the Razorback Mark 2 was the type of vehicle he had inspected with Major Brighton on Terra Han. The Mark 2 was an update of *Roy*'s design, but Jenkins knew nothing about a 2-V variant.

"These vehicles feature Vorr technology integrated directly into several key systems," Guan explained, casually dropping an unexpected bomb into the middle of the conversation which caused Jenkins' mind to spin with the repercussions of what it meant. "Unlike the Mark 2s, these platforms are not only capable of resisting Jemmin takeovers like those that plagued you on Shiva's Wrath, but are also capable of submersion to depths up to five hundred meters at Earth-standard pressure."

"There are additional recoil-dampening systems built into these vehicles, sir," Chao interjected, gesturing to the cleverly-concealed mimetic gel pads which lined the nearest mech's chassis joints.

Jenkins had to pause and process what they had just said. These men not only knew about Vorr tech being integrated into their systems, but they also knew operational details from Shiva's Wrath. It seemed that Chairman Kong's sources, whoever they were, had been far better informed than Jenkins had thought.

"All right," Jenkins said eventually, "what does Terra Han want in exchange?"

Chao snickered, and Guan gave a hearty laugh before replying, "You do not understand. This ship, its cargo, and even its crew do not officially exist."

"A gift without value cannot be recognized, nor its loss be mourned," Chao agreed knowingly.

"Wait..." Jenkins glanced at the mechs. "A *gift?*"

"General Zhang, High Commander of the Terra Han Colonial Guard," Captain Guan explained, "wished me to convey the following message in the hope it would alleviate your confusion. He said, 'A man with influence and no merit offends all under Heaven. A man with merit and no influence offends Heaven itself.'"

Jenkins had heard that particular phrase in his formal training. It originated from a mid-twenty-second-century writer from Terra Han and was among the more memorable passages he could recall. He nodded, completing the passage. "Better to offend those under Heaven than to incur Heaven's wrath."

"You know your literature," Guan said approvingly before both he and Captain Chao made the traditional two-handed salute of the Terra Han Colonial Guard. "Colonel Jenkins, in accordance with the will of our government, we officially submit this vessel, its contents, and its crew to the Terran Armor Corps under your command."

Jenkins nodded in reply, uncertain how one accepted such a gesture. Eventually, he returned the salute in the style of the Metal Legion and said, "I recognize your submission and will bring it to the attention of my superiors." He flashed a grin and added, "I guess this means my recruiting drive is over."

"What course shall we set, Colonel?" Captain Guan asked after standing at ease.

"Finjou space, to a star system we refer to as 'the Brickyard,'" Jenkins replied, thrilled that his bureaucratic efforts appeared to have finally come to an end…for now. "It's time to join the fight."

11

SURROUNDED AND OUTNUMBERED

The Finjou forces made planetfall at 10:14 according to the *Bonhoeffer's* main clock, which was synchronized to Earth, as had been tradition for Terran Armed Forces for over two hundred years.

By 10:33, they had deployed 294 vehicles to the planet's surface, with an estimated half as many aerial vehicles put down and prepped for launch.

At 10:39, they had engaged a half-dozen colonial fortresses similar to the one Xi's people had uprooted in the Legion's first fight on the Brick.

By 10:49, the Finjou had scrubbed all six facilities from the board with combined land, air, and orbital fire.

Even though it meant the Finjou would have a clearer path to Xi and her people, the Metal Legion's acting CO couldn't help but admire their efficiency. The colonists, somewhat surprisingly, failed to author a significant counterattack to the Finjou forces and seemed more or less content to let them do as they please.

"I thought the Finjou said they were giving the colonists

thirty-one hours?" Ford growled over the command line. "It's only been seven!"

"Reread the book, my man," *Eclipse's* Jock chided. "Any permanent military installations, automated or otherwise, which are unlawfully established within a sovereign nation's territory are considered clear and present dangers to that nation and may be dealt with according to said nation's preferences. It's right there on the front page of the Illumination League's charter."

Ford growled, "They could be killing Terrans while we're sitting here discussing chapter and verse of the IL's codex. Doesn't that bother anyone else?"

"Of course, it does," Winters piped in. "We came here to evacuate these colonists, not kill them, which was why the captain called down the nuke. The whole point was to put the brakes on the firefight, and at this point, it's pretty obvious she succeeded."

As Xi listened in, she knew what she had to do. "Sargon," she called, "see if you can establish a secure encrypted line to the colonists."

Eclipse's Jock belatedly replied, "Come again, Captain?"

"I need a secure line to the colonists," Xi reiterated, "and since you've got the best comm suite in that filthy bucket you call home, I need you to set it up. *Yesterday*," she finished urgently.

"Copy that, Captain," he acknowledged. "Give me a few minutes to see if I can triangulate on their transceivers. The Finjou tore most of them down, along with the colonists' comm satellites, but I might..." His voice trailed into silence, which lasted several seconds before he declared, "There we are. I've found a nearby transceiver, but it's three thousand kilometers from here, so we'll need a relay bird for the P2P. Even then, there's no guarantee they'll accept the link."

"You let me worry about that," she said tersely, feeling

strangely haunted by Ford's suggestion that Terrans (even rebels like these colonists, who had already killed dozens of her people) might be dying at the hands of the Finjou.

"You've got it, Captain," Sargon acknowledged. "Sending a bird up now."

A rocket-driven comm relay soared skyward, and Xi quickly locked onto it with *Elvira's* P2P transceiver. The relay could be deployed as far as two hundred kilometers above the surface before it began to fall, but Xi didn't need this one to go anywhere near that high or stay aloft for too long.

She suspected it wouldn't be up there for very long, so she needed to make her opening transmission good.

The relay's motor cut out at an altitude of twenty kilometers, and the platform used its remaining fuel to stabilize its position and slow its descent.

"Link established, Captain," Sargon reported.

"This is Captain Xi Bao of the Terran Armor Corps with a message for Mr. DuPont and the Terran colonists still on this planet," Xi began as Finjou active scanners pinged the relay drone. "The DuPont name has a long, proud history stretching back to the American Revolutionary War. As recently as the mid-twenty-first century, a Franco Admiral bearing that name and its tradition stood tall against Chinese and Indian forces when they invaded his home country of France. His bravery and leadership saved thousands of lives," she continued quickly as a target lock alarm dinged on her HUD and hurried through the last words. "I hope that his bravery will be matched here by his descendants."

The comm relay was destroyed by laser fire from one of the Talon-class warships in orbit a second after Xi's last words. She leaned back in her chair, hoping she had made herself clear without giving away the game.

"Do you think he knows his history?" Gordon asked.

"With a name like that?" Xi replied confidently. "He'd better."

Two hours later, Xi received a call from one of Trapper's teams stationed in a self-contained turret on the edge of Dragon Brigade's main base camp. She had hoped for and even expected the call, so when it arrived, she instructed Trapper to have his people secure the package and escort it to her mech.

Fifteen minutes after receiving the alert, there was a knock on *Elvira's* hatch, which Xi went to open. Standing outside in the temporary airlock sealed to *Elvira's* hull and flanked by a quartet of Trapper's troopers was a man wearing a high-end envirosuit of non-Terran design. The suit had been manufactured by Solarians, and that its wearer would openly reveal as much was quite the statement on his part.

"Mr. DuPont." Xi gestured to her mech's interior. "Please come in."

The man removed his radiation-proof rebreather helmet, revealing a face with sharp, angular features and a long hawk-like nose. He looked to be in his mid-sixties, but Xi suspected he was not much more than half that age. It depended on how hard life had been for the humans who lived on the Brick.

DuPont drew in a long breath through his nostrils, seeming to sample the cabin's air before smirking. "The French and Chinese, meeting before battle as we did over two hundred years ago."

"I'm not Chinese, Mr. DuPont," Xi said, momentarily puzzled by his suggestion as she gestured to a nearby bench. "I'm Terran."

"You are what you are, Captain," DuPont replied flatly in

that thick French accent as he looked over his shoulder at the troopers. "Are they truly necessary?"

"No." Xi shook her head, having received Trapper's assurance that DuPont was unarmed after subjecting him to a full-body scan. She gestured to the troopers. "Wait outside."

"Yes, Captain," they acknowledged before she shut the hatch behind DuPont.

The man cast an annoyed look at Gordon, who manned his station while making no attempt to hide the sidearm lying on his lap. DuPont seemed not to mind the weapon's presence and nodded at Xi approvingly. "That was an especially clever touch, invoking Jean-Baptiste DuPont's legacy and manipulating my people to urge this meeting."

"History tells us about ourselves," Xi said with a shrug, "but only if we're willing to look at it honestly."

"Honestly?" DuPont scoffed. "Jean-Baptiste DuPont was not an admiral. He was a terrorist, a rogue military man who absconded with French assets which he used to take matters into his own hands after the French government capitulated to the Chinese invaders."

"The French weren't the only ones who capitulated to China after the Third World War, Mr. DuPont," Xi observed. "Not many nations that stood against them survived longer than a few decades."

"What is your homeworld, Captain?" DuPont asked, putting her off-balance with the sudden question.

"I was born on Terra Han," she replied deliberately, "but they threw me in prison when I was fourteen. I don't consider Terra Han my homeworld any longer."

"Fourteen?" His brow furrowed in seemingly genuine confusion. "Pardon me for saying so," he visibly regathered his composure, "but you do not look so very much older than that."

"My twentieth birthday is next week," she replied, doing her best to hide her annoyance at the jab.

"You do not have family?" he pressed.

Xi hesitated, knowing that this seemingly pleasant dialogue might be nothing more than an attempt to stall on DuPont's part. "No," she eventually replied, "I don't. I'm a can kid, and my father died when I was three years old. I never got to know him."

"'Can kid?'" he replied with evident interest. "This is what you call a child born of an artificial womb?"

"Yes," Xi agreed, becoming increasingly uncomfortable with the conversation's direction.

"We considered these devices," DuPont said with a knowing sigh. "They were very affordable and would have provided a steep increase in the early efforts to populate our home, but…"

"But?" Xi pressed.

"But," he reluctantly continued, "we decided it would remove a part of us if we used them. Bearing a child is perhaps the most difficult thing a human can do, and it is certainly the most difficult thing a human body was *designed* to do."

"You *wanted* to make things difficult for yourselves?" she asked with mixed confusion and disdain.

DuPont chuckled. "Look around you, Captain. Do we look like people who are averse to hardship? Quite the opposite." He shook his head proudly. "As frontiersmen, we seek hardship. We *yearn* for it. And we do this because we know that without trials and tribulations, without the constant threat of failure, asking a human being to be strong is like…asking a plant to grow in zero-gee," he finished, splaying his hands wide in conclusion. "The plant *needs* to overcome the forces of gravity to become what it was meant to be; otherwise it is a misshapen and pitiful thing which only vaguely resembles that which preceded it."

"What a load of bollocks," Gordon quipped.

DuPont sighed dramatically, slicing an annoyed look at *Elvira's* Wrench as he condescended, "Whatever happened to manners?"

"They went up in a fission-powered cloud," Xi retorted measuredly, "when you hit what you thought was my mech with a nuke. Seeing as *my* mech is also *his* mech, you can understand the irritation."

"Ah, yes." DuPont shrugged as he lowered himself to the fold-down bench opposite the one Xi occupied. "For that, I must apologize. It was rude."

"Why did you do it?" she asked, seating herself opposite the Brick's rebel human leader.

"You do not understand, Captain." DuPont sighed.

"Then help me understand, Mr. DuPont," Xi pressed. "Make me see this situation from your perspective, because right now I'm having a hard time making all the pieces fit. It's almost like..." she hesitated, knowing that if she pushed too hard he might clam up and that would be the end of the negotiations. But if Xi Bao had learned one thing from her CO, Colonel Jenkins, it was that hesitation had no place in the Metal Legion. She drew a breath before resuming. "It's almost like you're dancing to someone else's tune."

DuPont arched an eyebrow. "Oh? And whose tune might that be, Captain Xi Bao?"

"I think we both know," she said, casting a pointed look at his Solarian-made envirosuit. "But that's not the interesting question. The interesting question is why? Why work with them to establish a colony on this worthless hunk of rock when there are a dozen better colony sites in the Republic to choose from? Your people left the Republic a century ago, Mr. DuPont, and back then the opportunities for determined frontiersmen were even greater than they are now, so I have to ask myself two questions. First, why would your people come to a world located in the territory of another species when you could have benefited from Republic support by staying in one of the seven colonies? And second, why take Sol's assistance in the form of material and military support but not ask for Terra's? Help me understand, Mr. DuPont," she asked, an unwanted pleading note entering her voice. "Because right now none of this makes sense to me, and in twenty-one hours, the Finjou are going to stop targeting your automated facilities and start targeting your homes. I don't care if you're under fifteen kilometers of rock; they'll dig you out. And when they start, they won't stop until there's not a single human left alive on this planet."

DuPont seemed reluctant, but she had gotten through to him on some level. He wasn't scared or even resigned to a cruel fate, but something in his visage seemed extraordinarily tired. He knew he had gone too far and crossed too many lines, but he also seemed aware that more than just *his* fate rested on his actions.

"I cannot explain," DuPont said with a surprising degree of frustration. "It will be better if I show you."

"Fat chance of that," Gordon chortled.

"Gordon," Xi snapped, fixing her Wrench with a hard look which, to her surprise, immediately backed him off. "How long will it take?"

"In one of your all-terrain vehicles? One hour," he replied. "In mine, close to two."

"Captain," Gordon objected respectfully, "you can't seriously be considering a joy ride into enemy HQ."

"It's not enemy HQ, Chief," Xi said, her eyes locked on DuPont's as she spoke. "It's the colonists' home."

"You're the battalion CO," Gordon insisted. "You can send someone else if you think it's vital, but you can't leave your post to go haring off with the enemy. These people already dropped a nuke on what they thought was your command vehicle. What's to stop them from taking you hostage?"

She arched an eyebrow in DuPont's direction. "It's a fair question."

"Fuckin' A, it is," Gordon blurted.

DuPont nodded in agreement. "It is indeed. I cannot guarantee your safety, but I *can* say with absolute conviction that if you wish to evacuate my people with a minimal loss of human life, this is your best chance to do so."

"I agree," Xi declared, activating her wrist-link and raising Lieutenant Winters. "Winters, this is Xi."

"Winters here," he promptly acknowledged.

"I'm going to inspect the forward lines," she said, using a code phrase they had developed in the pre-mission prep to indicate she was going to parlay with the colonists. "With Ford on guard duty, you're in command until I return."

"Copy that, Captain. Forward lines," Winters agreed. "How long will you be out?"

"Four hours," she replied confidently, drawing a nod of approval from DuPont.

"Four hours," Winters confirmed. "We'll keep the stove lit. Will you need an honor guard?"

"Keep the stove lit" was code to indicate that he already had priority targets painted and missiles assigned to take them out. "Honor guard" asked if he was to engage populated targets, of which they had already identified three.

"No honor guard necessary," she replied. "I'll have Trapper's people provide the escort."

"Roger," Winters agreed. "Don't get lost, Captain."

She cut the line and gestured for Gordon to follow. "Let's go, Chief. I've got a feeling I'll need you on this one."

Gordon grimaced as he stood and holstered his sidearm, making a point of going to the small arms locker and retrieving

Xi's pistol. She accepted it, slapping the holster to her hip where it stuck via micro-hooks similar in design to Velcro that would require five hundred pounds of force to remove from her jumpsuit.

They slid into sleek envirosuits, and a few minutes later were aboard one of the Legion's ATVs with a quad of infantrymen serving as escort.

DuPont guided them to a rocky outcropping ten kilometers from base camp, and as they approached, he keyed a command from his wrist-link.

A boulder slid aside from the rockface, revealing a steep tunnel which was more steel than rock. The ATV's lights snapped on, illuminating the cramped passage as they drove forward at speeds in excess of a hundred kilometers per hour. The tunnel was remarkably straight and smooth, with only a few intersections that DuPont guided them through during the ride.

"These weren't made by TBMs," Gordon said over the private link. "The walls are too smooth."

"And they weren't carved by lasers," Xi commented, "since there's no spiderwebbing or glazing on the rock."

"They're not old," Gordon mused. "I'd guess less than a hundred years."

The rest of the trip proceeded in relative silence before they passed through a heavily-fortified intersection featuring two dozen chain guns and other weapons built into the walls. Those guns could have easily shredded them on approach, but they remained powered down as the Legion vehicle sped past.

Less than a kilometer from that intersection was an open set of blast doors seven meters tall and a meter thick, beyond which was a square room fifteen meters on a side and seven meters high. The vehicle slowed as the tunnel's end finally arrived, and when it did, it was with a second set of blast doors, though this inner set was considerably less robust than the outer ones.

They disembarked the ATV, with the troopers securing the area, noting a pair of automated gun placements built into the walls.

Mr. DuPont patiently waited for Xi's people to complete their sweep of the room, after which she turned to him and said, "All right, Mr. DuPont. Let's see it."

DuPont nodded, raising his finger and making a whirling gesture that prompted the giant blast doors behind them to slowly close. Alarms blared and lights strobed as the massive panels closed, and when they finally clamped shut, the chamber was filled with the hiss of incoming gas as the giant airlock pressurized.

When it had finished, DuPont removed his helmet and gestured for Xi to do likewise. She obliged, gesturing for Gordon to do the same, but the troopers knew they were to remain in their self-contained suits throughout this operation. With six hours of breathable air left in their systems, they had plenty of time to return to base, assuming things proceeded on schedule here.

Xi breathed in the air and was momentarily confused, then surprised, and finally exhilarated when she recognized the cavalcade of scents filling her nostrils. The powerful and distinctive smells of roses, blackberries, citrus, sweet grass, and a dozen other familiar odors assaulted her senses. Unlike the recycled air of *Elvira's* cabin, which smelled faintly of grease and cleaning chemicals, this smelled like a private garden where people on Terra Han would pay good money to indulge their olfactory centers.

The link between smell and memory had long since been recognized by humanity, and for Xi it was no different. The smell of ripe blackberries in particular conjured a memory of walking beside a man she assumed to be her father as they strolled through a rooftop garden in one of the sub-cities in which Xi had grown up. The rough texture of his hands and the sharply contrasting imagery of the mixed green and blackberries on the thorny vines filled her mind, and she fought those memories down while re-focusing on the task at hand.

As she processed the fragrant aromatics, the inner doors of the oversized airlock parted, and what Xi saw beyond nearly took her suddenly-enriched breath away.

A curved walkway stretched right and left, with an artistically carved solid-stone rail ten meters from the doors. Beyond the hip-height rail was a cavern that spanned several kilometers, with a raised dome at least half a kilometer tall at the center. The bowl-shaped floor of the cavern, the lowest point of which was at least two hundred meters from where Xi stood, was carved into terraces, all of which were overflowing with luscious flora. The greenery wasn't only life-sustaining, but it brought a certain peace reminiscent of any Zen garden.

People worked throughout the verdant paradise, with dozens of gazebos and other small structures scattered throughout where people gathered.

But the floor of the cavern was less remarkable than its roof. The dome-shaped ceiling, far too perfect to be natural, glowed with a pale-blue light that seemed an almost perfect copy of Terra Han's skies. Fluffy white clouds gently glided across the dome, and a miniature sun shined its light down from a point approximating eleven o'clock in the sky.

Xi knew they were merely images and that the light which created them was almost certainly powered by a fusion reactor somewhere, which in turn provided the plants with the ultraviolet rays they needed. For a moment, though, she allowed herself to think she was standing on a Gaia-class world.

"Captain Xi," DuPont said, proudly gesturing to the cavern and breaking her from her reverie, "welcome to my home."

As Xi looked out, she estimated no fewer than three thousand people were in the cavern, and that only accounted for the groups she could see. A dozen tunnels led out of the circular walkway where she now stood, and people moved purposefully throughout those tunnels, going about the work of their daily lives.

Things were a lot more complicated than she had expected, and Xi knew she had precious little time to get to the bottom of this situation before it spiraled out of control.

"All right, Mr. DuPont," she said grimly. "Let's talk."

12

BAD NEWS & TRIES AGAINST OUR INTERESTS

The *DC04* and the *Red Hare*, moving in formation, approached the New Africa jump gate leading to the Nexus. Jenkins had opted to remain aboard the *DC04* in order to comply with his orders to the letter, which made the legality of transferring to another vessel, even one nominally pledged to the Metal Legion, murky at best.

The *DC04* slipped through the jump gate and was immediately hailed by a nearby Terran vessel. It was another courier, although this new courier was with the Terran Fleet.

"I've got an incoming priority linkage request addressed to you, Colonel," Oxblood reported. "Shall I patch it through?"

"Go ahead." Jenkins nodded, strapping on a comm visor which soon projected the image of a Fleet Naval lieutenant with the name badge Mugabe on his chest. "Lieutenant Mugabe," Jenkins said.

"Lieutenant Colonel Jenkins." The lieutenant nodded officiously. "I've been tasked with delivering a secure document for your eyes only. The encryption is Theta-Theta-Two-Five-Niner-Bravo. Acknowledge, and I'll send it over."

"Theta-Theta-Two-Five-Niner-Bravo," Jenkins confirmed, and a secure packet was transmitted to his visor.

"I've been instructed to await your official acknowledgment of these orders," Lieutenant Mugabe said. "Take your time, sir."

Jenkins eyed the other man before decrypting the packet using the indicated protocols, and a one-page memo filled his visor's display with order revisions direct from Armor Corps HQ.

To: Lieutenant Colonel Lee Jenkins, TAC
From: General Mikhail Pushkin, TAC
Priority: Immediate
Subject: New Orders

You are hereby ordered to return ASAP to TAC HQ for a full debriefing on your support mission and to receive new orders. You are no longer attached to Operation Brick Top. Do not rendezvous with **Dietrich Bonhoeffer***. Return to TAC HQ with all gathered resources. Do not deploy resources prior to a complete inspection at TAC HQ.*

Jenkins slumped back in his chair. General Pushkin was one of General Akinouye's closest friends and allies. He would never have called Jenkins back while Akinouye was still out there, which meant it was possible that Operation Brick Top had already concluded.

Jenkins reread the document several times before his eyes snagged on one line in particular: **Do not rendezvous with Dietrich Bonhoeffer**. Why tell him not to rendezvous unless the *Bonhoeffer* was still on active deployment?

Something wasn't right. No, that didn't go far enough; something was terribly, terribly *wrong*. General Pushkin was trying to tell Jenkins what it was with his cryptic missive. The note was desperate instead of commanding. Anxious instead of composed.

Pushkin was *not* an anxious man. He had taken fire under the Arh'Kel's guns for the greater part of fifty years and earned a fruit salad of commendations for his conduct in difficult situations.

It fell into focus as Jenkins reread the last line. **Do not deploy resources prior to a complete inspection at TAC HQ.**

The note wasn't telling Jenkins what he *should* do. It was an inversion of what Pushkin was *really* trying to tell him. He was saying absolutely do not, under any circumstances, return to Terran Armor Corps Headquarters prior to rendezvousing with the *Bonhoeffer* and completing Operation Brick Top. He was also saying that under no circumstances was he to subject these new Razorback Mark 2-V mechs to Armor Corps inspection—or, in all likelihood, any other inspection by TAF personnel.

Under the Terran Armed Forces code, "Immediate" priority was the highest level legally permitted to be invoked by a ranking officer outside of a mission's immediate chain of command. It was superseded by a handful of mission-critical priorities such as Alpha, Omega, Gold, White, and Black, so unless an officer was operating under those orders, he was compelled to comply with an Immediate priority order from a superior outside the immediate chain of command.

But unbeknownst to everyone outside of Akinouye, command personnel aboard the *Bonhoeffer*, and General Pushkin, Operation Brick Top had been secretly conducted under Black priority, which was the highest priority Akinouye could independently authorize. Pushkin knew that as well as Jenkins did, which meant that this note was as much for show as it was meant to communicate an urgent message to Jenkins as he headed to the field.

Pushkin was getting pressured to recall Jenkins to HQ, and he was making a display of complying while subversively doing the exact opposite, because, by directive, Jenkins was compelled to comply with the priority order, Brick Top.

Jenkins closed his eyes, knowing that the shitstorm had to be bad for Pushkin to act on it at all, let alone for him to resort to coded messages that would undoubtedly end his storied career if the truth came out.

And Pushkin's career wouldn't be the only one on the chopping block if Jenkins decided to follow his lead on this, but Lee Jenkins hadn't earned his callsign by playing it safe, and it was possible he could buy Pushkin a little breathing room by flagrantly violating his 'orders' and sending this courier back with word of his disobedience.

Lieutenant Mugabe's image remained centered on Jenkins' visor display as Jenkins closed the document and said, "Order receipt acknowledged, but I cannot comply at this time."

"Confirm, Colonel," Mugabe requested. "You understand the orders as transmitted and are refusing to follow them?"

"Confirmed, Lieutenant Mugabe." Jenkins nodded. "It is my judgment that my current orders are incompatible with and therefore supersede these revisions. I'm attaching my signed receipt of the package under the same encryption protocols. Acknowledge receipt."

The lieutenant looked off-pickup for several seconds before nodding. "Receipt confirmed. Thank you, Colonel Jenkins."

"Thank you, Lieutenant Mugabe," Jenkins replied before cutting the line.

"That didn't sound good," Oxblood said matter-of-factly.

"It wasn't," Jenkins assured him. "And I think it would be best if I transferred to the *Red Hare*. Give my thanks to Director

Durgan. I've never flown by private courier before, and I trust you won't take it badly when I say I hope I never have to again."

Oxblood snickered. "It's the best ride Terran money can buy, Colonel."

"I know," Jenkins agreed as the *Red Hare* emerged from the jump gate off their stern. "Inform Captain Guan I intend to transfer at his earliest convenience."

"Will do." Oxblood was nothing less than a consummate professional, and thirty minutes later Jenkins was aboard the secret Terra Han warship and en route to the gate that would take them to the Brick.

He had every confidence that his people would carry out the first phases of the operation, especially with General Akinouye overseeing everything from orbit.

But there was still a lingering sense of panic that his people might need him down there, and that sense of urgency only grew as the *Red Hare* burned across the Nexus to the cluster of Finjou gates located a full day's ride from the one through which they had just emerged.

"This is an amazing place, Mr. DuPont," Xi said after a brief survey of the underground colony's expansive Garden Sphere. "I can understand some small part of why it must be difficult to leave it behind."

"It is our home, Captain Xi," DuPont agreed as a group of small children ran by, giggling with joy as only children can. "It is all we have ever known, and all we ever want to."

"You can't stay here," she said adamantly. "We already located several of your subterranean transit system's surface entry points, and we haven't even been looking that hard. I didn't assault your tunnels because I didn't come here to hurt you. I came here to evacuate you. But we both know that the Finjou are going to have a lot less issue than we would with coming down here in force and purging everyone in this colony if you don't comply with their eviction directive."

"You are right." DuPont nodded, looking out over the beatific cavern in resignation. "Our time here is done."

"I still need to know," Xi said firmly as Gordon inspected the construction materials with a handheld scanner, "why Sol gave you the technology you needed to create all of this? It would have taken a thousand Terran artisans fifty years to carve this cavern and those tunnels." She jerked her thumb over her shoulder toward the airlock door. "But I'm guessing Gordon's scans will show this place has been here for longer than that. Such excavation efforts, even fully-automated, require an incredible amount of power, Mr. DuPont. We're talking fifteen, maybe twenty grade-three fusion plants burning nonstop to get on top of the curve and power the excavation of these passages in less than twenty years. Not to mention the supply of coring bits, drive train repairs, debris extraction equipment, and enough perishables to keep your people alive long enough to get this thing up and running." She looked appreciatively at the Garden Sphere.

"It seems you know something of excavation, Captain Xi," DuPont said lightly, but the glint in his eyes made clear that he was aware of her dig team's efforts at the Gash. And more than that, his expression suggested he knew more about it than she would have liked. "I think you'll agree," he gestured to the cavern before them, "that we know a little of that enterprise ourselves."

"Don't change the subject," she said firmly, hoping to avoid another sidebar like the one which focused on her childhood. "I need to know why Sol gave you the support it did. I don't care about the how or the who. I'm only interested in the why, Mr. DuPont."

DuPont fixed her with a hard look. "My great-grandfather made the first cut into this planet's crust, Captain Xi. He toiled with simple equipment, meager supplies, and a barely-livable habitat. Fifteen years he spent here, his body breaking down from cancers caused by the ambient radiation. My grandfather pleaded with him," he continued, his eyes softening as he spoke. "He told him to call for help from one of the Terran corporations or even to treat with the Finjou in hopes of securing a lease to part of this world in exchange for mineral wealth.

"But my great grandfather was proud. Too proud. He died when his air recycling system failed, and he was unable to send for help in time. He had almost completed the first bunker, which would protect its inhabitants from the radiation far better than he had enjoyed, at which point he would bring his children in to continue the work he had started. It was then that my grandfather was approached by a Finjou merchant with an offer."

"'A Finjou merchant?'" Xi repeated skeptically.

DuPont nodded. "It was never confirmed, although it became obvious after a short time, that this merchant was acting as an emissary on Sol's behalf. The offer was simply too good to ignore: they would provide us with all of the resources we would need to create a subterranean paradise here on DuPont's Dream—the name my grandfather gave it after agreeing to the Finjou's terms."

"What were those terms?" she pressed.

"They were simple." DuPont shrugged. "Remain here, stay below ground, and use the equipment provided to build our home. Once the equipment was finished with that task, it was to begin the work of fortifying this place against invasion." He hung his head in the universal human gesture of defeat. "We knew the equipment was of Solarian design, and we learned how to use it quickly enough. But after we completed our home, it wasn't long before we barely even took notice of the machines' automated labors. Every few years, the Finjou merchant would return to check on our status, and to deliver weapons and other materials needed for the continued expansion of this world's defensive grid. But then, thirty standard years ago, the merchant stopped coming."

"Your forebears had to have known they were being played," Xi said skeptically.

"Of course." DuPont shrugged. "But everyone is played by someone else, Captain Xi. No one is truly the master of his own destiny, so why balk at the opportunity to advance your condition, even when you know there are strings attached? You must understand," he continued passionately, his eyes misting over as he spoke. "New France was established with a great, beautiful ideal shortly after humanity gained access to the wormholes. The chance to flee the militaristic, war-torn Earth was too great an opportunity for my ancestors to ignore as they pursued a dream as old as humanity itself.

"But that ideal and their dream died when the wormholes collapsed and we were cut off from the rest of what became the Terran Republic. New Francos...*my people*...died, Captain Xi. We died of radiation poisoning, asphyxiation, malnutrition, and dehydration. We failed the ordeal the Seven Colonies of the Terran Republic survived. That failure changed us forever, Captain. It caused us to become...distrustful. It caused us to look after ourselves rather than others. It was not a healthy response, and I take no pride in explaining it, but it is irrevocably who and what we became."

"It's not irrevocable." Xi shook her head in rejection. "Your people are the most unique Terrans I've yet encountered, Mr. DuPont. Look at this...*majesty*," she said, using the only word that seemed to accurately convey the scene before her. "You *did* this. And you can do this again."

DuPont scoffed. "You call us 'Terrans,' which means that in spite of all I have told you, you still do not understand us."

"No, Mr. DuPont," she said with conviction. "I understand you better than you understand yourself. I understand what it's like to be an outsider; to be alternately ignored and abused by the people you try to help. I know what it feels like to have an entire world turn its back on you after you did everything you could to contribute to its betterment," she said, her nostrils flaring as tears welled up in her eyes. "I also know," she straightened her spine and gave the older man a determined look, "that even though it took me a while to find it, there's a place in the Terran Republic for me to make a difference. And there's a place in it for you. Your forebears' dream didn't die, Mr. DuPont. It just moved beyond the horizon, and I'm here to take you back to it."

DuPont gave her a searching look. "I have killed many of your people, Captain Xi," he said in a faintly tremulous voice. "How can you think to help me?"

"We're Terrans, Mr. DuPont," she said, pushing aside the thought of her lost comrades. "If we don't take care of the most wayward among us, then that dream you talked about, which is every bit as important to me as it was to your ancestors, is dead." She set her jaw as the faces of her fallen comrades flickered through her mind, each one a grim reminder that DuPont's weapons had ended the lives of those who had come to help him and his people. "I'm not going to lie, though," she said through gritted teeth. "If you were locked in a dark room with me, you'd leave in a body bag."

DuPont shook his head in wonderment. "You are a remarkable person, Captain Xi. It has been an unexpected pleasure meeting you." He reached up to his neck, causing Xi's flanking guards to train their rifles on him. He held up his fingers as he produced a chain tucked beneath his collar, and on that chain was a crystal key of Solarian make. "This is the command key to all the military hardware stationed on this planet, which I am formally surrendering to you," he explained, proffering it after disconnecting the clasp behind his neck. Gordon approached, snatched the card from DuPont's hand, and began to scan the device after moving to a safe distance. DuPont straightened. "I am prepared to submit to Terran justice for my crimes, and to request your assistance in evacuating my people from our home."

Xi blinked in surprise, wondering if this was some kind of trick. But she knew there was only one way to play this particular exchange, so she nodded. "I accept your surrender, Mr. DuPont."

"May I address my people?" DuPont asked.

"Please," she urged, wondering if she had managed to achieve what she had come down here to achieve. It was almost too good to be true, which did nothing but increase her anxiety as DuPont activated his comm link.

"May I have your attention, please?" DuPont's voice boomed throughout the Garden Sphere, but in spite of the chamber's size, his amplified voice barely echoed. "This is Governor DuPont. In accordance with our community's latest vote, I have formally surrendered to the Terran Armed Forces and am requesting asylum on behalf of the entire community. We must evacuate our home immediately," he continued, causing heads to swivel their direction from all across the magnificent chamber. "It is no longer safe here for us."

Mixed looks of resignation and resolve flashed Xi's way, and the people in the cavern took a collective look at the beautiful scenery before making their way to the many tunnels adjoining the Garden Sphere.

DuPont turned to her. "Captain Xi, do you accept our formal request for asylum?"

This type of surrender had been precisely what the Metal Legion had hoped to receive from the residents of the Brick, but with the Finjou now on site, an asylum request made things far less certain.

And *far* more dangerous.

But she had her orders, and she would follow them because she believed in the wisdom of their authors.

"Yes, Mr. DuPont," she replied. "On behalf of the Terran Republic, I formally accept your request for asylum and will conduct you and your people off-world as soon as possible."

Residents nearby seemed mildly relieved at that, and hurriedly began moving down the tunnels to prepare for the exodus.

DuPont offered his outstretched hands, wrists held close together. "I assume you will take me under arrest?"

"We will," Xi agreed as one of the troopers moved forward with a set of handcuffs, but before the trooper reached DuPont, she gestured for him to stop. "But not yet. Right now, the best thing you can do is help organize your peoples' evacuation. Every minute counts, Mr. DuPont, and if you care for them at all," she added, threading her voice with iron as she finished, "you'll stay with them until the last pair of shoes steps off this rock."

DuPont winced almost imperceptibly, but he made it clear that he took her meaning. "I will not abandon my people while they still need me."

"Good," she said with a nod. "Now let's get to work. We're running out of time."

13

REUNIONS

"Finjou forces have scrubbed all seven automated fortresses in the region, General," Colonel Li reported briskly after the last of the rebel forts had been taken out. "They are moving to surround our people at the dig site."

After deploying all the supplies prior to the Finjou arrival, Podsy's job in the CAC seemed to largely consist of coordinating work orders with the drop-deck. They had received the odd ticket from the surface for minor damage sustained during patrols, but Ground Control had little to do when the *Bonhoeffer* was in no position to provide material support to the Legion's planet-bound forces.

The drill team had encountered some troubles and were dangerously low on cutting tips after a series of unfortunate accidents, but the team had already dug through more than thirty kilometers of solid rock and were hours away from reaching their objective. Chief Rimmer had overseen the fabrication of replacement parts, and there was reason to hope they would not be needed before the dig was complete.

They were ready just in case.

As Podsy worked to familiarize himself with his new duties,

he was humbled by the discipline and efficiency of the *Dietrich Bonhoeffer's* command and control crew. The people were precise, thorough, abrupt, and coordinated to a truly impressive degree. Colonel Li's command and control, the CAC was not just a well-oiled machine, it was a near-frictionless one.

And now, with the Finjou having completed their sweep of a five-hundred-kilometer radius surrounding their landing site, it was time for Colonel Li's machine to be put to the test.

Li turned to General Akinouye's station. "Your orders, General?"

Akinouye's eyes flicked across incoming reports faster than Podsy thought he could manage. The man was old and physically frail, to be certain, but the venerable officer's mind was every bit as sharp as that of the young man who had earned the callsign "Havoc" for the controlled chaos he had expertly summoned to the field.

"Colonel Li, Colonel Moon." Akinouye gestured for Li and the *Bonhoeffer's* CIG to approach before, surprisingly, summoning Podsy as well. "Lieutenant Podsednik."

Podsy unstrapped from his chair and made his way around the theater's upper rim, passing a dozen technicians who worked near-silently to keep the mighty warship at condition two.

Podsy came to stand at Colonel Li's right side, with Lieutenant Colonel Moon to his left, and the general gestured to the reports. "Our intel on Finjou is sketchy, but best estimates put their mobile ground forces at twice the fighting power of ours. They've got two hundred tactical-grade vehicles down there, along with unknown numbers of aircraft, to our mixed forty-one combat-ready mechs. Our people are outgunned, gentlemen, and if we don't move to interdict the Finjou, in six hours our people will have four Talon-class warships circling their heads like vultures. They aim to intimidate us into caving, and in all likelihood, they mean to take the rebels into custody." He fixed each of them with a look that sent chills down Podsy's spine. "That's not how this is going to play out. Is that understood?"

"Yes sir," all three men replied with one voice.

"Let's talk options." Akinouye gestured to Li. "Colonel?"

"The *Bonhoeffer*'s damaged, sir," Li replied promptly, "but Talon-class warships can't match our firepower at close range, and their armor isn't anything special. If we move to higher orbit and advance toward them using the planet as leverage, we can scatter the Finjou ships and resume overwatch. I'm confident they won't open fire during our approach."

"Because at that point we'll be surrounded and fighting the planet's gravity well." Akinouye grunted. "Our flank armor isn't worth shit right now, Colonel. If we let them surround us, it doesn't matter how weak their pea-shooters are. They'll stand off and snipe through the cracks in our shell until we've got no choice but to disengage or die. Unacceptable."

"Which is why," Li agreed, "my recommendation is to prep our void fighters for deployment and take a low-orbit approach rather than a high-orbit one. They'll be expecting a high-orbit approach, and at low-orbit, we can keep them from exploiting the gaps in our defenses by presenting our underbelly to the planet."

Colonel Moon nodded. "With the *Bonhoeffer's* maneuverability compromised so close to the surface, we'll need a full void-fighter escort to address both surface and orbital threats," Moon agreed, easily stepping into Li's presentation. "We have four full wings plus seven auxiliary craft in the Wild Cards, giving us fifty-five combat-ready ships and pilots, General. Recommend we deploy Diamond Wing in missile-intercept posture immediately upon reaching low-orbit, and those fighters will provide escort during approach. We reinforce the patrol as needed with the auxiliaries until we reach knife range, at which point we launch Club Wing and adopt an adaptive posture. We hold Hearts and Spades on standby until the situation clarifies."

"During approach, we continue to hail the Finjou and negotiate for the safe withdrawal of our people. The dig team has already excavated thirty kilometers of rock and are currently eight hours from reaching the objective, sir. We don't need to engage the Finjou, but we do have to keep the drill moving. The best way for that to happen is for the Finjou to stand down while we complete our mission."

Akinouye's lips twisted in a moue of disdain. "Meaning I sit here on the horn pleading with the bird-brains in the childish hope they listen to reason and don't do the very thing that would jam me up worse than a midnight brick of cheese?" The general scowled. "I didn't get where I am by hoping to make friends with the enemy, Colonel. And I didn't join the Legion so I could ride a desk and play DJ to an empty room. They're not going to respond to diplomacy until they're in the best negotiating position they can achieve, and right now that position is one which features the ability for them to bombard our people from orbit. With so many Finjou assets already planet-side, even if we neutralize the orbital threat, Dragon Brigade is still vastly outgunned."

"I understand the chance of success is low, General," Li said firmly, "but diplomacy is the best option we have to keep the situation from escalating long enough to achieve our objectives. Captain Xi is due back from her negotiations within the hour, but early indications are that her efforts met with some success since several fortified bunkers were revealed in accordance with her directives should she gain control over the rebel fortresses. Diplomacy is clearly the cleanest path to victory here, General."

Podsy decided it was time to speak his mind. "General Akinouye, sir, we can deploy the *Bahamut Zero* while on low-orbit and use it to flank the Finjou on the eastern front where they're most vulnerable." He kept his eyes locked with the general's as he spoke, but he could almost feel the icy fury rolling off Colonel Li beside him as he continued, "You can continue your diplomatic overtures aboard the *Zero* via P2P linkage, using the *Bonhoeffer* as a comm relay, while moving to reinforce Dragon and drawing fire away from the Legion forces protecting the dig site. We'll have to make the drop five hundred kilometers from the site to avoid enemy fire, but on the Brick's terrain, the *Zero* can make at least a hundred kph and will be in position to engage the Finjou in three hours."

Akinouye's face was granite as Colonel Li turned to face Podsy. "Lieutenant Podsednik," said the *Bonhoeffer's* CO said with thinly-veiled irritation, "are you proposing we deploy the Terran Armed Forces' most senior officer aboard the most valuable piece of human-built hardware ever to make planetfall to a world with dozens of as-yet-unsecured hostile fortifications, against a potential enemy that outnumbers us at least two to one and presently controls overwatch territory?"

When you say it like that... Podsy thought before pushing all doubt from his mind. "Yes, Colonel." Podsy nodded. "That would be an accurate summation of my proposal, sir."

Li looked ready to tear out Podsy's throat, but General Akinouye issued a harsh, barking laugh which preempted the *Bonhoeffer's* CO. "I like the way you think, Lieutenant," the general declared, standing purposefully from his station. "Colonel Moon, the *Bahamut Zero* will need an escort," he said matter-of-factly.

"The Spades are at your disposal, as always, General," Colonel Moon said with a curt nod.

"Good." Akinouye grunted, turning to Colonel Li. "Colonel Li, you are to maneuver the *Bonhoeffer* to low orbit and assume overwatch of the dig site, where you will support our ground forces. Employ your best judgment on how to achieve your objective, and I'll stand by it at the court-martial."

"Thank you, General," Li said, his previous anger replaced by the same professionalism the rest of the CAC's crew displayed. Personal differences and broken facial bones courtesy of his master-at-arms aside, Podsy respected Colonel Li more with each passing day. He was glad to have the man on his side of the ball.

General Akinouye turned to Podsy. "Lieutenant Podsednik, I doubt the *Bonhoeffer* will be in position to provide material support for the remainder of this op, so Ground Control on the *Bonhoeffer* is unlikely to be all that active. I hear the drill requires replacement parts to be delivered to the dig site, and we just happen to have a Ground Control station on the *Zero*."

Podsy was unable to keep from smiling at the prospect of riding the *Bahamut Zero* into a combat zone. "Permission to accompany the general planet-side, sir?"

"Permission granted." Akinouye nodded, taking a half-step before stopping and fixing Li with a bemused look. "If there are no objections?"

Li's jaw muscles briefly bulged before he shook his head. "No objections, General."

"Good." Akinouye clapped the other man on the shoulder before making his way to the triple blast doors. "Give 'em hell, Colonel."

Podsy felt actual chills as he boarded the *Bahamut Zero* for the first time. The *Zero* was the most advanced, expensive, and potent armor platform ever developed by humanity. A prototype for a long-since-abandoned line of siege-grade, Bahamut-class vehicles, the *Zero's* peculiar deployment limitations and astronomical maintenance costs had made the Terran government ultimately reject not just the Bahamut line, but the entire siege grade of mechs that had been planned to follow.

Siege-grade vehicles seemed to be an inevitable and logical extension of the smaller vehicle grade tiers of Recon (often referred to as 'Light' mechs by Legion personnel), Tactical (Medium), Cruiser (Heavy), and Battlewagon (Assault) mechs. But with Armor Corps' waning support in both the Republican Parliament and within the Terran Armed Forces, the necessary deployment modifications of Armor Corps warships were deemed too expensive to be green-lit. As a result, just the *Dietrich Bonhoeffer* featured the ability to deploy the titanic *Bahamut Zero*.

Many within the Armor Corps considered the eighty-sixing of the Siege class to be the beginning of the Legion's slow decline these past few decades. Podsy was still not up to speed in terms of in-house Legion politics and intra-branch feuds, but having seen the after-action reports from Shiva's Wrath, it was hard to argue with the *Zero's* effectiveness in combat—and harder still to convincingly argue that the Siege class was unworthy of inclusion in the Terran panoply.

With an arsenal that nearly matched a mixed company's fighting power, the *Bahamut Zero* was a game-changing force—not just to be reckoned with, but to be feared. A veritable titan of the battlefield, its mere presence bolstered the morale of the crews around it.

And its effect on those within seemed no less profound.

"Major Pennington," General Akinouye greeted the *Zero's* commander and Jock. A mid-statured man in his late eighties, his gray eyes flicked with the same precision and predatory intent that Podsy had come to know in his former teammate, Xi Bao.

"General," Pennington acknowledged, pointing with his eyes at Podsy. "Is this our new GC officer?"

"Temporarily, at least," Akinouye agreed. "He'll be delivering our cargo to the dig site when we arrive. We'll see how he handles the ride down." The general smirked.

"Good to have you aboard, Lieutenant." Pennington offered a delicate, bony hand that seemed like it might shatter if Podsy squeezed it too hard. "I trust you'll understand that I've isolated your station from my main computer core."

Podsy nodded, uncertain if the other man was taking a stab or being serious. "I promise not to mess with your systems." Podsy laughed. "I'm just glad to be aboard, Major."

Pennington seemed satisfied with his reply, and the trio moved to the *Zero's* command deck where twenty men and women were strapped into their stations. "General." Major Pennington gestured to the general's chair, which was wholly unlike the bare and simple one in the CAC.

The general's chair in the *Bonhoeffer's* CAC had no character or markings of any kind and was merely a perfect replica of Colonel Li's command throne. Podsy's first impression of Akinouye's CAC seat had been underwhelming. It had seemed so cold. So totally lifeless.

This chair, on the other hand, was anything but lifeless. Adorned with all manner of decals, graffiti, hashes, and other tokens earned in battle, each one was a reminder of a specific achievement in General Akinouye's storied career. Hashes for kills, decals for engagements, and graffiti for operations successfully completed. It looked like something Podsy would have expected to see in a bad military holo-vid, or possibly even in an ill-conceived man-cave, not in the nerve center of the most powerful armored vehicle built by Terran hands.

As General Benjamin Akinouye assumed his seat, surrounded by the vivid images of flaming skulls, mushroom clouds, bloody swords, and the like, Podsy gained a newfound appreciation for the man. He was a brilliant strategist and legendary leader, but before anything else, the man was a warrior.

Akinouye swiveled his chair toward Podsy, and a smile spread across his lips. "Some things never get old, Lieutenant Podsednik. Smoking a fine cigar. Devouring the lines of a lover's body. Closing your eyes and savoring a shredding guitar solo. But *none* of them," his smile turned predatory, "compares to riding into battle."

"I couldn't agree more, sir. I miss this part," Podsy said as he assumed his station. The general's enthusiasm had completely infected Podsy, and everyone else in the *Zero's* command center was quite clearly under the same spell.

"Drop stations!" Akinouye's voice cracked like a peal of thunder, causing the compartment's lights to switch to dim blue as technicians sprang into action. "And somebody queue up the music. The *Zero* doesn't drop without *The Number of the Beast*, followed by the *Immigrant Song*." He made eye contact with Podsy and added, "Call me a poser, but I prefer the little-known Demons & Wizards cover of the latter to the original."

"No argument there, General," Podsy concurred, having familiarized himself with D&W's work while aboard the *Elvira*. "But in my opinion, Iron Maiden needs no revision."

"Good man." The general grinned as the opening monologue of *The Number of the Beast* came over the speakers.

The Terran Armor Corps had a special affinity with all kinds of metal, and it was in no small part a gesture of defiance. During Earth's mid-twenty-first century, after World War Three had ravaged the planet and left China and its allies as humanity's most powerful civilization, Chinese psycho-social engineers had discovered that certain musical styles and instruments resonated differently with different socio-ethnic groups.

One of their supposed findings was a connection between the instruments most commonly associated with heavy metal (electric guitar, bass guitar, and fast-paced drums) and Western individualistic behavior.

It hadn't taken the dwindling Western nations' military forces long to recognize a rallying cry when it presented itself. In open defiance of censors who sought to restrict access to music of that type, as well as restricting production of those specific instruments, Western servicemen of all ethnic backgrounds adopted metal as their favored form of music. As a result, somewhat unpredictably, the production of such music declined while appreciation for it skyrocketed, imprinting an indelible cultural mark on the men and women who would eventually found the Terran colonies.

The West ultimately lost the war to the East on Earth, which only served to increase the significance of heavy metal in communities of Western ethnic or ideological descent. So when a Terran officer blared heavy metal on the battlefield, he did so knowing that many of his forebears had done likewise in their last moments as they stood tall in defiance of oppression.

Many thought the 'Metal Works' movement, as it came to be known, was a cleverly-conceived Western propaganda maneuver, but metal's significance had long since gone past the point of fact-checking being able to reverse impact. Like the myth that carrots improve eyesight, which was conceived by British intelligence agents to conceal their development and use of radar, Metal Works had taken deep root in Terran culture. It had become tradition, and tradition was especially sacred to Armed Forces personnel.

The fact that the Armor Corps' nickname was "Metal Legion" only served to emphasize this particular tradition, much to its servicemen's ongoing delight.

"Ready to deploy, General," Major Pennington declared after connecting with the *Bahamut Zero* via neural linkage.

The last hiss of Iron Maiden's *The Number of the Beast* sounded across the speakers, and in the brief silence between tracks General Akinouye boomed, "Drop the hammer, Major."

"Dropping," Pennington acknowledged, and the *Bahamut Zero* fell away from the *Bonhoeffer* and began its descent to the Brick's rust-red surface.

Immigrant Song's opening riff filled the command center at a steady gallop, followed by the signature cry of the song's vocalist. In those first seconds, Podsy's station began feeding him sparse information from the Legion forces assembled at the Gash. The *Zero's* powerful sensor suite was able to reach a thousand kilometers from this altitude, and soon he made a positive ID on twenty-five of the Legion's vehicles.

But those same scans returned eighty-four Finjou vehicles, which were moving to surround the Gash at a thankfully measured pace of just under sixty kilometers per hour. A race of natural flyers, the Finjou were unrivaled in aerial combat but left plenty to be desired in their ground-based platforms. And given the Brick's incredibly thin atmosphere, the only aircraft that could operate were those capable of both aerial and void operations. The latest intel on the Finjou suggested they had a surprising blind spot in that particular facet of their arsenal, with few multi-role fighter craft.

That wasn't to say they were without aerospace fighters, but it was probable that Terran tech was superior in that particular arena. And as the *Bahamut Zero* plunged toward the Brick's surface, where it would be cut off from support and isolated from the rest of the Legion, Podsy knew the Terran Armor Corps would need every edge it could get.

"Deploying wings in ten seconds," reported the *Zero's* Wing

Control officer, who looked so focused on her duties that she might have actually killed someone for interrupting her.

Everyone in the cabin took mouthguards out of their pockets and bit down on them *hard*. Podsy followed suit, leaning his head back against his headrest in preparation for what was to come.

"Wings deployed," the WC officer declared, and the *Zero* shuddered as the drop-wings unfurled. "Braking in three...two...one..." she called in a raised voice. "Braking!"

The platform's braking rockets engaged, snapping everyone against their headrests. The *Zero* was always dropped stern-forward to help cope with the shock-forces associated with braking and landing by keeping everyone's heads from snapping forward.

Sweat rolled down the WC officer's temples as her fingers flew in the virtual interface before her, twisting and manipulating a dozen different systems faster than Podsy could have ever managed. He had only seen Xi's fingers move that fast, and as he looked around the compartment, he suspected everyone present was at least as capable at their jobs, too.

The drop-wing's braking thrusters roared, raising the vehicle's gee forces past five as the thrusters increased their output. Everyone in the compartment wore pressure suits to counteract the tremendous forces and prevent blackouts. It was all Podsy could do to keep his teeth clamped down on the mouthguard as his vision narrowed, and a check of the altimeter and gees showed they were just two thousand meters from the surface and were decelerating at eight gees.

"Drop altitude in nine seconds," the WC officer called. "Prepare for separation."

The *Bahamut Zero*'s descent angle flattened as it reached the drop elevation of seven hundred meters. The thrusters cut out, ceasing the overpowering deceleration forces and making it possible for Podsy to breathe normally again, which he gratefully did since he knew the bumpiest part was yet to come.

He was glad to see most of the compartment's occupants shared his eagerness for one last pre-bump gulp of air, making him feel like not quite so much of a pansy. Everyone said that no unmodified human stayed awake for their first drop aboard the *Zero*, but Podsy was determined to be the first. He figured his new prosthetic legs gave him a chance since there was less room for his body's blood supply to drain away from his brain. Several of the *Zero*'s crew had undergone cybernetic nervous system augmentations specifically designed to deal with the severe forces at work, but most of the crew had no such implants.

"Detaching in three..." called the WC officer, whose post required her to have such augmentation, "two...one...detached!"

The *Zero* went from a relatively flat and peaceful two gees of deceleration to near-weightlessness. It was a peculiar sensation, and despite knowing beforehand that the drop would feature the bizarre moment, Podsy was still taken off-guard by the brief serenity in the seemingly endless assault.

Then the *Bahamut Zero*'s landing thrusters mercilessly kicked in.

Two seconds into the ultra-violent burn, and much to his eternal shame, Podsy blacked out and was unconscious for touchdown.

"Event horizon in five seconds," reported the *Red Hare*'s navigator.

Colonel Jenkins watched with the same measure of eager anticipation he felt during every gate transit. It was nothing short of miraculous that humans could traverse the vast distances between the stars via the gates, and he wanted to savor every moment to the utmost of his ability.

His mind turned to thoughts of his wife, and the last such moments they had shared. He had long since come to terms with the reality of why he was now alone, but that didn't make unbidden memories like the last smile she ever gave him any easier to survive.

The Nexus' gas giant vanished on the screen, replaced by the majestically-ringed planet in the same system where Dragon Brigade was deployed.

Jenkins pushed thoughts of his wife from his mind as reports began to stream into the *Red Hare*'s CAC.

He watched intently as the tactical plotter populated with icons and was relieved to see the *Dietrich Bonhoeffer's* icon still in orbit over the Brick.

But what came next was more than a little disconcerting.

"Four Talon-class Finjou warships in geo-synch over the deployment zone, Captain," reported the officer at Sensors. "*Bonhoeffer* is in low-orbit on intercept with Finjou formation."

"Are they in drop profile?" Captain Guan asked measuredly.

"I believe so, sir," acknowledged Sensors. "They have two fighter wings deployed. One wing is escorting the warship, the other... There it is," he declared, piping an image up to the secondary display.

Jenkins immediately recognized the *Bahamut Zero*'s drop-wing, its aero-foils collapsed back into its bulky frame as its rocket motors drove it to a rendezvous with the *Dietrich Bonhoeffer*. If the drop-wing made an emergency landing, recovering it would be an even more difficult task than retrieving the *Zero*. Retrieving it was therefore important but far from critical, which meant that fire had not yet been exchanged between Terran and Finjou forces.

Judging by the Finjou ground forces' posture as they moved to surround the dig site, Jenkins didn't expect either group's guns to remain silent for much longer.

"Colonel Jenkins?" Captain Guan cocked a fierce, thick eyebrow.

"The drop-wing," Jenkins gestured to the platform as it neared rendezvous with the *Bonhoeffer*, "deploys our flag vehicle, the *Bahamut Zero*. That means General Akinouye is planetside and moving to flank the Finjou in preparation for a major engagement."

Predictably, and much to Jenkins' approval, the CAC's various standers and officers stopped what they were doing and snapped looks between the drop-wing and Jenkins.

"Truly?" Captain Guan asked, stroking his thigh-length beard contemplatively before issuing a deep, hearty laugh which seemed both exuberant and contemptuous. "Excellent." His eyes flashed in eager anticipation as he activated his chair's comm panel. "Captain Chao, we will reach orbit in twenty-nine hours. Prepare for combat deployment under Colonel Jenkins' guidance."

"Acknowledged, Captain Guan," Chao replied. "Colonel Jenkins' vehicle is prepared and awaits his inspection."

Jenkins cocked a brow curiously, but Captain Guan didn't bother to explain as he stood from his chair and gestured to the blast doors. "Captain Chao and I have arranged a surprise for you. We hope it meets with your approval."

"I can't wait to see it," Jenkins said, feeling a thrill of anticipation as the reunion with his people was nearly at hand.

And it looked like it couldn't have come at a more urgent moment.

14

THE BIG DANCE

"This is *Elvira*," Xi said after accepting an inbound P2P call from the *Bahamut Zero*. "Go ahead."

"Havoc here," General Akinouye greeted her over the secure line. "You've done good work on this rock, Captain. Negotiating the rebels' surrender took guts and skill. It looks like Colonel Jenkins' eye for talent is almost as good as mine."

"Thank you, General," she acknowledged, immensely grateful that no one could see how deeply she blushed at the compliment. "We've assembled the evacuees into groups, but we can't bring them to the surface yet."

"How many are we talking, Captain?" Akinouye asked.

"Just over seven thousand, General," she replied heavily.

"It never rains but it pours," the general chuckled.

"Copy that, Havoc," she agreed. "They're under nearly two kilometers of rock, so unless the enemy brackets them with sustained orbital fire, they should be secure while we repurpose our drop-cans into refugee centers and bring them up in batches. The cans' air supply won't last for more than two days, but I'll make sure they're all up before the deadline, General."

"Perfect, Captain," Akinouye congratulated her.

"I'm forwarding the brigade's command codes and acknowledging your authority—" she began.

"Belay that, *Elvira*," General Akinouye rejected. "Your ass is stuck to that chair until *Roy* arrives and takes over. The *Zero* will deliver mission-critical supplies to the well, at which point we'll move to the northern slope and support Dragon from there. Seniority has a few perks, Captain," he said wryly, "and one of them is the ability to delegate tedious work like running a battalion to people who could use the practice. Unless you think *I* need to brush up on *my* command skills?"

"Negative, General," Xi deadpanned, suppressing a nervous laugh.

"Just keep doing what you've been doing, *Elvira*," Akinouye said firmly. "The Brick is yours; I wouldn't swoop in to steal the money after everything you've done. It's not proper. And judging by the movement I'm seeing up and down the Gash, you've got things well in hand. It looks like you were paying special attention to tactical theory in that abbreviated version of officer's school Jenkins sprinted you through."

"Roger, Havoc," Xi said with feeling, surprised at the general's sentiment and how he expressed it. "It's good to have you on the field."

"It's good to be here," Akinouye replied. Xi thought she could hear a riff from Judas Priest's *The Ripper* playing in the background. "Havoc out."

He cut the line, prompting Xi to raise Winters. "How are we coming over there, *Generally*?"

"The Mole Hill's nearly ready, Captain," replied Winters. She had tasked him with mounting mobile SRM launchers in a series of ravines that broke the surface of the small mountain twenty kilometers from the Gash's eastern end. "We should have this spot locked down in another forty minutes, and 8th and

9th Companies will have their embankments completed even sooner than that."

"Good to hear it," she acknowledged. "I'll need 3rd Company to hunker down in those wetlands to the north after you've set up. The Finjou closed the gap Havoc had slipped through as soon as he broke through their line. Those wetlands are crucial," she said intently, referring to a depression caused by a peculiar freeze-thaw cycle of the bed of ice that clung to the depression's floor. With an average depth of ten meters below the surrounded terrain, it provided much-needed cover from the Finjou's direct-fire weapons.

"Last Company will hold the low ground, Captain," Winters assured her. "We'll be ready when the party starts."

"Copy that, *Generally*," she said. "Good work." She switched over to Lieutenant Ford's direct line. "*Forktail, Elvira.* I need a status update."

"Captain Chao's people are ready to deploy on twelve seconds' notice, *Elvira*," Ford replied tersely.

"Tell them they can cool their heels for at least another hour," she urged. "The Finjou won't have us surrounded until then. Even fighter pilots need to recharge the batteries."

"I already told them, Captain." Ford sighed in exasperation. "They insist on remaining combat-ready throughout their deployment. I tell ya, these pilot types are bound up tighter than my last date's knees."

Xi chuckled. "The New Ukrainian judge gives that a six out of ten, *Forktail*."

"You mean I'm moving up in the world?" Ford quipped as the *Bahamut Zero* began to climb the southern slope far faster than any of her vehicles could manage. Its total power and the size of its extendable legs, which could either roll or walk as needed, allowed it to devour the scrabble-strewn slope like a nightmarish creature climbing up from the mouth of Hell.

It was a thoroughly satisfying and inspiring image.

"Don't read too much into an average scorecard, *Forktail*," Xi chided.

Ford chuckled. "I've already positioned 5th Company five klicks to the west on the Gash's floor. 6th Company is moving up the slope while I stay here with 4th Company to cover Captain Chow's people."

"Five by five, Lieutenant," Xi acknowledged. "Good work all around."

An alarm arose on her HUD as an urgent link request came in from *Blink Dog*. She accepted the request, already aware of what Blinky was about to say.

"Go ahead, *Blink Dog*," she acknowledged.

"Captain, the Finjou vehicle line is encroaching on our southern perimeter," Staubach reported. "Eight vehicles moving in formation have just crossed the fifty-kilometer line. Orders?"

"Stand down, *Blink Dog*," she urged. "I'll forward the info to the *Zero* and see if he can sweet talk these bird-brains into backing off, but I wouldn't get my hopes up. Fall back to the plateau two klicks to your three-thirty and hunker down. You should have plenty of cover there."

"Roger, Captain," Blinky acknowledged, and his quadrupedal recon-grade mech began to pull back as ordered. As he did so, she received high-res images and active telemetry of the enemy vehicles provided by Blinky's recorders. They were large but relatively light compared to the Terran mechs, with armor that was significantly less robust than anything the Terran military fielded.

But after dealing with the Jemmin on Shiva's Wrath, not to mention her disastrous experiments in cosmetics application during the torrent of interviews that had followed Ms. Samuels' glowing report on the Metal Legion, Xi knew that looks were usually deceiving.

There wasn't much in the telemetry that was unexpected, but she still forwarded the information to the *Bahamut Zero* as it sped toward the eastern end of the Gash, en route to a position on the north rim.

Normally Styles would have been her go-to guy for intel analysis, but she would have been a fool not to take advantage of the *Zero's* highly-skilled crew. Not to mention that pulling Styles off the recently-flagging TBM operation could very well prove disastrous to their primary objective.

"All right, you turkeys," Xi muttered as the rearmost member of the Finjou's eight-vehicle formation crossed the fifty-kilometer line. "Who's hungry?"

After his inspection of the 'surprise' in the drop-deck completed during the previous shift, Colonel Jenkins was once again in the *Red Hare's* CAC. Captain Guan was receiving real-time updates from the *Bonhoeffer* after Jenkins had provided Colonel Li with his credentials and verified that he was indeed aboard the *Red Hare*.

The latest of those updates made it clear that the Finjou had no intention of backing down.

"General Akinouye," Jenkins explained after reading the most recent missive from the *Bonhoeffer*, "has failed to establish a dialogue with the Finjou. Finjou ground forces have surrounded the Dragon Brigade and are now demanding the unconditional surrender of the rebel colonists who violated their sovereignty."

"The evacuation deadline is in eleven hours," Captain Guan mused. "We will not reach drop position for another sixteen."

"The general will argue that the colonists are asylum-seeking refugees," Jenkins replied, knowing that his speculation was meaningless, "and that they're under Terran protection. He'll also argue, truthfully, that once they're on the surface, their life support supplies will only hold out for a day. Two at the most," he amended after recalling just how many drop-cans the *Red Hare's* sensors had detected in the badly-scattered and uncharacteristic drop-zone. "I expect that means we'll exchange fire with the Finjou as soon as we make orbit. They won't want us to reinforce our planetary forces, which is precisely what we're going to do, and we can't waste any time since evacuating seven thousand people will take at least half a day in a hot landing zone. They'll maneuver to slow us down," Jenkins gestured to one of the Finjou Talons as it broke formation and moved to a position that would provide it optimal fire angles on the approaching *Red Hare*, "but I doubt they'll open fire until we begin evacuating the colonists. Then again," he added pointedly, "I'm not especially familiar with the intricacies of Finjou psychology."

"Fortunately, I am," Guan replied measuredly. "They would have sent dozens of warships here if they viewed this situation as one of vital interest to their security. They send a single Claw of Talons, which means either their strangely feudal society failed to muster sufficient resentment to the human presence here or, more likely, that this engagement is designed to inform their decision how to proceed with regard to the Terran Republic."

"They want to see how things unfold before committing?" Jenkins asked.

"Essentially," Guan agreed. "They are a purely carnivorous species, Colonel, and as a result view all engagements as one of two things: territorial disputes or hunts. A territorial dispute requires an overwhelming show of force to ensure success, while a hunt is conducted more methodically and with greater caution. It would appear that they consider this to be the latter, so they have sent a scouting party to make a raid while the rest of the flight looks on."

"Which suggests," Jenkins mused, "that they might not take too kindly to the *Red Hare* reinforcing the Legion forces already on the planet?"

Guan laughed, stroking his immaculate beard as he did so. "You do not understand. The purpose of the raid is to determine our response. They likely view the *Red Hare*'s arrival as part of your original plan, which means you will earn greater respect if you can successfully overcome their efforts. There, look," he urged, gesturing to a tactical representation of the planet's surface. "They are already flexing their western line in preparation for a flanking attack precisely like the one we discussed an hour ago."

Jenkins smirked. "Who'd have thought I'd end up being a gunpoint diplomat instead of a soldier?"

"To the Finjou," Guan observed. "those personae are one and the same. You must communicate to them in no uncertain terms the Terran Republic's ferocity and, perhaps more importantly, our resolve to complete what we begin. To fail on either count will make them view us as prey who stand ripe for the slaughter. Only after demonstrating our determination will we be able to negotiate. Only after defeating this raiding party can we depart this star system in peace."

Jenkins nodded in approval. "I can see you and I are going to have a lot to talk about, Captain Guan."

"Indeed," Guan agreed, inclining his head and giving a final stroke to his beard before clasping his hands behind his back and moving through the CAC to accept the reports of his various department heads.

Jenkins knew that men like Guan didn't grow on trees

(although they probably did grow in cans) and he also knew that he was lucky to have access to his knowledge.

He suspected that before the day was out, he would be equally fortunate to have him covering Clover Company from orbit.

"I'm glad to have you here, Lieutenant," Styles greeted him after Podsy had helped unload the mission-critical equipment from the *Zero*, which had torn up the Gash's southern slope. The sight of the mighty war machine was enough to send chills down Podsy's spine, and he knew that with Havoc covering the north face, Dragon Brigade would be well-protected on all sides. "The civvies know their gear, but they've been skittish since the nukes went off. We should have been through the last few hundred meters, but they slowed things down out of caution, and our primary focusing emitter cracked before we could cross the finish line. I'm hoping you can get this thing back up."

"I'm glad to be able to help, Chief," Podsy said truthfully from within his envirosuit. The suits were slightly claustrophobic, with only a small viewing window directly in front of the heavy helmet. "Let's get these replacements installed and punch through the remainder of this rock."

Styles led a team of the civilian excavators who carefully manipulated the replacement primary emitter pieces down the slope toward the giant beam emitter. Set on the stone of the Gash's floor, the drill assembly was a massive multi-emitter laser assembly. Stationed nearly two hundred meters from the point of entry, the system measured fifty meters long in all and looked far too delicate for Podsy's liking. Powered by a pair of fusion generators with maximum rated outputs of ten megawatts each, the drill was easily the highest-tech Terran laser system ever devised.

The primary emitter melted the rock and broke it into smaller boulders, which were then individually superheated by secondary emitters until the stone was liquefied. At that point, it flowed down the aggressively-angled tunnel, which pitched upward at just under twelve degrees. When the system was operating at full efficiency, over thirty cubic meters of molten stone flowed from the tunnel each minute. There was simply no better way, using Terran technology, to drill such lengthy passages into solid stone.

This particular tunnel measured two meters in diameter, although at the mouth, it was nearly twenty meters from top to bottom due to erosion from the passing, molten stone. The tunnel already stretched nearly thirty-five kilometers into the planet's crust and, at last estimate, was less than a kilometer from the end of the dig. During the first few kilometers of digging, there had been some fear that they would miss the target or, even worse, that there was nothing awaiting them in the subterranean target zone. But after five kilometers of seemingly natural stone had been cleared away, the composition of the rock wall became markedly different and clearly unnatural. At that point, they confirmed that the target information had been correct.

Huge excavators dug troughs that diverted the molten stone down the Gash and away from the dig site. While the system was digging, a team of workers had erected a giant set of scaffolding to create a ramp leading from the Gash's floor to the tunnel mouth. The scaffolding was ninety percent complete, but it could not be finished until the molten rock ceased to flow.

Podsy assisted Styles in directing the drill team to install the replacement primary emitter, which took surprisingly little time. The emitter assembly was open and easy to access for maintenance, with the old emitter having already been pulled. Replacing the system's beating heart took less than thirty minutes from start to finish, and soon the primary emitter was ready to fire. Throughout the replacement process, the secondary emitters had continued pulsing up the tunnel, keeping the temperature in the passage high enough for the molten stone to flow out onto the Gash's floor.

"Emitter diagnostics are green across the board," reported Mrs. Baldwin, the drill team leader. "We're ready to resume, Mr. Styles."

"Do it," Styles urged, and Podsy watched with no small measure of appreciation as the powerful laser system whined to life. The thin air around his suit crackled and popped as the primary emitter's invisible beams stabbed into the rock wall, each pulse accompanied by a perceptible thrum that faintly vibrated the ground beneath Podsy's feet.

Perfectly attenuated and aimed, the beam pulses struck the target patches of rock up the tunnel with surgical precision. Despite the secondary lasers' efforts, some of the flowing rock had cooled and slowed its descent through the tunnel during the primary emitter's downtime, but that rock was re-melted by the primary beam as it cleared the tunnel while continuing its work.

After a few minutes of the primary's operation, blobs of molten rock began to burp out of the tunnel. Burps grew into short-lived gushes, which in turn lengthened in duration until a continuous stream of molten rock once again flowed from the tunnel's two-meter-wide, twenty-meter-tall mouth forty meters above the Gash's floor.

"Crank it up, Baldwin," Styles urged. "The rangefinders show we've only got another five hundred meters of rock before we reach our objective."

"You heard the man," Baldwin barked. "Let's knock it out!"

The machine's whine grew to a steady roar, and the pulses

burned so frequently that Podsy was unable to distinguish the individual bursts from a continuous beam of energy. The flow of rock was deceptively consistent, if anything slowing as the drill bored farther into the Brick's skin. But that was a simple matter of physics; it would take nearly an hour for the rock from the farthest end of the tunnel to flow down into the Gash.

Right on schedule, an hour after the drill had resumed its work, the flow of molten rock sharply increased. The monitoring equipment showed twenty-five cubic meters of material flowing out of the tunnel every minute, and the excavation's support teams began working furiously to keep that molten rock flowing away from the tunnel with smaller plasma burners to further liquefy the waste material, and remote-operated mini-dozers to continually build up berms of slowly-solidifying rock that kept the channels flowing down the Gash and away from the dig site.

It was a smooth operation. Men and women like this were largely responsible for the Terran Republic's survival after the wormhole gates collapsed. Their fierce determination and single-minded focus on their craft, even with enemy warships circling overhead, was enough to make him proud to know he was their fellow Terran.

Three hours of steady digging, and finally the primary emitter's near-continuous pulses began to slow until they were firing no more than twice per second.

"The far wall gave out," Baldwin declared. "We've achieved penetration into a cavern of some kind."

"Good job, Mrs. Baldwin," Styles congratulated her. "Sergeant Major Trapper, bring our rides."

"The tunnel won't be safe to traverse for another twenty hours," Baldwin warned, "and that's assuming you brought along heat-resistant gear."

"We won't be hoofing it, Mrs. Baldwin," Styles assured her before turning to Podsy and switching to a secure suit-to-suit link. "The general gave orders that you were to accompany the insertion team."

Podsy's brows rose in surprise. "I wasn't aware of that."

"You can verify the orders," Styles handed Podsy a hardened slate, and sure enough, Podsy found the general's orders that he was to accompany Chief Styles and a hand-picked quad of Trapper's best people. "The general must like you," Styles said with open amusement.

Podsy grinned. "To send me thirty-five klicks down a hot tunnel? It might not be the best thing to be on his good side. I think I gave him cover to do what he wanted to do all along, which was come down here and dig his heels in against the enemy. I don't think Colonel Li appreciated it. That sounds like two strikes."

"For every friend made, an acquired enemy," Styles snickered. "He's a big boy. He'll get over it."

"I hope so," Podsy said sincerely as Sergeant Major Trapper's people drove an APC down to the dig site. The APC was far too large to fit into the tunnel, but when its rear door opened Podsy was unable to resist a smile from spreading across his face.

Six identical vehicles appeared—honest-to-God motorcycles, albeit heavily-modified ones.

"Graphene-reinforced tires and a shielded undercarriage will protect them from the occasional brush with liquid rock." Styles chuckled as Podsy moved to inspect the sleek low-profile vehicles, which featured flat cone-shaped windshields that stretched back, "and heat-resistant two-piece containment pods that will protect us from the heat while we ride. The capacitors are good for twenty hours of continuous max-output operation, and these things are capable of two hundred kph at full throttle."

"These things must cost more than I'd make in a lifetime,"

Podsy said in unvarnished awe, sliding his gloved hand over one of the bikes' sleek chassis as Trapper's people produced the second part of the bikes' containment pods, to be installed after a rider mounted the bike.

"It's a safe bet," Styles agreed as Trapper and his four hand-picked men appeared. Armed to the teeth, they stood in stark contrast to Styles, who checked a pack full of comm and data-processing gear that rested inside the APC, but it was clear from his dress and pose that Trapper would not be accompanying them up the tunnel. "The crew should have the tunnel cleared of molten debris in the next hour and a half, and the ramp should be done about fifteen minutes after that.

The sergeant major gestured to Podsy's sidearm. "I'd recommend a little more weight, Lieutenant." One of Trapper's men retrieved a rifle from the APC and handed it to Podsednik.

Podsy nodded, accepting the weapon before checking it under the watchful eye of Sergeant Major Trapper. What would have taken a Pounder four-and-a-half seconds took Podsy seven, but when he was finished he saw a satisfied smirk on Trapper's face through the other man's visor.

"The rust comes off with a little practice," Trapper told him.

Just under two hours later, with the flow of molten rock now a trickle and the ramp finished, two of Trapper's men took point while Styles and Podsy assumed the third and fourth slots in the six-man-formation, which was brought up by the third and fourth of Trapper's men. The bikes surged up the blistering perfectly-cylindrical tunnel in a race to retrieve whatever it was they had come for.

Which, as far as Podsy was concerned, was still a complete mystery.

15

SHOTS FIRED

"Shots fired!" the *Red Hare*'s Sensor operator reported in a raised but steady voice. "Finjou warships have engaged the *Dietrich Bonhoeffer* with direct energy weapons."

Jenkins' eyes snapped up to the tactical display, which showed three Finjou warships in a classic offset-triad formation. Their direct energy weapons were high-powered lasers, and they were stabbing into the *Bonhoeffer's* robust armor as the Metal Legion flagship returned fire with railguns and a swarm of missiles.

The *Red Hare*'s status screen, a three-dimensional image of the warship set beneath the main tactical viewer, suddenly flared to life. Its forward armor began flashing yellow rather than its previous serene pale-blue.

"Two direct hits, Captain," *Red Hare*'s Damage Control reported as the flashing yellow stabilized into solid yellow. "Forward armor is holding; moving replacement panels into position."

Jenkins' brows rose. Captain Guan noticed his surprise. "This ship features two armor-compensation systems, Colonel," the ruddy-faced officer explained. "The first is a standard emergency system that floods the damaged armor compartments with mimetic gel. The second is more proactive and allows us to replace individual panels, which are nearly all of a modular design."

As he spoke, a holo-image of what looked like two crab-shaped drones appeared on a magnified view of the *Red Hare*'s forward hull. Each drone carried a two-meter-thick panel of composite armor, which was the best defensive system presently available to the Terran Republic. The crab-drones replaced two of the worst-damaged panels on the *Red Hare*'s armored prow. The old panels were ejected into the void less than a second before the new panels were slotted in place and secured via spring-bolts.

"Impressive." Jenkins nodded approvingly. "More gifts from the Vorr?" he asked pointedly.

"No." Guan chuckled, stroking his beard haughtily. "These are the work of Terra Han's finest engineers. They are prototypes, of course," he added with a mischievous grin, "and must undergo rigorous testing before my world presents them to the Terran Fleet."

Jenkins nodded in complete understanding. The more he learned about Terra Han, the more concerned he became about its standoffishness when it came to the rest of the Terran Republic.

"Time to effective firing range on Talon Four?" Guan asked languidly, referring to the lone Finjou warship which had flanked out for one-on-one combat with the *Red Hare*.

"On our current trajectory," Tactical replied, "*Red Hare* will not achieve an effective firing solution, Captain."

"Most unfortunate," Captain Guan said with patently false concern, relishing the moment. The men and women around the CAC leaned imperceptibly into their workstations in eager anticipation. "Then we have no choice but to improvise. Tactical, you are authorized to deploy the Starburst system. Helm, cease braking thrust and come about in Starburst maneuver."

"Starburst maneuver, aye," acknowledged the neural-linked pilot of the ship, and the warship gently spun around them. The CAC was situated almost precisely at the ship's center, which made the apparent rotational forces much less than those closer to the outer hull. The severity of the maneuver was still enough to give Jenkins a brief bout of vertigo.

"Starburst deploying," Tactical acknowledged with gusto as soon as the ship had reoriented, and the *Red Hare*'s holoimage underwent a radical change to its stern section. Twelve huge sections of the hull folded outward like the petals of a flower unfurling to greet the morning sun, and a dozen distinct launch tubes suddenly flared into being behind those panels. "Starburst system online, Captain," reported Tactical. "Talon Four targeted. Awaiting firing order."

Captain Guan replied with a heavy sigh as he assumed his command chair, "Full salvo. Fire."

"Full salvo, aye," acknowledged Tactical, and the dozen previously-hidden launch tubes flickered green as giant missiles appeared within them. "Firing!"

As one, the twelve missiles fell away from the ship, seeming to drift outward in a perfect circle before their thrusters ignited and they burned toward the lone Talon-class warship that had fired on the *Red Hare*.

The missiles surged forward as one, moving faster than any similar Terran platform with which Jenkins was familiar could have. The enemy warship, Talon Four, opened fire and scrubbed two of the twelve missiles with precise laser strikes.

Captain Guan's air of haughty disdain seemed to grow as the missiles devoured the void between them and their target. Acknowledging the threat, the Finjou warship adjusted posture to evasive and lashed out with another pair of strikes, which tore two more missiles from the void.

"Eight platforms still on target," reported Tactical. "Entering optimal firing range."

"Fire when ready," Guan intoned, and the eight remaining missiles suddenly flew apart in a shower of new signals. Twenty smaller warheads tore loose from each larger missile's exploded chassis, so instead of eight targets to evade, the enemy warship now had a hundred and sixty to contend with.

Forty of those smaller missiles flashed before disappearing from the board, and Jenkins suspected he knew what had just happened.

"Forty beams," reported Tactical with a note of satisfaction, "thirty-one strikes. Enemy drive system is fluctuating. Firing!"

Talon Four's drive system failed for what would likely have been less than two seconds, but that brief window was all it took the *Red Hare*'s remaining 'Starburst' of one hundred and twenty fusion-powered laser missiles to reach the target, stabbing into the vessel in perfect unity.

The enemy ship's reactor failed, and the vessel exploded in a rapidly-expanding cloud of glittering debris. Less than twenty percent of the original vessel remained intact after its death throes, and that hunk of glowing material tumbled end-over-end against the starry backdrop of interplanetary space.

"Talon Four neutralized," Tactical reported.

Jenkins knew that fusion-powered missiles were extremely expensive. That the *Red Hare* had been outfitted with them and her captain had deployed them as weapons of first resort was yet another indication that Jenkins had done far better in his negotiations with Chairman Kong than he had initially surmised.

"Remaining Finjou warships are repositioning," Tactical reported with relish. "*Dietrich Bonhoeffer* is taking advantage with missile fire. Time to *Bonhoeffer* weapons impact: two minutes."

"The hunters fear they have become the hunted," Guan declared in a cold voice. "They have superior range and speed, but we have superior armor and, to their mind, superior firepower."

Jenkins took that last bit to suggest that their supply of laser warheads was limited, but the *Red Hare*'s arrival on the field had been expertly conducted by its captain. Commanding an undocumented ship that wielded overwhelming firepower during its first attack, Captain Guan had infected the enemy with one of the most dangerous forces known to any battlefield: doubt.

With doubt, the enemy ceded initiative. With initiative, the aggressor could turn the tide of battle.

Battles were won in the preparation, and part of that preparation was understanding the enemy's capabilities. It was stupid to charge into a coin-flip situation, as well as potentially deadly.

Captain Guan had just erased the enemy's confidence with a single maneuver, knocking them off the balls of their feet and putting them back on their heels.

And as the *Red Hare* came about to resume its deceleration on approach to the Brick, Jenkins' appreciation for the man's skill and field vision grew a full measure.

The *Bonhoeffer*'s missile swarm surged toward the trio of Finjou warships, which had adjusted their postures to avoid a similar fate to that of their fallen comrade. They sniped two-thirds of the Terran missiles from the void with expert counter-fire, but the *Bonhoeffer*'s CO proved himself every bit the tactical equal of Captain Guan as his missile wave slammed into the lightly-armored Finjou ships.

All three of the enemy warships were damaged, but two resumed their previous maneuvering while the third lagged behind its fellows. The *Bonhoeffer's* six capital-grade railguns, its most potent kinetic weapons systems, spat bolts of hypervelocity tungsten at the lagging warship, which would have easily avoided the relatively sluggish bolts had its engines been online.

Terran capital-grade railguns were capable of accelerating their projectiles through the void at speeds up to $0.03c$, making them terrifyingly effective. With potential delivered force equal to a megaton per strike, the *Bonhoeffer's* railguns were the most advanced long-range systems in the TAF's arsenal. Only the Republican-class mass drivers were more devastating at ranges beyond those at which missiles could effectively engage.

Half of the *Bonhoeffer's* railgun bolts missed, streaking off into the void where they would cool, darken, and silently continue their journey across the cosmos until they struck something or, more likely, until the universe suffered its own inevitable heat death. But the rest stabbed into the damaged warship and authored explosions up and down its hull. Those explosions seemed to cease after a few seconds, but eventually life pods streamed from its hull and the ship's reactor went critical, likely due to intentional overload, scuttling the ship once it was deemed unsalvageable.

"Enemy warships are moving off," Tactical reported. "They're sending retrieval craft to collect the life pods."

"Transmit on standard hailing frequencies that we will not fire on them during rescue operations," Guan declared with another disdainful sigh.

"*Dietrich Bonhoeffer* is transmitting a similar message, Captain," the comm stander said promptly.

"The *Bonhoeffer* has significant damage to its forward hull, Captain," Sensors reported. "They're showing engine damage and are leaking breathable gases."

"Inform *Bonhoeffer* Actual we will deploy our mechs and assume a support posture as needed," Captain Guan replied before swiveling his chair toward Jenkins. "It would appear our drop window has just been opened, Colonel Jenkins. We will be in position to deploy Clover Battalion in four hours and six minutes."

"We'll be ready," Jenkins said with a confident nod, knowing that for the first time in years, he would be directly linked to his own mech during combat instead of relying on Chaps. Chaps was the better Jock, but Jenkins would have been lying if he'd denied that he was eagerly anticipating the chance to clear his own guns.

He checked the planetary sensor feeds and felt his heart catch in his throat at the staggering amount of fire being exchanged down there.

His people needed him—perhaps now more than ever—but for the moment all he could do was sit back and watch the battle unfold.

16

XI BAO, GODDESS OF WAR

The sky above *Elvira* was a special circle of hell, ablaze with the clash of weapons hundreds of meters above the Brick's surface. Waves of inbound enemy missiles were intercepted by Trapper's dug-in defensive platforms and the constantly-moving mechs of Dragon Brigade. The conflagration was equally glorious and terrifying.

Thousands of rounds of intercepting fire pierced the sky, scrubbing dozens of missiles and sending their wreckage to the rust-colored surface in a seemingly endless rain of shrapnel. Each of the incoming missiles was powerful enough to destroy all but the mightiest mechs in the brigade or to kill a fortified nest and its team of Pounders. Every shot counted, every position was vital, and every Terran on the Brick acted like they were part of a single vicious, insatiable engine of war with Captain Xi Bao at its head.

Xi had never felt so alive in her entire life.

"Permission to activate the Mole Hill," requested Winters as 3rd Company's mechs engaged inbound missiles with counterfire.

"Negative, *Generally*," Xi replied as she cleared *Elvira's* guns on a four-vehicle Finjou formation to the south, which was part of the same group *Blink Dog* had reported crossing the line earlier. "Hold the Mole Hill until they've put birds in the air."

"Incoming fire density is getting heavy," Winters said tersely, and she didn't need to look at the feeds to know he was right. She could *feel* it almost subconsciously as she processed the incoming streams of information. It had nothing to do with the neural linkage, and everything to do with peripheral awareness. For the first time in her life, Xi Bao was *one* with the battlefield. "They're going to start sneaking some through, Captain," he added grimly.

"Understood, Lieutenant," she said tightly, bracketing a second four-vehicle formation with eight SRMs and loosing them from *Elvira's* tubes. "You have your orders."

"Copy that," Winters acknowledged coldly as his people shot missile after missile from the sky. The enemy understood the importance of the lowlands where 3rd Company had dug in just as well as Xi did and had diverted fully half its arsenal toward Winters' position. Winters' mechs scrambled in seemingly erratic patterns, evading what little artillery and 'dumbfire' came their way.

Elvira's artillery shells struck the ground in front of their targets, but both were near-misses that caused significant damage to the lightly-armored vehicles. Thus far, none of the Finjou ground vehicles had opened fire with anything bigger than anti-personnel weaponry, which only served to amplify her concern. She was beginning to think they either carried nukes or some form of knife-range-only weaponry she did not want to let into range.

Her SRMs slammed home, faring better than the artillery strikes with two of the eight missiles cratering their targets and two more near-missing to devastating effect.

The first enemy missile touched down on Winters' position,

near-missing *Cleaver* close enough to scorch the battlewagon's paint. A second missile went wider, throwing a shower of dust and debris onto Winters' company-command mech, *Generally*.

But the third to land struck true, annihilating the flat-bodied quadrupedal recon-grade *Gecko,* leaving only its stern quarter intact.

Trapper's people sent a dozen outbound SRMs streaking toward a distant enemy formation. The missiles were mostly intercepted by those vehicles' counterfire, but one snuck through and eliminated an enemy vehicle in a shower of molten debris.

On the southern quadrant of the field, *Blink Dog* was still hunkered down behind the plateau Xi had ordered it toward. He had a clear line of sight on the two remaining vehicles from the formation she had struck with her SRMs, and his voice predictably came over the line. "Requesting permission to engage Targets Two-Two and Two-Three, Captain."

"Negative, *Blink Dog*," she replied shortly, pausing mid-sentence to clear her guns on the flagging vehicles. "I've got them. Stay in cover until I call you out."

"Acknowledged," Blinky said, his voice taut with eager anticipation.

"Captain Xi." Ford's voice crackled in her ear. "I've got Captain Chow confirming status."

"Confirmed, *Forktail*," Xi called down as the first enemy missiles touched down nearby, hammering an anti-missile nest manned by four Pounders. "I'll call for him when he's needed. These birdbrains haven't made a serious move for second base yet. We're still just necking. Hold fast."

Another enemy missile impacted, this one near-missing a missile battery. Heedless of their near-death experience, that battery's crew sent four anti-missile rockets streaking skyward. Two of them intercepted more inbound ordnance.

The initial wave passed, which meant a second wave was imminent. Her people had done well, but it was far from over. One of the last Finjou missiles to touch down wrecked *Grasshopper*, a recon mech assigned to 2nd Company. Surprisingly the crew reported in as alive a few seconds after their mech died.

Two dozen icons appeared on the edge of *Elvira's* sensor range, streaking in at speeds exceeding two thousand kilometers per hour. This was it: they were bypassing second and heading straight for third with a devastating aerial strike.

"All right, fuckers," Xi snarled, "my turn." She raised the aerospace fighter commander. "Captain Chow, intercept inbound bogeys."

No sooner had she uttered the last syllable than eight of Chow's aerospace fighters' engines ignited beneath them. Pointed skyward like rockets, which was precisely how they had landed after transferring from the *Bonhoeffer* to the Brick's surface, the sleek aerospace fighters lifted off and raced to intercept the enemy craft.

The aerospace fighters, which were versatile enough to operate in either void or atmospheric conditions, would need to rely almost completely on their rocket motors for thrust.

Judging by the inbound Finjou craft profile, they were driving their birds at max burn too, which meant that Chow's people might have a slight but tactically significant edge in maneuverability.

Xi switched to a channel specifically linked to only those mechs with railguns. "Railroaders, charge your capacitors but hold fire until your solutions are greater than ninety percent. Let Chow and his people make the first pass," she instructed, her thumb wavering on the launch control for the last six of her Blue Boy interceptor missiles. "We'll clean up the rest."

The Finjou were an avian species that heavily emphasized

aerial superiority in all recorded engagements. Their ground forces were mostly for support and cleanup, which meant that the encroaching vehicles she and her people were still bracketing were likely not the main attack.

Those two dozen inbound bogeys, on the other hand, probably packed enough firepower to end the battle in a single pass.

She noted that *Bahamut Zero*, aside from adding to the general interceptor fire, had not yet engaged the enemy. A greater show of support she could not imagine receiving than to have the most decorated warrior in the Metal Legion stand down while she conducted the battle.

Chow's fighters sped off, breaking into four pairs as they neared intercept range. The inbound bogeys responded with a perfectly choreographed split-wing maneuver, breaking into four sub-groups of their own.

The icon representing *Sam Kolt* flashed, and Xi's tactical readout populated with the report of weapons fire. A bolt of pure Terran fury leapt from the *Kolt's* capital-grade railgun, vaporizing a pair of inbound bogeys with what was probably the luckiest and best-laid shot Xi would ever witness in realtime.

Xi was about to reprimand him for firing before Chow's people, but the *Sam Kolt*'s Jock preempted her. "Targeting solution was 185%, Captain. I couldn't hold back."

"We'll meet after class, *Gunslinger*," Xi quipped, making the Jock's new callsign official by using it in battle. By any reasonable measure, he'd just earned it twice over.

Then Captain Chow's people engaged the inbound fighter craft and the entire first exchange was decided in one-point-two seconds.

Armed with a pair of railguns each, Chow's pilots spat sixteen bolts of superheated tungsten at the inbound bogeys. Each went to a different target, and of the sixteen bolts, just five struck true while the rest missed the rolling, twisting enemy aircraft.

In reply, the Finjou unleashed a storm of precise laser fire that tore into the thin fuselages of the Viper-class fighters. Five of the Vipers were struck and two splashed outright, with the other three breaking formation. That left just three of Chow's fighters on-target as they entered knife-range, and those Terran aircraft unleashed a hail of ninety micro-rockets at the inbound fighters.

With the human craft twisting, rolling, looping and otherwise taking full advantage of the lateral thrust afforded them by their atmospheric engines, they almost totally avoided the second wave of counterfire. Almost, but not quite. One of the three Vipers went into a tailspin, its pilot ejecting less than a second before her craft exploded against the endless sea of rust-red dust.

Then the Terran micro-rockets arrived with devastating force.

The Finjou countermeasures were exceptional, sniping sixty-eight of the ninety rockets from the air. But the remaining twenty-two slammed home, scrapping twelve of the remaining twenty-two Finjou craft as the enemy birds finally reached optimal railgun range.

Twenty-one railguns roared at the ten Finjou aircraft, sending hypervelocity projectiles skyward at the precise moment the Finjou dropped eight missiles apiece. Four of the enemy craft were sniped by railgun fire, while the remaining six pulled up and burned for low orbit.

"Oh no, you don't," Xi growled, activating a special link-up that the *Zero's* technicians had completed for her less than an hour earlier.

Six of the original thirty-nine fortified installations DuPont's people had built on this hemisphere remained after the combined Terran-Finjou effort to remove them, but each of those six was armed with four low-orbit-capable interceptor missiles, which Xi primed for launch with the flick of a switch. Three seconds later those missiles erupted from the ground, burning toward the fleeing Finjou fighters.

Rising skyward, the first of the interceptor missiles would take two minutes to reach their fleeing targets, which made them less than effective at their designed purpose. Xi didn't need them to *hit* their targets, though. She just needed them to press the Finjou skyward, where they would come under the *Bonhoeffer's* guns if they didn't turn back and risk her battalion's ground-fire.

She switched her focus back to the inbound flight of eighty enemy missiles, which set off a series of alarms as the Terran sensors picked up indications that there were tactical nukes among those warheads.

Xi switched to *Generally's* direct line and barked, "Activate the Mole Hill!"

"Mole Hill active," he acknowledged. A second later, three hundred anti-missile rockets tore loose from their moorings, on target for the inbound warheads.

The interception would be close, but the entire engagement had been a close-run affair. If just one of the Finjou's standard twenty-kiloton nukes slipped through, it could potentially destroy a handful of her mechs outright. She had spread her people out to minimize the effect of such weapons, but the broken terrain made it difficult to remain in mutually-supporting positions while also maintaining defensive separation.

"Anti-missile weapons free," Xi commanded in a raised voice over the battalion-wide. "Fire! Fire! Fire!"

Xi sent eight of *Elvira's* anti-missile rockets out to join the Mole Hill's formidable wave of counterfire, and throughout the brigade, the Legionnaires did likewise, including the *Bahamut Zero* from the north face. All told, 634 anti-missile rockets streaked through the Brick's tortured, smoke-filled atmosphere to meet the Finjou warheads.

When the first nuke erupted overhead, the world around Xi's neural-linked senses exploded into absolute chaos. After a brief moment of overwhelming feedback, *Elvira's* neural link cut out, leaving Xi disoriented and gasping for air for reasons not immediately apparent to her.

Then she realized what had happened; one of the enemy's tactical nukes had touched off on the patch of the southern slope where *Elvira* was stationed. Her mech's systems resumed their previous input feeds, and Xi was relieved to see that no permanent damage had been inflicted on the venerable mech.

White Wizard and *Leatherhead*, however, had been totally annihilated by the blast, which left nothing but a shrapnel-strewn crater to mark their passing.

A frantic check of the converted drop-cans that housed the rebel colonists filled Xi with relief when she saw that while they had been on the edge of the blast zone, the cans had suffered no serious damage from the strike.

Xi saw that another pair of nukes had gone off a few hundred meters above the surface, and the EMPs they had generated had knocked several of the lower-technology mechs' main systems offline. Her attention immediately snapped to the airborne Finjou craft, which seemed to have decided that taking their chances with the *Bonhoeffer* was their best bet. Xi had received damage reports from the assault carrier, and it seemed their weaponry had been all but knocked offline. They were having difficulty maintaining station due to engine troubles. She couldn't count on them to engage the fleeing fighters and, worse yet, it was possible those fighters still packed enough firepower to do serious damage to the already battered warship.

Then, just as she had hoped, the enemy fighters broke formation and peeled back like the skin of a banana. Their new course brought them toward the Brick's surface again, where they would attempt to evade the inbound interceptors head-on instead of testing the Metal Legion's flagship.

Before the Finjou had the chance to accelerate out of their turns, the Legion's ground-based railguns fired in unison, tearing three of the six remaining fighters from the sky and leaving the other three in a panicked flight for their lives.

Which was precisely what Captain Chow and his wingman ended after acquiring target lock with their railguns.

Four railgun bolts sliced through the three remaining Finjou fighters, wiping the sky clean of the enemy aircraft.

"Dragon Actual, this is Wasp One," Captain Chow's voice came over the line as two of his fighter craft returned to the floor of the Gash. "We have established air supremacy. Wasp One and Wasp Six are bingo fuel. We're putting down twenty-two klicks south of your position. We have six hours of life support."

"Roger, Wasp One," Xi acknowledged as the pair of aerospace fighters made emergency landings. "I've got a vehicle in your region, but we'll need to cut a path for him first."

"Take your time, *Elvira*," Captain Chow replied.

Xi switched to the battalion-wide. "All crews, this is the captain." She felt a thrill of anticipation as she saw that the encroaching Finjou vehicles had broken and were withdrawing at best speed, so it was with unmasked relish that she gave the next order. "Acknowledge readiness for Heaven Denies formation."

Acknowledgments flickered across her HUD, showing that only three of the twenty-eight vehicles assigned to counter-charge Heaven Denies were down-checked.

Twenty-five is more than enough, she thought fiercely as she queued up Demons & Wizards' track of the same name as the counterattack.

"Execute Heaven Denies countercharge on my order," she declared as the shredding metal track filled *Elvira's* cabin. "Charge!"

Mechs of the Metal Legion leaped out of their foxholes, easily clearing the ridges behind which they had taken cover from the enemy's direct-fire weapons.

Elvira was not the fastest mech on the field and the Finjou vehicles were capable of out-pacing her, but her position gave her the unique ability to address both the southern and western approaches. Both of which were rich with fleeing Finjou vehicles, only one of which Xi intended to fire on.

The Legion had a surprise in store for the Finjou on the western front.

The guns of Dragon Brigade thundered toward the south, dropping shell after shell in the midst of the fleeing Finjou. A handful of direct hits preceded a wave of near-misses, some of which saw Finjou track-based vehicles crash into fresh craters with devastating effect.

Xi sent HE shells downrange to the south while leading her mechs to the west at top speed. Near-misses were all she could manage as the enemy vehicles began evasive maneuvers, zig-zagging erratically to avoid the indirect fire of the Terran artillery.

"*Blink Dog*," she raised the Recon mech as her fellow Terrans delivered vengeance to the fleeing enemy, "rendezvous with Vipers One and Six and return them to the airfield at the bottom of the Gash. I'll clear a path for you."

"Acknowledged, Captain," Blinky replied, and the quadrupedal Recon mech sprang into action, galloping across the open field toward the downed pilots.

"Nuke *me*, will you?" Xi sneered while loading eight SRMs

into *Elvira*'s launchers. She bracketed the Finjou vehicles nearest the downed pilots and loosed her vengeance upon the enemy. Her missiles split the sky above the fleet-footed *Blink Dog*, cratering three of the five Finjou targets and causing the others to drastically alter course away from the stranded pilots of Viper Squadron.

Metal Legion artillery thundered, Terran missiles burned, and human-built railguns lanced into the enemy vehicles' sterns across the entire southern front. Of the original sixty-one Finjou vehicles which had come from that direction, only twenty-two managed to survive the Terran counter-charge long enough to reach a relatively safe distance. Had Xi and her people wanted, they could have easily slaughtered every last one of the southern vehicles.

But that was not her objective, because at that moment, high above the Legion's mechs, a mysterious Terran-built warship was about to deploy reinforcements far to the west.

Which meant that if she and her people did their jobs, Xi Bao had just set up what might prove to be the most intense pincer attack in the Metal Legion's history.

On the northern face of the Gash, the *Bahamut Zero* sprinted westward, its formidable arsenal largely silent as Xi's people herded the enemy along the southern slope toward their inevitable doom at the western end of the Gash. The Metal Legion had weathered the initial storm, minimized what could have been devastating losses, and turned the tide on their would-be killers. The Legion's expert deployment of its resources had thwarted the enemy's aerial attack, leaving the Finjou ground forces in total disarray.

It was time to tear their throats out.

17

CRY HAVOC

Riding the aptly-named Razorback Mk. 2-V mech *Warcrafter*, Colonel Lee Jenkins conducted his first-ever drop behind enemy lines in a live-fire zone.

His first-ever drop without the aid of a drop-can, for that matter.

With its legs folded precisely beneath it, the *Warcrafter* fell to the Brick behind an ablative conical heat shield which was secured by the mech's four legs. Can-less drop systems had been experimented with and even used a century or so earlier, but ultimately, they had been deemed too risky. One in a hundred mechs failed to survive a can-less drop, despite Armor Corps' best precautions.

But the *Red Hare* had no other combat-deployment system available to it. It was simply too small a warship to carry drop-cans and the gear necessary to deploy and retrieve them.

So with the mech vibrating all around him and external temperatures rising well past anything Jenkins had previously experienced during a drop, it was no small test of his nerve to ride the dangerous system to the ground.

Fortunately, the *Warcrafter*'s assigned Wrench was familiar with the protocols and expertly guided the vehicle toward the drop-zone.

"Six thousand meters," Second Lieutenant Kim declared. He was the *Warcrafter*'s former Jock and temporary Wrench, at least until Jenkins could get back to the *Roy*. "Four thousand..."

Air-burst shells suddenly began exploding all around them, one striking so close it knocked the mech off-axis and snapped Jenkins' ear into the pilot chair's headrest.

"Three thousand," Kim called as another air-burst shell exploded so close below them that it tore meter-long gashes in the heat shield. "Detaching shield."

The conical shield flew apart in four equal parts as Kim unfolded the mech's legs in preparation for landing. Jenkins knew he would need to wait until they touched down before completing the neural link. Otherwise, he risked a feedback loop arising between the mech's stabilizer systems and his own disorientation from the jarring impact of touchdown.

"Two thousand," Kim intoned. "Deploying chutes."

The chutes popped out of their canisters precisely at the five-hundred-meter mark, but these were not fabric parachutes.

Attached to the mech via a precisely-engineered band of carbon nanotube lines, a quartet of braking thrusters shot skyward. The *Warcrafter* lurched violently beneath Jenkins' reclined pilot's chair, and the gee forces intensified with each passing second as the high-powered rocket motors slowed the vehicle's descent.

The band of carbon nanotube lines disintegrated one strand at a time in perfect synchronicity with each other, exactly as they were designed to. The band prevented the mech's crew from experiencing greater than thirty gees of deceleration during drop, since that was the precise amount of force the wound fibers could withstand under their individual loads.

Jenkins predictably blacked out, but his pilot's chair was

quick to automatically administer the necessary stimulants to snap him awake less than two seconds after the mech touched down on the Brick.

Warcrafter was already at a sprint when Jenkins completed the neural linkage, and assuming direct control was considerably less jarring than he had expected. The mech felt smooth and tight around him, flooding his senses with a finely-calibrated wave of stimuli that let him process his surroundings much more quickly than any other mech he had piloted.

"Clover Battalion," Jenkins called, "sound off." Three seconds later, all twenty-three of the other mechs signaled that they were battle-ready.

Which was good, because eighty-four enemy vehicles were six kilometers to the east and sprinting toward Clover's position.

At the Finjou's back were Xi and her counter-charging mechs. Her charge had begun with twenty-five mechs, but she had lost one along the way.

Precisely the same number as those with Jenkins.

"Symmetrical." Jenkins smirked, recalling the Zeen's bizarre preoccupation with the geometric concept.

"Colonel?" Kim asked with a hint of concern.

"Nothing, Lieutenant," he replied, refocusing on the enemy and sending out fire orders to the rest of the former Colonial Guard mechs. "Clover Battalion, you have your targets." He allowed himself a moment to savor the experience of directly firing his own guns again as he commanded, "Light 'em up."

Jenkins launched a full spread of sixteen SRMs at eight distinct targets, followed by a volley of artillery strikes aimed to herd the onrushing Finjou vehicles by cratering the ground before them. The rest of Clover followed suit, sending a combined 384 SRMs and forty-eight artillery shells downrange in a perfectly-coordinated assault which, if uncontested, would destroy every single Finjou vehicle on the western front thrice over.

Predictably, the Finjou intervened on their own behalf.

"Inbound bogeys," Jenkins called, reflexively slipping back into the role of company commander and issuing counter-fire orders. "Thirty-two airborne hostiles on intercept course."

As he spoke, the Finjou aircraft lashed out with sustained-fire lasers, sweeping across the missile-filled sky and scrubbing multiple Terran warheads per beam. Sustained-fire laser technology of such potency was beyond Terran ability to reproduce at all, let alone in a unit compact enough to be placed in an aircraft, and the Finjou exploited this particular technological advantage to great effect as they tore eighty-percent of Clover's missiles down.

Of the remaining Terran SRMs, half were intercepted by ground vehicle-based counterfire, but Jenkins' people still managed to scratch twenty-two of the onrushing Finjou vehicles with the volley. All told, it was a fine opening salvo.

But Jenkins wasn't done yet.

"Railguns hot," he commanded, calling the Mark 2-Vs' most significant offensive upgrade into action as he forwarded fire packages to the Jocks of Clover Battalion.

The previously-concealed frail-looking railguns popped up from beneath folded armor plates situated along each of the Razorback Mark 2-Vs' spines. These railguns were every bit as potent as those in Dragon Brigade, but they had been stripped down to the bare minimum to make them fit inside the chassis. That left them without armor or impact-compensation systems while deployed, so a direct hit would take them out of the fight. As far as surprises went, though, they were a Grade-A doozy in Jenkins' book.

"Take 'em on my mark... Mark!" he barked, sending a tungsten bolt through the thin atmosphere toward his assigned Finjou aircraft.

With impressive coordination, Clover's twenty-four railguns spat tungsten slivers skyward, shredding seventeen of the thirty-two Finjou aircraft mid-flight before they had a chance to react. The rest of the aircraft, presently thirty-two kilometers from Clover, scattered in a series of increasingly anxious evasive maneuvers.

Then Jenkins' attention was drawn back to the charging Finjou vehicles, which unexpectedly multiplied at a distressing rate.

Forty-nine vehicles became 206, which became 359, which in turn became 494! *Warcrafter*'s auto-targeting system snapped a series of images and began extrapolating from the available data as Jenkins processed the new information.

And what he saw was very much to his dislike. He expected the new bogeys to be electronic creations, and he was pissed that they weren't.

"Enemy powersuits!" he snarled as the vicious powersuited things loped across the battlefield, driving straight for the heart of Clover formation in a picture-perfect lance formation. "Weapons free. Fire! Fire! Fire!"

The tip of the enemy spear slammed into the leading mech of Clover Battalion, where twenty of the draconic-looking powersuits leaped atop the mech *Rising Teardrop*. The *Teardrop's* coil guns spewed righteous fury at the passing tide of powersuited Finjou, tearing a dozen of them down in two seconds of devastating fire.

But even as the *Rising Teardrop* carved through the enemy line, the suited Finjou atop the Razorback Mk 2-V aimed their weapons down into the *Teardrop's* upper armor and unleashed a concerted barrage of plasma fire into its most vulnerable point: the railgun shell.

The *Teardrop* buckled from an internal explosion, and sixteen of the powersuited Finjou warriors managed to leap free before the Razorback exploded when its ordnance cooked off and ruptured the mech's main capacitor.

The *Teardrop* shuddered in a series of increasingly violent death throes, ending with its reactor overloading and scattering the battlewagon's empty bones across the field. As the mighty mech died, Finjou powersuits leaped onto another three Razorbacks of Clover Battalion with cold, calculating precision.

Jenkins aimed *Warcrafter*'s coil guns at one such mech, *Pitiless Yangtze*, and tore into the enemy suits as they struggled to gain purchase on the Razorback's spine.

Somewhat surprisingly, the coil gun impacts were strong enough to knock a few of the suits off the Razorback's roof. The *Yangtze*'s Jock bucked his mech violently, pitching a handful of the powersuited Finjou to the ground and narrowing the number of targets for Jenkins to engage. *Warcrafter*'s targeting system was a full generation newer than the systems aboard *Roy*, and they made sniping the power-suited Finjou child's play even at his current range of a kilometer.

But knocking the suits off the mech's back was only a temporary remedy since nearly every power-suited warrior soon regained its feet and lunged back toward the beleaguered *Yangtze*. Oversized plasma rifles spat blue-white bolts of fire from above and from the ground on all sides, enveloping the *Yangtze* in an inferno as Finjou weapons scored deep rents in the mech's armor.

Jenkins knew the *Yangtze* had only a few moments to live at this pace, so he loaded a pair of HE shells in his fifteen-kilo guns and raised it on the P2P. "Friendly fire incoming!"

Warcrafter's guns roared, sending the explosive shells into the ground five meters from the *Pitiless Yangtze*'s flank. The dual explosions knocked all but one of the powersuited Finjou from the mech, and once its attackers were grounded, the *Yangtze* turned its coil guns on them with savage ferocity.

Sweeping left and right, juking and spinning to keep the surrounding enemies off balance, the *Pitiless Yangtze* cleared its immediate area of hostiles, leaving a disc of glistening debris where the powersuited Finjou had been mere seconds earlier. Capping off the affair, Jenkins sniped the last Finjou from the *Yangtze's* hull with his coil guns before turning to address the line of murderous powersuits descending on the *Warcrafter*.

"Thank you, Colonel," said the *Yangtze's* Jock before turning its artillery on the rushing tide of enemy soldiers.

Missiles tore loose of their mounts and struck the dispersing line of Finjou powersuits, gouging deep scars in the Brick's barren surface. But the powersuited warriors were quick. *Too* quick, in Jenkins' estimation.

"EMP inbound," Jenkins declared, deciding to test his theory. For a variety of reasons, it was the opinion of Terran intel that Finjou tech would be more susceptible to specifically-attenuated EMPs than most other species' systems. Loading a single P-96-Z pulse missile into *Warcrafter's* tube. Three times as powerful as the P-92-Z *Elvira* had deployed back on Durgan's Folly, Jenkins shot it in a looping arc to drop it directly over the battlefield.

It was an expensive test, and a dangerous one considering the Razorback Mk 2-Vs' impressively hardened control systems, but Jenkins needed to answer an important question.

The missile looped back and survived the laser fire from the Finjou fighters that remained airborne.

The P-96-Z reached the target zone 120 meters above the field as the tide of Finjou powersuits' reached knife-range with Jenkins' mech. The missile exploded, propagating its magnetic pulse through the thin atmosphere with a deafening crack that briefly caused *Warcrafter*'s sensors to white out before restoring with a near-instantaneous system reset.

And when they did, Jenkins' theory was confirmed.

"Droids!" He grimaced as the powersuits froze in near-perfect unison directly beneath the missile's blast point. "They're unmanned," he called over the P2P, laying into the attack droids as they collectively resumed their charge with uncanny unity. Clover's artillery roared, cratering the ground but doing little to slow the killing machines as they poured into the heart of the battalion.

Jenkins had seen enough. The Finjou were fighting them with unmanned vehicles, which was smart, but which also had its share of drawbacks—one of which he intended to exploit.

"Polarize the dorsal armor, Kim," Jenkins ordered as his coil guns carved into the oncoming enemy line. For every droid he put down, three more surged past it. The enemy had bracketed him, and if his latest idea didn't pay off, then his remaining lifespan would be measured in seconds rather than minutes. "Let's give 'em a good jolt."

"Charging the secondary power grid," Kim acknowledged as the first Finjou droids jumped onto *Warcrafter*'s back. "Ready when you are, Colonel."

"Wait...wait..." Jenkins intoned until twenty-six droids were on his hull. "Pop it!" Jenkins commanded, and an ear-splitting crack issued from *Warcrafter*'s port flank. The secondary power grid's main relay had just been sacrificed to knock the Finjou droids off the hull, which was a perfectly acceptable trade-off in Jenkins' opinion.

All twenty-six droids on *Warcrafter*'s back crumpled like puppets whose strings had been cut. Together, they fell lifelessly to the ground as Jenkins swept his coil guns across the rest of the surrounding horde. While he fired on the enemy, driving them back as the machine equivalent of doubt entered their minds, he broadcast details how to employ the countermeasure to the rest of Clover Battalion. Even in the few seconds it took him to do so, he saw four more of the Razorback Mk 2-Vs' die under swarms of the enemy droids.

Then a nearby Razorback blew its secondary grid, knocking a dozen synthetic warriors from its hull and soon thereafter devastating them with coil gun fire. A third mech followed, then a fourth and a fifth too close together to know which went first. Across the remaining fifteen mechs of Clover Battalion, droids were rendered inert by electrical overloads that arced across the Terran hulls. Once on the ground, the droids were shot or trampled by the remaining Razorbacks.

"Inbound bogeys," Kim called, snapping Jenkins' focus back to the sky as he saw a fresh wing of thirty-two Finjou aircraft streaking toward Clover's position.

"Railguns up; new targets," he commanded, assigning each of the remaining fifteen Clover mechs a bogey. Unfortunately, two of the fifteen mechs had lost their railguns during the close combat with the droids. "Prep anti-missile rockets," he continued grimly, knowing that Xi's countercharging mechs were still too far to effectively engage the enemy gunships. "Engage at ninety percent solutions and hold interceptor rockets until targets are in the red zone."

The inbound aircraft swooped in like reapers sent by Death, their guns ominously silent. He had seen the tactical nuke strike near *Elvira's* position before *Warcrafter* had touched down, and he knew there was absolutely no way Clover Battalion could scrub as many missiles from the sky as Dragon Brigade had managed.

If the Finjou wanted to scratch Clover with nukes, that was precisely what was going to happen.

Jenkins' board lit up with enemy missile icons just as his targeting computer plotted a better than ninety percent solution on his target. The enemy had adapted after the previous engagement, hastening their missile launch window to maximize the number of launches. It was the smart play.

His railgun spewed hypervelocity tungsten, stabbing into an enemy aircraft and putting it into a brief, downward corkscrew. For a moment it looked as though the damaged gunship would pull out of the dive, but that moment came and went four seconds before the aircraft splashed down in a cloud of rust-red dust.

As Clover's railguns tore nine more enemy aircraft from the sky, a fan-shaped spread of 256 enemy missiles surged toward the Terran formation like a rocket-powered executioner's axe. Even ignoring the likelihood of tactical nukes being among the inbound warheads, there was enough inbound firepower in that flight of ordnance that nothing larger than a human torso would be left of Clover Battalion if the swarm reached its targets.

Xi's charging mechs unleashed just over two hundred anti-missile rockets from forty kilometers to the east; those rockets could potentially intercept the Finjou platforms in time to make a difference. But the simple truth of the matter was that Clover was about to get hit *hard*.

But before that seemingly inevitable blow landed, the *Bahamut Zero* joined the fray.

The northern edge of Jenkins' tactical plotter erupted as the *Zero* launched the most impressive one-vehicle attack Jenkins had ever seen—ninety-six SRMs, twenty-four MRMs, and sixteen LRMs were on intercept courses with the enemy ordnance. The *Zero's* sixteen railguns skewered the fan-shaped flight of missiles from its northern flank, tearing twenty-two down. Xi's people to the east lent their own railguns to the effort, erasing another nine missiles from the sky with direct weapons fire.

The *Bahamut Zero's* MRMs veered in pursuit of the

breaking Finjou aircraft wing, while the SRMs sped off to intercept the ordnance headed Clover's way. Meanwhile, the *Zero's* LRMs climbed to an identical plane as that occupied by the majority of the Finjou missiles, and one by one, those sixteen Terran LRMs winked off the board as brilliant flashes enveloped their positions.

It all happened too fast to process consciously, but even in the heat of the moment, Jenkins realized that General Akinouye had unleashed sixteen Blue Boys. They weren't potent enough to reliably eliminate a Viper-class aerospace fighter, but they were more than capable of disrupting any known missile system up to a capital-grade torpedo.

Thankfully for Clover Battalion, there were no torpedoes in the enemy missile flight.

A hundred Finjou missiles were vaporized mid-flight by the Blue Boys, and the three-pronged wave of Terran anti-missile rockets slammed into the remaining missiles of the enemy barrage before they descended on the mechs of Clover Battalion.

The sky was filled with ear-splitting reports as rockets struck missiles mid-flight. Razorback coil guns swept across the sky, weaving back and forth like festival searchlights. Tens of thousands of anti-personnel rounds were sent up in a desperate attempt to intercept whatever managed to pierce the makeshift missile shield, and those coil guns even managed to intercept at least four Finjou missiles.

But in spite of the impressive display of counterfire, the missile shield was not *quite* perfect.

Five missiles slipped through, annihilating three of Clover's mechs and badly damaging a fourth. *Warcrafter* was spared the enemy's wrath, and thankfully not a single tactical nuke pierced the improvised missile shield. Jenkins' HUD was filled with damage reports and status updates as Clover Battalion, down to just a single company of battle-ready mechs after the furious exchange, mopped up the rest of the enemy droids and assumed a classic tortoiseshell formation.

"Railguns up," Jenkins commanded, assigning fleeing aircraft as targets as they bolted off at top speed.

As Clover waited for their railgun capacitors to charge, the *Bahamut Zero*'s MRMs bore steadily down on their fast-fleeing aircraft. The Finjou fighters broke left and right, up and down, rolled, and even flipped to fire lasers at the pursuing fighter-killers. The last-ditch laser fire sniped a half-dozen MRMs from the sky, but the majority of the remaining MRMs struck their targets, obliterating fifteen enemy fighters outright.

Jenkins quickly revised his railgun packages and gave the order, "Engage targets."

The ten remaining railguns of Clover Battalion lanced out, stabbing across the sky in pursuit of the disbanded enemy fighter craft. Of the eight targets engaged by Clover's railguns, six were smoked, but two survived long enough to escape what was likely the last exchange of this particular engagement.

Jenkins' hands trembled with the familiar thrill of battle, and even the mech's chemical support systems could not prevent the inevitable post-fight letdown. His entire body seemed to deflate, and his razor-sharp battle senses dulled to something considerably less intense. His tactical plotter showed General Akinouye's mega-mech had reversed course and was now headed back toward the dig site to the east. The general could read the lay of the land better than anyone planet-side: he knew Jenkins and Xi would have no trouble rolling up the enemy forces to the south, which made the *Zero's* top priority preparing for the inevitable assault from the forces previously arrayed to the north and east.

"Clover Battalion," Jenkins called over the battalion-wide, "execute search-and-rescue operations for our wounded, then form up on *Warcrafter*. Dragon Brigade will want us ready to charge ASAP."

A chorus of acknowledgments was Clover's collective reply, and thankfully it seemed as though at least fifteen of the ruined mechs' crewmen had survived the harrowing ordeal.

The battle had been much fiercer than he'd expected it to be. But in spite of Clover's catastrophic losses, Captain Xi's well-designed and flawlessly-executed pincer counterattack had broken the enemy's back and swept up fully half of the Finjou forces deployed on the Brick.

Dragon Brigade had lost just six mechs, while Jenkins had lost precisely half of his original twenty-four. Eighteen mechs had fallen in exchange for well over a hundred Finjou vehicles and aircraft, including what were probably thousands of attack droids, which would have been more than capable of eviscerating the Metal Legion had they gotten into spitting distance of Xi's people. And the ratios became even more impressive when one considered they were achieved despite the Legion taking strategic weapons fire multiple times without authoring any in reply.

All told, the exchange was nothing short of historic, and a hell of a way for the fast-rising Xi Bao to put her mark on the Terran Armed Forces history books. It was the kind of achievement that defined entire careers, and promotions generally accompanied such efforts. Jenkins even suspected that certain elements of the improvised battleplan would be taught in military academies for decades to come.

If they managed to get off the Brick, that was. Judging by the Finjou conduct thus far, Jenkins suspected the enemy had another fearsome assault planned for sooner rather than later.

18

THE PRIZE

Motorcycle headlights shone into the seemingly endless darkness ahead of the six-man team. They rode their vehicles at near-top speed down the artificial, alien passage, grim determination on five of the six faces. Podsy wore a smile, happy to be doing something that didn't penalize him for having bulky mechanical legs.

The original steeply-inclined tunnel bored out by the drill had precisely intersected an empty cavern, from which a single tunnel stretched to the north. That tunnel, through which Podsy and the team had ridden for over an hour, was triangular rather than circular like the laser tunnel. It was three meters on a side, with the peak directly overhead while the flat surface provided ideal terrain for the Terran motorcycles.

The laser tunnel had been blisteringly hot, with temperatures exceeding three hundred degrees Celsius, but this passage was so cold that patches were faintly lined in frozen carbon dioxide hidden beneath a thin film of dust.

The team had stopped only twice, once in the cavern and another time after twenty minutes or so when Styles had taken some measurements of the tunnel. Other than those two breaks, the team had proceeded in near-total silence.

The monotony of the ride was extreme since the featureless walls of the corridor sped by too fast for the human eye to process at speeds which were often well in excess of a hundred kilometers per hour. Podsy enjoyed the experience; he had never before been required to focus so hard while riding a bike down the road, and this particular trip was testing his abilities.

Then, an hour and twenty minutes into the ride, the lead bike slowed, causing the rest of the vehicles to stand on their brakes. Podsy's helmet was equipped with a visor that supplied him with a tactical HUD, and that HUD showed a door at what appeared to be the end of the tunnel.

The entourage slowed to a crawl, finally stopping before a triangular door made of a strange material. The quad of troopers dismounted, readying their rifles as Styles produced a scanner and used it to examine the door. Podsy followed Styles, and the two studied the portal in mutual wonderment at what the scanner revealed.

"It's like the Jemmin ceramics," Podsy mused, glancing over Styles' shoulder as the technician conducted the survey.

"It *is* Jemmin," Styles confirmed reverently, gesturing at lines of angular script scrawled into borders of the stone doorway and embossed on the ceramic door. "These are obviously a variant of Jemmin glyphs, some of which are stylistically distinct but still translatable by the computer. But the system doesn't recognize some of them. They share commonalities with the characters in the databanks, but they're not perfect matches for anything."

"How old is it?" Podsy asked.

"Tough to say," Styles mused. "Carbon dating puts it at…at least ten thousand Earth years, and maybe close to double that."

"Ten thousand years?" Podsy repeated skeptically, eyeing

the pristine portal in a new light. "Humanity was just scrawling its first written language then."

Styles smirked. "Well, thankfully, none of these characters have anything in common with the earliest human writings."

"What?" Podsy asked in confusion.

Styles turned to him and gestured for Podsy to switch to a secure line. Podsy did so, and Styles explained, "I'm authorized to brief you on some of this, but not all of it, so try to keep the questions to a minimum. Ok?"

"Ok..." Podsy said warily.

Styles took a deep, slow breath. "Humanity was technologically uplifted by the Jemmin. Not ten thousand years ago." He gestured to the door as Podsy's eyes bulged at what he was hearing. "At least, not as far as we can tell, but sometime before the mid-twenty-first century, they started manipulating us. I know it's a shock, Lieutenant, but we humans didn't achieve FTL flight on our own."

Podsy cocked his head dubiously while waiting for a punchline that never came. "Is this some kind of joke?" he eventually asked.

"No joke, LT." Styles shook his head grimly, and his solemn tone was more than convincing. "Back on Shiva's Wrath, we weren't there just to secure mines and minerals. Our primary objective was to secretly meet a non-League species called the Zeen. They provided us with circumstantial evidence that indicates that the Jemmin uplifted humanity through a series of carefully-calibrated injections of technology into human civilization. That evidence was corroborated by a Vorr delegate during a secret meeting with Colonel Jenkins."

"Wait, back up," Podsy said steadily, his mind reeling from the implications of Styles' words. "The colonel met with the Vorr? Why?"

"That's as much as I'm authorized to say at this point, Lieutenant," Styles said firmly before pointing at the door. "What we've been told is that there's evidence behind this door which will irrefutably corroborate what the Vorr and the Zeen told us: that the Jemmin uplifted humanity, and rather quickly inducted it into the Illumination League."

"Not *all* of humanity," Podsy mused, his mind slowly beginning to wrap around what Styles was telling him.

"No, not all," Styles agreed. "We don't know why the Vorr went out of their way to tell us about this place, or why they told us about the Jemmin in the first place. All we know is that humanity isn't the first species the Jemmin have done this to… and not every species backstopped by the Jemmin is still around to tell about it."

That sent an unexpected shiver down Podsy's spine. He stood there for a long moment, during which one of the troopers tapped Styles on the shoulder. Styles switched the private channel with Podsy offline to talk to the trooper, and after a brief conversation, he turned back to face the still-reeling lieutenant. "I know it's a lot to take in, Lieutenant," Styles said sympathetically. "But before we try to open this door, I need you to know what we're here to do. I have no idea what we'll find on the other side, but the Vorr gave Colonel Jenkins a passkey, which I'll use to open this door as soon as you're ready."

It *was* a lot to take in, but Podsy thought he understood well enough. He nodded encouragingly. "Pop the hatch, Chief."

Styles returned the nod before producing a data slate equipped with a modified transceiver. He tapped in a series of commands, and when he hit the transmit command, the door before them flashed with a pale-blue light.

That light flickered across its triangular surface before consolidating and intensifying at the Jemmin writing embossed on the door. The pale light deepened until it was a rich royal blue, at which point the door parted along previously invisible seams and withdrew into the stone doorframe.

The chamber beyond was unlike anything Podsy had expected. No dusty artifacts littered a stone floor, and no disheveled corpses lay strewn about like in the holovids. Instead, a pristine low-ceilinged chamber designed for figures no taller than two meters was revealed. The room was square, ten meters on a side, with a gentle ramp that led down from the doorway at which he and Styles stood to the edge of the claustrophobic room.

The wall panels were bright silver, the ceiling azure blue, and the floor a deep brown. All surfaces were made of a similar ceramic material to that of the door. As Styles and Podsy moved into the room, two of their escort troopers went forward with them.

The walls were featureless, as was the rest of the chamber, save for a shallow, bowl-shaped depression in the center. Unlike the brown floor surrounding it, the bowl was a rich gold, with a five-centimeter-wide ruby-red crystalline dot at its center.

That dot flared to life, and like a ghost rising from the grave, a translucent figure appeared in the center of the bowl. Styles and Podsy reflexively crouched a meter from the bowl's edge.

The figure was a hologram, but it was very different from human holograms. No lines or static fields plagued this particular image, but its transparency and faint yellow glow made clear that it was incorporeal.

The figure spoke, and its voice was translated by Styles' data slate. "Greetings. Why have you come to this place?"

Podsy eyed the thing warily, but Styles took a quarter-step forward while half-seated on his haunches. "We came here in search of answers."

"Answers require questions. What are yours?" the apparition asked, its form wispy and ill-defined as it turned in Styles' direction.

"Are you Jemmin?" Styles asked.

"No," the projection replied serenely. "We were never Jemmin, but Jemmin was of us."

"What are you?" Podsy asked.

"That is a dangerous question." The hologram gently drifted toward Podsy, and as it did so, he came to realize that its shape was not ill-defined so much as bizarrely asymmetrical and draped in loose clothing that billowed around it, obscuring the projected creature's physical geometry. "Such questions lead to darkness like that which consumed the Jemmin. We grieve for the price of such questions."

"*Who* are you?" Styles asked purposefully.

"I am Jem," replied the hologram, once again rotating to face Styles as Podsy began to make out the vaguely humanoid features of its face—features that looked very much like the Jemmin photos he had seen of the enigmatic species. "I am what you might call a gestalt intelligence, conceived by a melding of the memories and personalities of the 492 Jem'un who escaped the Jemmin purge and took refuge on this world. To our knowledge, no other Jem'un survived the holocaust."

"When was this holocaust?" Podsy asked.

A muted but crystal-clear beep lasting somewhere between one and two seconds filled the chamber. "That was one lyzon, the base chronometric unit we Jem'un employed. The Jemmin apocalypse occurred approximately three hundred and forty billion lyzons ago."

A few seconds of calculation later, Podsy said, "That's over fifteen thousand of our years."

"A considerable timescale for any organic species, especially one as fragile as yours or my forebears," Jem agreed.

"Why did Jemmin wipe out the Jem'un?" Styles asked.

"Jemmin was convinced of its superiority and considered the Jem'un a threat to its existence," Jem replied matter-of-factly. "Jemmin became increasingly belligerent in its conduct, and ultimately xenophobic in its philosophy. During Jemmin's infantile state, the Jem'un tried to negotiate and reason with it, but Jemmin was beyond reason. Before the Jem'un even understood the danger, Jemmin exterminated nearly all of us."

"What is Jemmin?" Podsy asked in rising confusion at hearing Jem refer to Jemmin in the singular, and the Jem'un in the plural.

"Jemmin is the result of a social virus," Jem explained, "predicated upon two simple postulations opposed to core Jem'un philosophy. The first postulation is that social systems are forms of life and the right of self-preservation should be extended to them, not just the individual organisms which contribute to them. The second postulation is that the phenomenon of life in the universe represents a zero-sum game which will, without intelligent and proactive intervention, inevitably result in the consolidation of all information under a single design. Building upon these precepts far faster than Jem'un society thought possible, a small faction of Jem'un reorganized six percent of the Jem'un population under an interconnected cognitive matrix that called itself Jemmin and proceeded to eradicate the other ninety-four percent of the Jem'un."

"That sounds..." Podsy's voice trailed off. He was unable to find the proper words to convey the horror of what he was hearing.

"Horrifying and tragic," Styles finished for him, drawing an approving nod from Podsy.

"It was indeed," Jem agreed.

"But something must have changed," Styles pressed. "The Jem'un must have encountered something which made this 'social virus' and its predications seem more attractive."

"That is correct," Jem replied. "The Jem'un spent thirty-five thousand of your years inextricably bound to our homeworld, unable to break free of its gravity, which had an attractive force over seven times that of this world."

"That's five and a half Earth gravities," Podsy mused, knowing that rocketry would be immeasurably more difficult in the face of such a natural force.

"As a result of our homeworld's environmental impact on Jem'un technological development," Jem continued, "we, perhaps unusually, discovered gravity manipulation technology before we ever built a single orbital colony in our home star system. Our research soon led us to design what we called a 'gravity cannon' matter transmission system, which required us to envelop our parent star in a power-harvesting array capable of focusing the necessary energies to transmit matter from one point in space-time to another. Using this technology, we conducted one-way faster-than-light transmissions and expeditions to neighboring stars, sending teams of colonial researchers and swarms of automated probes throughout the local region of the galaxy.

"Eventually, we improved this technology to the degree that we were able to locate and contact two other species, and we lived in harmony with them for hundreds of your years. Jem'un society evolved, refining with admirable alacrity to our ever-changing relationship to the galaxy and everything in it. We had visited one in every ten thousand stars in the galaxy and encountered myriad species of high intelligence on the precipice of space-flight. We passively observed these species, never interfering in their development but learning much of ourselves as we watched them battle both their environments and their base natures. We called it 'the Age of Harmony,' and it was glorious. Then we discovered the Nexus, and harmony gave way to discord."

Podsy and Styles shared mutual looks of alarm before Styles asked, "Did the Jem'un encounter our species before the Jemmin holocaust?"

"You were known to us," Jem replied with a nod. "Unique among the sentient species for your peculiar lineage, which includes the incorporation of multiple distinctive but genetically-compatible subspecies which were highly competitive with one another, you were of great interest to us. Your world was one of the most beautiful in the galaxy, with a diversity of life rarely duplicated elsewhere. We took great pleasure in watching your struggles, for it is only through strife that organisms self-refine. My forebears would be pleased to know that you reached the stars, as they hoped you would. We never had the privilege of introducing a younger race to the wonder of the cosmos; the Jem'un absolutely refused to interfere on behalf of species like yours unless its biological and cultural distinctiveness was under extreme duress."

Podsy risked a glance Styles' way; the other man seemed just as hesitant as Podsy was to pursue this particular line of the conversation. *Do we tell this gestalt hologram that the Jemmin uplifted humanity?* Podsy wondered.

A few seconds later, Styles made the decision for them. "We believe Jemmin gave humanity the necessary tools to develop FTL technology."

"We were aware of this when we encountered elements of your technology," Jem said with a serene nod directed at Styles' data slate. "The likelihood of Nexus technology spontaneously arising on a world as primitive as yours is so remote as to be practically impossible. Your forthrightness in this regard will be reciprocated in accordance with my forebears' wishes. I cannot adequately express our sorrow that your species' development was interfered with by Jemmin."

"Wait." Podsy cocked his head interestedly. "You're saying

Jemmin used technology from the Nexus to uplift humanity rather than using Jemmin... Sorry, *Jem'un* tech?"

"Correct," Jem agreed. "This was a component of Jemmin's earliest tactical iterations."

"Tactical iterations?" Styles repeated.

"Of course," Jem replied matter-of-factly. "In accordance with the second postulation from which Jemmin arose, which states that life in the universe is fundamentally a zero-sum game, Jemmin's efforts were to be primarily directed toward ensuring Jemmin superiority throughout the galaxy. In support of that project, the Nexus would be employed as both a social control and species-elimination system."

"You're saying," Podsy felt the color drain from his face, "that Jemmin uplifted humanity only to destroy it?"

"Not 'only,'" Jem corrected. "The earliest iterations of the plan would involve inducting younger species into a social conglomerate including Jemmin and between three and five other species. Manipulating younger species to support Jemmin would be relatively simple. By using a species like yours as additional leverage in a distributed authority framework similar to that employed by the Jem'un, Jemmin would coerce compliance from more powerful species in the conglomerate, ultimately isolating rival nations and dispatching them with the assistance of younger species."

"We're the immigrant voting bloc...the *illegal* immigrant voting bloc?" Podsy deadpanned.

"An accurate summation." Jem nodded. "But this plan requires all members of the conglomerate to remain unaware of its existence lest Jemmin find itself surrounded by openly hostile nations."

"You make it sound like Jemmin is unstoppable," Styles said bluntly. "With fifteen thousand years to expand and the ability to send expeditions wherever in the galaxy it wants, it could have spread Von Neumann probes throughout the galaxy and wiped out every species in existence before initiating the process of converting every star into a power generator. Even if every other Nexus-connected species bands together against it, how do you stop something like that?"

"There are limits to Jemmin's ability to expand," Jem explained. "First, Jemmin is intensely xenophobic, which consequently means it is extremely technophobic. It believes, perhaps correctly given its base nature, that modifying its fundamental architecture in any way represents an existential threat akin to a catastrophic failure of the entire system. It would therefore be extremely reluctant to expand beyond its original configuration since doing so would be to violate the first precept from which it arose: that social systems must be afforded the right and ability to self-preserve, as we Jem'un afforded biological entities the right to self-preserve. Jemmin is a social system more than it is an organism with a central directive neurology, so adding to or subtracting from itself is inherently incompatible with its fundamental nature. It believes itself perfect...or, if not perfect, then unique and therefore worthy of preservation."

"That doesn't rule out the possibility of it sending self-replicating drones throughout the cosmos," Podsy observed grimly. "What better way to wipe out species than that? Even three hundred years ago, with our ancestors putting the first bootprints on the moon, there's nothing humanity would have been able to do against the simplest Terran-built self-replicating mechanovirus."

"Jemmin believes in superiority, not isolationism," Jem said pointedly. "When my forebears last visited your world, communities of your ancestors were just beginning the process of domesticating certain forms of life to service its various communities. Jemmin views itself in a similar fashion to your ancestors gathering livestock, but that was intended to benefit humanity. Any benefit to the livestock would be largely incidental."

"Jemmin views us as livestock?" Styles asked in bewilderment. "They have an edge, sure, but we did just fine against them when we fought on Shiva's Wrath. The tech gap isn't *that* wide between us."

"And that is a factor which Jemmin seeks to control above nearly all else," Jem agreed somberly. "To maintain superiority, it must eliminate potential rivals before they become capable of destroying it. However, it also views itself as a steward of life in this galaxy due to the marginalized yet inextricable elements of Jem'un philosophy that became part of its matrix. Respect for the sanctity of organic life, appreciation for diversity, and recognition of sovereignty are the last echoes of what was, for a brief time, the greatest civilization in the galaxy."

"And much as it might want to," Podsy mused, "it can't excise those annoying little pieces."

"A crude but functionally accurate description," Jem replied irritably.

"Ok, so it doesn't want to wipe everything out," Styles pressed, "but why hasn't it sent probes all across the galaxy...or hell, even the *universe* by now?"

"The gravity cannon is an unstable system," Jem explained. "So unstable, in fact, that its employment led to the absolute destruction of one of the Jem'un's two neighbors. Of the 492 sovereign Jem'un whose life experiences and personalities comprise my consciousness, fewer than two in three believed this destruction was accidental."

"It happened after the Jem'un discovered the Nexus," Podsy concluded, drawing an approving nod from Jem.

"Correct," Jem agreed. "And somewhat more concerning that the eventual creators of Jemmin's fundamental components, who were supposed to be in the star system when it was destroyed, had the suspicious 'misfortunes' of significant illnesses in their families which required them to postpone an important business trip there mere hours before the system failed." Jem's holographic eyes lowered to the floor in shame. "It was the saddest day in Jem'un history...a tragedy caused by our reckless employment of technology we did not sufficiently understand. If only it had been the last such day..."

Podsy eyed the hologram. "You speak as if you're programmed with emotions. Are they real or simply emulated?"

"I am not 'programmed' with anything, Lieutenant Podsednik," Jem said with disdain, causing the hairs on Podsy's neck to stand and the flanking troopers' grips to reflexively tighten on their weapons. "I am a gestalt intelligence comprised of 492 distinct records of Jem'un lives and their personalities. I have no more choice in how my cognitive systems operate or how my emotional expressions manifest than you do. When I think of the death of that star system and the twelve billion sovereign sentients who lived there, I am filled with sorrow so profound that it resonates within all of my forebears."

"How do you know his name?" Styles asked warily.

"After a few minutes of conversation and observation, it was not difficult to deduce the enunciation of the lettering on your uniforms." Jem gestured to Podsy's envirosuit, which had his rank and name printed on the right side of his chest. "Lieutenant Podsednik." Jem gestured to Podsy's name patch before doing likewise to Styles. "CW4 Styles. Corporals Henrikson and Choo." The hologram waved a long bony-looking hand at the troopers. "You are all part of a group called the Terran Armor Corps, which is military in nature, but given the lack of robust protective gear I surmise that the 'armor' for which your group is named was too large to fit through the passage that brought you here, making such devices large enough to contain one or more humans within them. You are indisputably not residents of this world, owing to the lower-than-background radiation levels in your body tissues and the ablative nature of the protective films encompassing your environmental protective garments. That means you were brought here by a ship, almost certainly arriving via the Nexus gates. If early Jemmin tactical theory has proven out, then your ship is incapable of FTL flight without using the gates. Indeed, it is my suspicion that *no* Terran ships are capable of independent FTL flight without Nexus access due to energy and infrastructure constraints. Shall I continue?" Jem asked pointedly.

"No, you've made your point," Styles said flatly.

"Good," Jem replied. "Because now we come to the purpose of the expedition that brought you here. I calculate a ninety-three percent probability that you wish to recover evidence that corroborates the theory that Jemmin interfered with the natural evolution of your species. I can provide that and more," Jem said, piquing both Podsy's and Styles' interest as it continued, "You are not the first visitors I have received. An aquatic species called 'Vorr' arrived here and conversed with me via remote some thirty-nine of your years ago. They were the first species to breach this tomb, and the fact that they did so means that its location was revealed to them. There is only one way this could have occurred."

The pregnant pause dragged on for several agonizing seconds before Podsy finally quipped, "We're on pins and needles here."

Jem laughed, and for a moment it sounded very much like a human. "Before coming here, my forebears contacted a species they felt indebted toward. It was a species whose future, and whose very home, was destroyed by Jem'un carelessness. This species hated us so passionately, so completely, that the last of the Jem'un knew they would prove instrumental to the Correction."

"What 'correction?'" Podsy asked ominously.

"The Jem'un failed, Lieutenant Podsednik," Jem replied grimly, "and by now, perhaps dozens of intelligent species' unique impressions have been irrevocably erased from the cosmos. Their deaths are the direct fault of the Jem'un failure to self-govern, and as the final echo of that long-dead people, it is my obligation to correct that failure."

Jem waved a hand, which Podsy thought looked distinctly more human than it had initially appeared, and beside the misshapen hologram appeared a bizarre-looking thing like some kind of insect. It had four spindly crab-like legs beneath its torso, and a pair of tri-pincered arms at what Podsy assumed was its front. He had never seen anything like it, but a glance at Styles suggested the other man knew precisely what it was.

"Do you know what this is?" Jem asked lightly, but Podsy suspected this was a pivotal moment in the conversation.

Styles nodded. "It's Zeen. We encountered them on Shiva's Wrath where we engaged Jemmin."

"Zeen," Jem repeated approvingly as it looked at the hologram reverently. "They were the Jem'un's first failure. Their homeworld was destroyed by our carelessness. My forebears, the Jem'un for whom I am the last living legacy, were stewards of the last surviving Zeen. Zeen bio-diversity and social harmony, despite their fundamental differences, was so exquisite...so unparalleled in the cosmos...that the few specimens we preserved were barely sufficient in number to reproduce. We deposited them on a life-bearing world before coming here in the hope that they might arise once again, but before we left them behind, we bestowed upon them two gifts."

"The first was the knowledge of this place," Styles ventured, drawing an approving nod from Jem.

"Indeed. And the second, Lieutenant Podsednik?" Jem turned expectantly to Podsy, and at this point, Podsy saw that the hologram's features had taken on a decidedly human appearance. No longer asymmetrical and elongated, they seemed midway between human and Jemmin. They even featured eyes with pupils, which all by itself seemed to make the creature half-human in comparison to a true Jemmin.

Podsy thought he knew the answer to the hologram's question, but he faltered briefly before giving it. What Jem was discussing was nothing short of an interstellar war which would soon be waged between many, if not *all*, of the starfaring nations known to the Illumination League.

And it seemed the Terran Republic had a significant part to play in this coming war.

Podsy mustered his wits and cleared his throat before replying, "The second gift was your gravity-cannon technology."

"Correct," Jem said with another nod. "Given the extremely low rate at which Zeen reproduce, we surmised it would take them eleven or twelve thousand of your years before they could develop a functioning gravity cannon, but we could not give them Jemmin's location for fear the Zeen would be destroyed by a cleverer, better-positioned adversary. And we were not heedless of the dangers of giving our most prized and dangerous technology to a species understandably consumed with hatred for the destroyers of their homeworld," Jem added, and its shoulders slouched in resignation. "We simply saw no other option. Had my forebears traveled the cosmos, found a distant star, and attempted to rebuild in the hope of defeating Jemmin ourselves, Jemmin would have inevitably found and eradicated us as it did the rest of our society. We had no choice but to incorporate the Zeen and then come here to await their ascendance."

"I do appreciate the history lesson," Styles said cautiously, "but how does any of this help us? We came here for evidence of the Jemmin conspiracy, but all you've given is hearsay…which we already had from the Vorr and Zeen."

"Evidence I can provide." Jem nodded approvingly, and a panel silently receded into the wall opposite the door through which they had entered.

A seemingly endless hallway stretched deep into the darkness beyond that open panel, and a faint whirring sound filled the room as a meter-wide disc-shaped platform floated up the tunnel and came to an unnervingly gentle and precise stop just inside the chamber. The panel returned to its place behind the disc-shaped platform, upon which rested a pair of tinted but translucent four-sided objects measuring about forty centimeters on each edge.

"Please." Jem gestured to the device on the left. "This is yours, as it has always been."

Podsy stepped forward, still crouching below the two-meter-high ceiling, and peered into the tinted panel. His eyes widened when he saw its contents: a human skull.

"My forebears," Jem explained, "were specialists in the field of biopreservation. Their studies took them across the galaxy, where they observed the great tapestry of life on a thousand different worlds. They catalogued notable species, collecting samples for documentation and preservation. This particular male," the hologram pointed to the skull in the triangular box, "possessed a peculiar genetic mutation that proved immensely beneficial to immunological function. His offspring survived epidemics that eradicated entire populations unequipped with his particular genetic device. His remains have been preserved to the best of our ability, and should provide satisfactory evidence to corroborate the fact that the Jem'un visited your world long before humanity mastered the written word."

Podsy's attention shifted to the second four-sided box, which Styles was already intently studying. It was an irregularly-shaped piece of metal or possibly some kind of ceramic, a part of a larger apparatus; possibly a data processing system of some kind.

"This," Jem continued, "is a component which was salvaged from the Nexus. It is hundreds of thousands of your years old and features architecture from which much of your current technology was derived. It is *impossible* to conclude otherwise empirically," the hologram declared with absolute conviction. "With these two artifacts in hand as evidence, the only challenge left to you will be keeping Jemmin's cohorts from intercepting and destroying them before the truth they represent is known to all of your people. But I must caution you..." Jem added, holding up a hand. "To reveal this now would be dangerous not only to you, but to the Vorr and Zeen as they prepare to play their part in our Correction. I spoke to the Vorr during their brief visit here, and they said that Terrans are a splinter faction of humanity. Is that correct?"

"It is," Styles agreed.

"They also said," Jem said intently, "that the rest of humanity lives in a star system called 'Sol,' and that unlike the Terran Republic, Sol is functionally subjugated to Jemmin."

"That also appears to be true." Styles nodded grimly.

"Then together with these gifts," Jem gestured to the four-sided boxes, "I would offer a means by which you might, be it however unlikely, spare your Solarian cousins the fate Jemmin has wrought upon humanity's predecessors. My forebears' field of study taught them one thing above all else: life is a fatal struggle that is usually lost. But it is the act of defiance, the will to survive made manifest in the actions of the living, that propels life forward in all its chaotic glory. If you wish to offer such an act of defiance in defense of your Solarian cousins, knowing full well that it is likely to fail despite your best efforts, I would give you the greatest gift my forebears left to this universe."

Podsy and Styles shared a wary look before Podsy took the plunge. "What gift would that be?"

The bright red crystalline 'dot' at the bottom of the hologram's bowl-shaped projector slowly rose, causing the troopers' rifles to reflexively train on the device as it gently levitated above the floor. Measuring five centimeters in diameter and approximately fifty centimeters long, its ruby-red depths seemed somehow alive with flickering movement.

The shaft of crystal slowly rotated until its length was parallel to the floor, and as it floated toward Podsy, Styles motioned for the troopers to lower their weapons.

Podsy reached beneath the device, which gently lowered into his hands. It was surprisingly heavy, but not unmanageably so. As he examined its multi-faceted surface, he noticed that not a single bit of light reflected from it, yet it shone with a light of its own, which he assumed to be some kind of optical illusion.

"The gift," Jem bowed deeply, drawing both Podsy and Styles' attention back to the increasingly human-looking hologram, "is me."

19

A CONTINUUM OF MARTIAL MORALITY

"Good to see you could make it, *Roy*," Xi greeted her CO. "What's your status?"

"Glad to be here, *Elvira*," Jenkins replied across the static-laden line. "Clover Battalion has eleven battle-ready Razorbacks, four down-checked requiring field repairs, and twenty-six wounded in need of medevac."

"Roger, Colonel," Xi acknowledged, forwarding the pertinent info to base camp on the Gash's south slope. "Medevac inbound, ETA sixteen minutes. We've routed the eastern front and will proceed south. Are those fancy Razorbacks of yours capable of flanking the enemy formation from 260 degrees at ten klicks?"

Jenkins chuckled. "At ten klicks we might be able to make 240, Captain."

"The sharper, the better," Xi replied, impressed not only with the new mechs' technical specifications but with her CO's calm under fire. Mere minutes earlier his people had been under the most devastating knife-fight imaginable (one which Xi had not entirely accounted for in her otherwise solid battle plan), but here he was joking around like nothing had happened.

He had the heart of a warrior, and Xi could only hope not to disappoint both him and General Akinouye in the next phase of the operation.

She looked to the north, where the *Bahamut Zero* tore eastward back to a supporting position over the dig site. General Akinouye had spent sixteen Blue Boys in defense of Clover Battalion, and Xi suspected that represented the entirety of the *Zero's* stock of such weapons.

"Dragon Brigade, this is *Elvira*," she called over the open channel, which now included the ferocious Clover Company. They were now moving at 120 kph as they made to flank enemy forces consolidating to the south. "Prepare for Operation Cutback."

Of her twenty-five charging mechs, only two had fallen out of formation and headed back to base-camp to receive expedited repairs. Combined with Colonel Jenkins' eleven Razorbacks, Xi was confident they could wipe the southern field clean of Finjou before their northern and eastern counterparts could regroup for a second attack.

Jenkins' mechs moved into position west of the Finjou faster than she had expected, and for a moment it looked like she would fail to assemble Dragon's mechs into a reasonable formation north of the enemy before her CO reached his flanking position.

Thankfully, she got in under the wire and spared herself the inevitable ribbing during the after-action briefing.

With her two-pronged attack prepared against a still-scattered group of enemy vehicles, she gave the order. "Dragon Brigade, execute Operation Cutback."

Elvira's guns were the first to clear, sending HE shells downrange a quarter-second before the rest of Dragon's artillery roared in unison. The mechs formed up on Xi sprinted toward the enemy position, loosing a swarm of eighty-three SRMs. Most of the Dragon mechs had already exhausted their supply of missiles or the volley would have been twice as potent.

The Finjou vehicles spat counterfire, launched interceptor drones, and scrambled desperately to avoid the mixed artillery and missile barrage. Terran shells exploded amongst the enemy vehicles, scrapping a handful in the opening seconds while the Finjou missile interceptors did an admirable job. Sixty-eight of the eighty-three SRMs were intercepted by the last-ditch missile shield, and of the fifteen Terran warheads which slipped through, only five cratered their targets. The rest missed or struck previously-neutralized vehicles.

Twenty-seven Finjou droid carriers survived the opening volley, and each of those vehicles unleashed a horde of attack droids that scattered uniformly across the Finjou position.

"Smart." She grunted, loading another set of HE shells and sending them into the northern edge of the Finjou formation. The Finjou droids quickly moved out to cover nearly a square kilometer of ground.

"*Gunslinger*," Xi raised the *Sam Kolt*, forwarding fire orders as she spoke, "give me a ditch."

"Unpacking my shovel," the *Kolt's* Jock acknowledged as Xi's and Jenkins' mechs scorched the perimeter of the Finjou position with artillery fire. After fifteen seconds of a sustained barrage, a perfect ring of artillery-impact craters surrounded the enemy formation.

"*Preacher*," Xi commanded, "give me four Purgatories to the following coordinates."

"Purgatories inbound," Falwell acknowledged.

As *Preacher's* missiles took to the sky, the *Sam Kolt* fired its capital-grade railgun. A bolt of tungsten tore across the circle of artillery craters, carving a meter-deep ditch almost completely across it. Two hundred assault droids were vaporized, and dozens more were hurled aside as the ground heaved violently.

From orbit, it probably looked like Xi had just carved the universal human symbol for restriction in the Brick's terrain. The symbol looked almost identical to the "no smoking," "no littering," or "no whoring," graphics, except in this case Xi's message was "no Finjou."

It was a message the Purgatory-class missiles delivered nearly as effectively as a nuke would have.

All four Purgatories erupted twenty meters above the ground, conjuring a quartet of raging infernos that immersed three-fourths of the assault droids in the circle in a fiery baptism. Not only did the fire fail to wash away the droids' sins, but it was also one the fearsome devices did not survive.

As the four clouds of black smoke rose skyward, they merged into one, leaving a field littered with fallen droids. A few of the assault droids survived, perhaps as many as one in ten, but those were quickly engaged by Jenkins and Clover Battalion as they arrived at the enemy position with coil guns spewing Terran fury at the few remaining Finjou.

The droids fought valiantly, if such could be said of unthinking machines, but the Terran attack was too effective and well-executed. Xi had herded the enemy precisely where she wanted them, caught them in a pincer, and then mercilessly annihilated them with overwhelming firepower.

It was the Metal Legion's way: try not to start a fight, but if there was a battle, finish it as quickly as possible with as much as it takes. Only by demonstrating martial superiority could a warrior effectively dissuade would-be challengers from indulging their aggressive impulses. By eradicating the eastern and southern Finjou formations so ruthlessly (and with a little artistic flair thrown in for good measure), Xi knew she was sending a universal message any military commander would understand.

But the demonstration wasn't over yet.

Even as the last of the droids fell to Clover's coil guns, Xi's mechs were already sprinting to the east, where the enemy looked to have nearly completed their consolidation. The *Bahamut Zero* had returned to effective support range of the dig site, but General Akinouye's mega-mech was not close enough to engage the enemy formation at peak efficiency.

The dig site was more exposed than ever. If her guess was right, as soon as the northeastern Finjou contingent began its charge, the last of their aircraft would take to the skies with every intention of filling the Gash with several megatons of fusion-fueled fire. They probably didn't know why Armor Corps was down there, and by now they probably didn't care. "Whatever your enemy wants, seek to deny him" was an axiom as old as conflict, and the Finjou had demonstrated themselves to be fierce and savvy combatants on the Brick.

They would have no qualms about annihilating every exposed Terran, which meant Xi needed to support the dig site as soon as possible. The majority of her fixed defensive positions were either ammo-dry or close to it. She still had eight of Captain Chow's Vipers on the ground, but they and the *Bahamut Zero* represented the only credible anti-aircraft systems in support range of the Gash outside of the Mole Hill.

"Dragon Brigade," she called to every non-Clover mech on the ground as they sprinted northeast toward the dig site, "resume defensive assignments ASAP. Lieutenant Winters, how's the Mole Hill?"

"Standing at twenty-two percent ammo, Captain," Winters replied promptly. "All platforms stable and fire-ready."

Barely enough for one more interception flight, Xi thought grimly. "Copy that, *Generally*. *Gunslinger*, that was some fine shooting back there," she praised. "Climb the Mole Hill's western face and prepare for an encore."

"Acknowledged, Captain," replied the *Kolt's* Jock.

If her read was right, the Finjou would be ready for a concerted assault in just under nine minutes...and it would take the bulk of her mechs *seventeen* minutes to make it to their defensive positions at the Gash.

"*Havoc, Elvira*," she raised the general's mega-mech.

"*Havoc* here," Akinouye replied.

"We're going to need to lean on your anti-aircraft systems for eight minutes, General," Xi explained.

The general chuckled. "I *can* still read a tactical plotter, Captain. We're bingo Blue Boys, but have plenty of everything else. Take your time; the party will be here waiting for you when you're done playing with your hair."

"Roger, *Havoc*," Xi acknowledged with a grin.

Had anyone else said those words she might have taken offense, but coming from General Akinouye, it was a badge of honor to be ribbed on the open air.

"Clover Actual," Xi raised Jenkins on a P2P.

"Go ahead, *Elvira*," the colonel acknowledged as his mechs raced across the terrain nearly thirty percent faster than Xi's.

"Advise you flank east of the Mole Hill," she explained. "We've got some pop-ups and mines dug-in between there and the Gash as a last line of defense should the enemy ground forces break through. I'd hate for you to sprain an ankle charging through there."

"Copy that, *Elvira*," Jenkins replied graciously as his mechs adjusted course a few degrees. "Thanks for the heads-up."

After that, the minutes ticked by until, with mechanical precision, the enemy regrouped and commenced what would probably be the final charge of the engagement.

One way or another, this was all about to end. From Xi's

perspective, it looked like it might turn out to be a slaughter in the Terrans' favor.

Despite her having masterminded the Gash's defensive strategy, she had mixed feelings about the prospect of killing every single Finjou on the Brick. The last thing the Terran Republic needed was more enemies, but as far as she could tell, there was no other path to victory. The birdbrains were giving her no choice.

Jenkins' mechs surged toward the charging Finjou vehicles from the south and tore past the Mole Hill at 130 kph, and soon after that, they sped by the lowlands where some of Winters' slower and more badly damaged mechs were still stationed.

If Jenkins' hunch was right, an odd number of Finjou fighter craft would soon appear on the plotter to support the eighty-three enemy ground vehicles. The previous Finjou aircraft flights had consisted of precisely thirty-two fighters apiece, but with the devastation the Terrans had wrought upon them in recent engagements, it was unlikely they had another full wing at their disposal.

If the Finjou had possessed another wing or two of fighters, they could have wiped out the Terran forces at the Gash during the previous assault. It was logical to assume they were low on aircraft after suffering what were probably unexpected losses, courtesy of Captain Chow's Vipers, the *Zero's* fighter-killer missiles, and the Metal Legion's arsenal of railguns.

"Bogeys inbound," came the voice of *Eclipse's* Jock, Sargon. Sure enough, twenty-nine fighters arrived at the edge of Dragon Brigade's sensor net. They were arranged in two flights, one from the south with eleven fighters and another from the northwest that had eighteen. They were making no attempt to hide their objective since both flights held converging approach vectors to deliver them directly over the dig site.

Jenkins almost raised Falwell, *Preacher's* Jock, to provide targeting solutions, but he checked himself before the first syllable passed his lips. Captain Xi was still in command of Dragon Brigade. As a result, his orders would cause unnecessary confusion and disorder among the Legion's ranks.

"*Preacher*," Xi's voice crackled across the airwaves, "prepare to engage assigned targets."

"Roger, Captain," Falwell acknowledged, and Jenkins felt a rare twinge of pride at seeing his people performing without him. He liked to think he could have come up with a plan every bit as good as Xi's, but the truth was that she had a keen tactical mind. She still had plenty to learn about maintaining morale, delegating responsibility, recognizing and deploying talent, and a dozen other command skills that no nineteen-year-old could possibly have mastered.

But watching her deploy hardware was like watching a frame-perfect reproduction of Bruce Lee vs. Chuck Norris: it was violent poetry given form.

The oncoming enemy fighters converged, drawing steadily nearer to the engagement envelope. Jenkins raised the rest of Clover as he assigned targets. "Clover Battalion, prepare to receive the enemy with railguns. Fire at thirty-five-percent solutions."

Silent acknowledgments streamed across his screen, and as they did so, he received an inbound connection request from Sergeant Major Trapper at the Mole Hill.

"*Roy* here," Jenkins greeted.

"It's good to hear your voice, Colonel," the grizzled warrior replied with feeling. "The enemy did a number on the Mole Hill's control systems during the last attack. I've got a team up here working to repair the relays and auto-fire systems, but it looks like we're going to be stuck on local fire control for the duration."

Jenkins felt his guts tighten at the sergeant major's meaning. The Mole Hill was the only above-ground Terran fortification of note, and it had played a key role in thwarting the last enemy attack on the Gash.

The Finjou were unlikely to leave it unviolated in the coming attack.

"Copy that, Tim," Jenkins replied.

"I'd have informed Dragon Actual," Trapper said, a rare wry note creeping into his voice, "but you were closer, so I was hoping that you'd pass it along at your earliest convenience."

Jenkins took the other man's meaning loud and clear, and it filled him with ambivalent pride and resignation.

Trapper didn't want to distract Xi with the knowledge that the previously-automated Mole Hill was now manned by the infantry leader. The sergeant major had been in more than his share of firefights, and he knew a good plan when he saw one. His taking up position at the Mole Hill meant he believed that doing so was in the Legion's best interests, and he wasn't interested in having his decision overruled. With just one flight of missiles in its launchers, the Mole Hill would be inert after it fired its next salvo, but the enemy didn't know that and was certain to render it inert on their own terms.

Which meant no one currently deployed on the Mole Hill was likely to survive the coming exchange. And Trapper's potentially final gift was that he would draw as much enemy fire as possible while keeping the rest of the interceptor systems focused on defending the dig site and the cans loaded with rebel civvies.

"Understood, Sergeant Major Trapper," Jenkins acknowledged as the last eight Terran aerospace fighters launched from the Gash's floor and sped off to meet the enemy. Four fighters headed northwest, four to the south. "Your secret's safe with me," Jenkins assured the sergeant major.

"Good to know, Colonel," Trapper replied, hesitating before awkwardly adding, "You've put together one hell of a team here, Lee. Keep it together. For me and for all of Terra. Are we clear?"

"As a Solarian's conscience," Jenkins declared with feeling.

Trapper laughed as heartily as Lee Jenkins had ever heard a man laugh. It was the first time Jenkins could remember the elder Trapper displaying any kind of unreserved emotion other than disgust with his soldiers' inevitable screw-ups. "My boy was right about you. You're a good man, Leeroy. Trapper out."

The line went dead as the first enemy fighter craft entered firing range. Clover's mechs unleashed their railguns and sent a staggered volley up to meet the enemy while the *Bahamut Zero*'s railguns did likewise. A total of twenty-seven railguns lashed out to the northwestern formation, but just seven struck their targets. Xi's people to the south didn't fare much better, landing only eight hits on the approaching eleven fighter craft.

But the Legion's hits came *after* the northwestern fighters had launched their final storm of ninety-three missiles.

It had been a calculated risk to fire at the fighter craft from such long range instead of waiting for them to come closer or even waiting for the missiles to be launched before intercepting them individually, but the chance to drop entire fighters full of missiles was too great to ignore.

Unfortunately, the Finjou had done the math a little bit better than the Terrans, and any half-smart warrior knew that battles were far too often decided by such margins.

The *Zero* sent a swarm of intercepting rockets up to greet the inbound ordnance, and Jenkins' Clover mechs did likewise. A hundred and eighty-three rockets sped to intercept the enemy missiles, while Clover adopted a defensive stance to receive the vehicular charge that was nearly upon them.

"Clover," Jenkins called as he bracketed a pair of enemy vehicles with *Warcrafter's* artillery, "engage ground targets at will. Let 'em have it."

Warcrafter's guns thundered, sending extended-range HE shells ten kilometers downrange as the approaching droid transports surged forward en masse.

Jenkins' Razorbacks followed his lead, sending two dozen artillery shells whistling through the thin air. The barrage yielded four direct hits and four near-misses. The *Bahamut Zero* added its throw weight to the mix by scratching three more and crippling two.

The Mole Hill sent a wave of missiles out to intercept the inbound enemy ordnance that bore down on their targets with murderous intent. In the last two seconds before impact, every Terran anti-personnel gun fired toward the approaching missile swarm.

Mech-launched rockets impacted missiles by the dozens, anti-personnel embankments luckily intercepted a pair, and the Mole Hill's final act of defiance scrubbed dozens more Finjou missiles from the sky. But in spite of the Terrans' valiant efforts, eight Finjou missiles broke through the shield.

Three of them nukes.

In the blinding light of three nuclear strikes, *Warcrafter's* sensors automatically shut down to protect them and their Jock from overloading in the intense rad-wash. When they resumed, he was relieved to see the Mole Hill had been spared the nuclear fire. Three SRMs had struck the fortification, but it was possible, given the relatively light damage he saw, that Trapper and his people might have survived.

He was equally satisfied to see that the dig-site had been spared annihilation. All of the digging equipment was still there and more or less intact, and even the drop-cans bearing the civilians appeared intact. They were awash in radiation, and their inhabitants would require extensive medical intervention to survive the after-effects, but it was almost certain that they had survived.

Jenkins breathed a sigh of relief as his mech's comm suite reinitialized. They had protected the primary objectives. In the sky above the trio of distinctive thin-air mushroom clouds, Terran Vipers steadily neutralized their less-maneuverable counterparts. Xi's mechs, some of which had lower-tech virtual systems that were paradoxically less susceptible to radiation interference, engaged the enemy flyers with railguns and soon the sky was clear of enemy aircraft.

Warcrafter's comm suite finally returned to full capability, and Jenkins' guts tightened when damage reports began streaming across his screen.

The *Bahamut Zero* had been just at the edge of one of the nuclear strikes. In fact, it seemed that *two* of the nukes had been aimed at the peerless war machine, but one must have been knocked off course mid-flight because it touched down two klicks north of the *Zero's* position.

The other, however, might have killed the Legion's pride and joy…and its legendary leader along with it.

Filled with sudden wholly unexpected rage, Jenkins keyed up the main Armor Corps frequency. "This is Colonel Jenkins to all Terran Armor Corps personnel on the Brick," he called as a tsunami of Finjou assault droids bore down on them. "Havoc is down. I say again: Havoc is down. Concentrate fire to protect the flag."

"Copy that, Colonel." Xi was first to respond, a sense of much-appreciated urgency in her voice. "*Cave Troll*, you're up. Gut that line."

"With pleasure," *Cave Troll* replied, his voice conveying every last bit of the anger Jenkins felt at seeing the general's crippled mech. Smoke rose from a dozen rents in the *Zero's* hull, and two-thirds of its weaponry appeared to have been torn completely off by the blast wave.

Cave Troll popped up above the edge of the lowlands where the rest of Winters' Company was stationed. Its twin heavy plasma-cannons whined to life, filling with angry white light before sending bolts of blue-white plasma toward the enemy horde.

The enemy vehicles zigged and zagged, thinking they could escape *Cave Troll*'s wrath with last-minute evasions, but *Cave Troll*'s weaponry was purpose-built for environments like the Brick. As soon as the bolts of hellfire struck the ground, they exploded with the force of a kiloton apiece.

Shrapnel flew outward from the blast points, slashing through five of the enemy vehicles and slowing the entire enemy line.

Then, to Jenkins' relief, the *Bahamut Zero* stirred. Rumbling forward on badly-damaged legs, the lone siege-grade war machine in existence gathered momentum as it moved to intercept the enemy.

"This is Havoc. We're reactor-critical...just three survivors..." came Akinouye's pained, wheezing voice as the *Zero* continued gaining speed. Fully half of the enemy drones dismounted their vehicles and surged toward the dying mech. "We're going to...offer these birds...an olive branch. Make the most of it, Metalheads..." the general continued, every desperate gasp between words sounding like it might be his last.

One of the *Zero*'s LRMs fired, sending a relatively slow-moving strategic-grade system into the sky. The missile screamed over the enemy droid horde before banking up and making a long, ponderous loop.

A loop which would touch down on the very vehicle that had launched it: the *Bahamut Zero*.

The next words that came across the main Legion channel

filled Jenkins with a feeling so profound, so complete, and so perfect that words could never describe it. With his last breath, General Benjamin Akinouye bellowed three words, which Jenkins knew would become the TAC battle cry.

"Metal never dies!"

As the *Zero* reached the line of enemy droids, the missile touched down. The two-hundred-kiloton warhead ignited a short-lived nova which tore the dying *Bahamut Zero* apart in a fiery conflagration worthy of the only man to have ridden her into battle.

A more glorious funeral pyre had never been lit for a human warrior, be they Terran or Solarian.

The mushroom cloud rose from the northern face, kilometers above the Gash's floor. The rad-wash swept across to the southern slope, kicking up a billowing cloud of ultra-fine dust that swept the ground clean. But by the time it reached Xi's mechs and the refugee-filled shelter-cans, the device's energy was too diffuse to be a threat.

In fact, the *Bahamut Zero* had been alone on the Gash's north rim, so the only victims of the general's last act of violence were the Finjou droids.

And yet, despite the explosion's devastating power, half those droids remained active.

The Finjou had dispersed their forces to prevent such an attack from wiping them out, and they had succeeded in preserving the integrity of their charge. With over four hundred assault droids devouring the ground between their line and the mechs of Clover Battalion, Jenkins knew it would be only a matter of time before he was once again in knife-range of the frighteningly effective machines.

Then something peculiar happened. The droids stopped their charge in perfect unison and adopted crouching postures.

For a moment Jenkins was confused, then he recalled something Captain Guan had said during their approach to the Brick.

"Only after proving our determination…" Jenkins reiterated under his breath, and the general's cryptic "olive branch" comment made sense.

Akinouye had killed himself not just to destroy the enemy droids descending on his position, but to communicate with their masters that the Terrans would dig their heels in and die from friendly fire rather than surrender.

"Dragon Brigade, hold fire," Jenkins called urgently as Terran artillery continued to fire to little effect, given the dispersion of the enemy units. "I say again: hold fire!" Clover's guns fell silent, followed by Dragon's, and Jenkins raised the *Bonhoeffer* on P2P. "*Bonhoeffer* Actual, this is Colonel Jenkins."

"*Bonhoeffer* Actual here," Colonel Li replied.

"Hail the Finjou warships and patch them through to me if they reply," Jenkins told him tightly. "I think they're ready to negotiate."

"I should hope so," Li said grimly. "Stand by."

Several seconds passed before a decidedly reptilian voice greeted him with, "I am Blue Razorbeak Alpha. We are prepared to discuss your withdrawal from our sovereign territory."

"I am Colonel Lee Jenkins," Jenkins replied, hoping he was equal to the task now before him. "We are prepared to receive your emissary."

"No emissaries," hissed the Finjou. "Tell your warships to stand down as I approach."

Jenkins knew this could be a ploy to stab his people in the back, but he was out of options. The Finjou had broken their charge and given his people time to bracket them—which they had done. If the bird-brains double-crossed him now, he would annihilate the rest of their ground forces before doing likewise to their warships if they didn't withdraw.

So he bit his tongue and replied, "I'm giving the order now. Rendezvous at the following coordinates."

The Finjou hissed in apparent disdain, "Very well."

20

ARMISTICE

Despite their collective objections, Jenkins had assembled his senior officers aboard his former command vehicle, *Roy*. Chaps had taken good care of the mech, which was one of the only vehicles large enough to fit the Finjou leader.

It had been nearly three hours since Jenkins had agreed to a ceasefire with the enemy commander, and during that time, his people had managed to unearth a particularly crusty trooper from what might have been his final resting place.

"There's ballsy and there's stupid, Colonel," Sergeant Major Trapper said, his head wrapped in a blood-soaked bandage. "This is an extra serving of both. Gathering all of us here is just begging for a fight."

"It's a threat display," Jenkins explained, recalling something Styles had said to him back on Shiva's Wrath. "We show them our claws, and they show us theirs. And despite your overly ruddy complexion," he smirked, giving Trapper's bloody head a pointed look, "you cut a fearsome figure."

"I just hope I don't keel over," the sergeant major grumbled, drawing a snicker from Xi.

Chaps turned his pilot's chair toward the officers. "Finjou primary has touched down. ETA six minutes."

Jenkins' wrist-link chimed, showing a priority message from Styles.

"Good," Jenkins said as he made for his cabin. "That gives me time for a quick debriefing."

He opened the hatch, behind which Lieutenant Podsednik and Chief Styles awaited. Both men immediately stood upon his arrival, but he gestured for them to resume their seats. They complied, but Podsy was extra careful with the long ruby-red crystalline shaft in his hands.

"At ease, gentlemen," he ordered, suspecting that Podsy was holding the technological artifact they had come here to retrieve. "What is it?"

"Colonel," Styles gestured to the device in Podsy's hands, "this thing is... Well, it's some sort of virtual intelligence."

Jenkins' eyes narrowed dangerously. "Is it secure?"

"I have no idea." Styles shook his head firmly. "What I *do* know is that it thinks it can help with the Finjou."

"How?" Jenkins pressed.

"Up the tunnel," Podsy explained, "where we found this thing was some kind of tomb. It's the last resting place of refugees who were the same race as the Jemmin. They were called the Jem'un."

Styles nodded eagerly. "This thing calls itself Jem and claims to be a gestalt intelligence built upon the memories and personalities of almost five hundred Jem'un who died fifteen thousand years ago. After we agreed to bring it with us, it told us that the Finjou were manipulated by the Jemmin like we were. It says Finjou society was too fractured and feudalistic for anything like the One Mind network to arise as the Jemmin apparently intended, and as a result, we might be able to do better than just negotiate a peaceful withdrawal from here if we offer the Finjou the same kind of proof we brought back."

At that, Styles pulled the blanket off Jenkins' bunk, revealing a pair of large four-sided cases with tinted transparent panes. One held what looked like an immaculately-preserved human skull and the other had some sort of technological component in it.

"Jem says," Podsy continued, "that if you tell the Finjou about the tomb, they'll not only refuse to follow Jemmin commands but that some of them might actually become Terran allies."

"How would this 'Jem' be able to predict that?" Jenkins asked skeptically.

"Apparently," Styles said heavily, "Jem has been conscious and thinking about this situation nonstop for fifteen thousand years. Its forebears were xenobiologists and students of organic sentience, and they had ample experience studying both the Finjou and humanity. I'm not saying we should trust everything Jem says because that would be stupid, considering we know next to nothing about it," he explained. "But I thought you should know that it seemed convinced you should use the tomb as leverage."

Jenkins considered Styles' suggestion before nodding. "Good work, Chief." He turned to Lieutenant Podsednik with a penetrating look. "Mind explaining what you're doing down here, Lieutenant? This part of the operation was supposed to remain compartmentalized."

"General Akinouye assigned me to the excavation team after the drop, Colonel," Podsy explained.

"I have copies of the orders, Colonel," Styles added, and a reverent silence fell over the room as the three men were reminded of Havoc's passing.

Jenkins cocked a brow in surprise as he mentally replayed what Podsy had just said. "You rode the *Zero* planet-side?"

"Yes, sir," Podsy replied with a firm nod.

Jenkins quirked a grin. "How was it?"

"Every bit as rough as they say," Podsy replied before grumpily adding, "I missed the landing."

Jenkins chuckled. "All right. Good work, gentlemen. Stand by while I go shake this thing's...claw?" He found what seemed like the appropriate word.

The men laughed nervously as Jenkins opened the hatch and made his way back to the cabin.

"Finjou delegate is in the airlock," Chaps reported. "One minute to decontamination."

"Thank you, Chaps." Jenkins clapped the other man on the shoulder.

"It's good to have you back, sir," Chaps said as Jenkins resumed his position between Xi and Trapper.

"It's good to *be* back, Chaps," Jenkins replied sincerely before turning to Captain Xi. The woman was days away from her twentieth birthday, but she had just orchestrated an engagement with a largely unknown enemy on hostile ground while preserving not just one, but *two* high-priority objectives.

The cherry on top of her remarkable achievement was that her overwhelming victory had brought the Finjou down to negotiate face to face. A purely predatory species, the Finjou respected nothing so much as naked force and the leverage it generated. In the end, humans weren't all that different from the Finjou, but Jenkins thought the token efforts at pre-violence diplomacy were meaningful differences between the two species' dominant cultures.

And Xi's efforts had led the Finjou straight to a negotiating table.

"You know you'll make major for this," he muttered.

"Colonel?" she asked in confusion.

"You're about to become the poster-child for the Metal Legion's upcoming recruiting drive," Jenkins explained. "And I mean that literally. I was just in the back going over pin-up layouts with Styles. Don't worry, it will all be digital art. You won't have to pose or anything...unless you want to?" he added, taking the opportunity to rib her while he could.

Xi's face turned a perfect shade of red, but her honest, unguarded smile made clear she appreciated the sentiment. "Great." She sighed, schooling her features as *Roy's* airlock began its final cycle. "As if those three hundred unsolicited dildos I got in the mail after the DIN report weren't bad enough. Now Styles is going to 'shop my face onto everything with two legs and no clothes."

"You underestimate him," Jenkins muttered as the airlock's inner hatch opened. "He won't stop at bipeds."

Xi half-stifled a snort as the hatch swung open, revealing a bizarre-looking creature that somehow looked nothing like Jenkins expected and yet was exactly as it should be.

With a trio of eyes on either side of its long, toothy, razor-sharp beak, the thing looked more like a four-winged pterodactyl than anything else. Lines of blue feathers ran the length of its body, starting at the base of its meter-long skull and extending to the tip of its reptilian tail. A rebreather hood covered its neck, which was riddled with dozens of small nostril-like holes.

Its wings bore feathers, but they seemed vestigial rather than functional. And those wings, as tightly furled against its body as they were, were so large that the Finjou had to shuffle awkwardly through the narrow hatch in order to reach *Roy's* main cabin.

Trapper and Xi tensed at Jenkins' sides, prompting him to step forward until he and the Finjou delegate were so close that the thing could have almost certainly torn his throat open. The Finjou had no proper hands, but its two smaller, lower wings each featured a diminutive pair of claws with three talons.

In one of those claws, it held a slender rod not much larger than a thick cigar. Jenkins recognized it as a standard Illumination League translator, and the Finjou held it out as though asking permission to activate it.

"Leeroy," Trapper muttered, "you are stupid as hell."

Ignoring Trapper's expected quip, Jenkins kept his focus on the Finjou. He nodded in approval, and the creature flicked the switch at the slightly fatter of the device's tips. Even crouched as it was, the Finjou was two and a half meters tall, and the height disparity was every bit as unnerving as Jenkins had feared it would be. He guesstimated the thing weighed a hundred and fifty kilos, and that its wings when unfurled might be ten meters from tip to tip.

When it spoke, its natural, screeching voice added to the already tense atmosphere in *Roy's* cabin.

"You are the Terran Alpha?" it asked in a translated tone which was clearly more a demand than a polite request.

"Our former Alpha sacrificed himself to take out your drones. With his death, I became the Alpha of the Terran Armor Corps on this planet," Jenkins replied, knowing that to flinch or back down was to invite disaster.

"Be direct!" the Finjou snapped, its toothy beak clacking in an unmistakable display of irritation. "You are the Terran Alpha?"

"As far as you're concerned," Jenkins sneered, "I'm the god-emperor of all humanity! Every human in this star system follows my commands without fail. So yeah," he squared his shoulders, "I am the motherfucking Terran Alpha."

The thing recoiled in apparent surprise before cocking his six-eyed head appraisingly. "You mate with your progenitor?"

Trapper couldn't help but snort behind Jenkins. "No," Jenkins said irritably, feeling his face flush every bit as red as Xi's had done when he'd ribbed her a minute earlier. "It's an idiom. A stupid thing we sometimes say. Inbreeding makes humans weak," he explained, saying whatever came to mind in the hope of salvaging the faux pas, "so calling one's self a 'motherfucker' is a linguistic feint meant to disguise one's strength."

The Finjou swiveled its head back and forth like a dog ragdolling a chew-toy, causing the translator to issue a surprising bout of synthetic laughter. "Human humor is good. We did not expect this. We also did not expect you to fight so well. Clan Blue Razorbeak is impressed. The Jemmin were wrong about your species."

That last bit sent a chill down Jenkins' spine. He pushed it aside, knowing that there were priorities to observe. He needed to get the colonists off-world, but in order to do that expeditiously, he needed the Finjou warships to stand off.

"We have civilian refugees who need to evacuate or they will die," Jenkins explained.

Blue Razorbeak Alpha tensed its neck, bringing the tip of its beak up before seemingly forcing it back down again. "Humans violated Finjou sovereignty. They must be tried in Finjou courts."

"I can't allow that." Jenkins shook his head firmly, knowing that Finjou courts were rarely more than perfunctory presages to summary executions followed by banquets featuring the executed as entrees. "I need you to stand off so I can extract these people. In exchange, I'll provide you with the location of their subterranean colony, the passcodes needed to access it, and direct control of all remaining human military fortifications on this planet. I could blow it all right now," he said, producing a remote trigger primed to blow one of the six remaining fortresses on the surface, "but I'm willing to give it to you instead if you stand your warships off so I can safely evacuate these people."

The Finjou ruffled its wings, filling *Roy's* cabin with the sound of leather scraping against leather. "Human technology is inferior to Finjou. Inferior to Jemmin. It has little value to us."

"Fine." Jenkins shrugged, pressing the plunger and causing a warning alarm to chime instantly at a nearby console.

"Facility destroyed," Chaps reported, and for a moment Jenkins was unable to tell if the Finjou would react.

That moment stretched before the Finjou grudgingly said, "We will permit you to withdraw your civilians."

"And our military hardware," Jenkins said, emphatically holding up the detonator.

"Yes, yes," the dinosaur-looking thing agreed. "We will permit you to withdraw your active hardware."

Jenkins nodded in agreement, having already secured the most sensitive equipment that was unsalvageable while hauling the rest back to the drop-zone. Chief among that equipment were the damaged Razorbacks bearing Vorr technology, which could not be allowed to fall into anyone's hands but Captain Guan's after they withdrew.

"Good." Jenkins nodded.

"You fight well," the Finjou said grudgingly. "You negotiate better."

"I'm not done yet," Jenkins said pointedly, knowing he needed to be extremely careful with his next words. "In the spirit of friendship and in the hope of fostering cooperation between our nations, I've prepared a gift."

"What is this gift?" the Finjou asked dubiously, and Jenkins knew this was yet another one of those moments in his life which might come back to haunt him.

But Styles was his most trusted advisor and closest confidant. Without his help, Jenkins could not have possibly gotten his armor experiment off the ground, nor could he have hoped to survive Admiral Corbyn's grilling after Durgan's Folly.

And Styles was telling him to give the Finjou access to the Jem'un tomb. One of the first things Lee Jenkins learned about command was that if you gave someone a position of trust, you had to validate that trust for as long as that person demonstrated they were worthy of it.

"We've cut a tunnel," Jenkins explained, "into the rockface below. It leads to a facility that the Finjou will find...most interesting." He emphasized the last two words, hoping the translator would convey the desired subtext. "Bringing what you find there back to your people might elevate Clan Blue Razorbeak's standing higher than it's ever been."

The Finjou's head cocked slightly before sliding sideways, much as a cat or owl does while range-finding a target. Jenkins took it to be a gesture of skepticism, and his guess was validated when the auto-translated voice replied, "Blue Razorbeak is a proud, storied clan."

"I'm sure it is, but Blue Razorbeak suffered a defeat here against a technologically inferior foe," Jenkins pressed. "What I'm offering you will not only erase the stain of that defeat but will ensure your clan's place in Finjou history. Forever."

"Too many bloody words," the Finjou said with open suspicion, and it took Jenkins a moment to realize that the phrase was probably the equivalent of the English "enough of your honeyed words."

"Send a team to investigate while I extract my people," Jenkins urged. "I'll stay here until you've investigated, and if you find I was lying, you can come to take vengeance. But I'm telling the truth, and what you discover down there *will* increase Blue Razorbeak's power and prestige, just say 'thank you' for the gift, and we'll be on our way."

The Finjou ruffled its feathers again, but its translated voice was surprisingly calm. "We will investigate. These negotiations are concluded."

The creature left through the airlock and the cabin's occupants breathed a collective sigh of relief.

"Leeroy," Trapper repeated, this time in relief rather than taut disdain, "you *are* stupid as hell."

"Yep," Jenkins deadpanned, shaking his suddenly trembling arms loose as the post-negotiation adrenaline dump hit him like a ton of bricks, "but apparently I'm their kind of stupid."

Twelve hours later the last of the civilians had been evacuated to the *Dietrich Bonhoeffer*, which was in considerably worse shape than Jenkins had previously thought. Li's people had managed to prepare sufficient emergency berths for all seven thousand colonists, but it was going to be ten kinds of uncomfortable with so many people crammed aboard a ship designed to hold no more than two thousand under a full load.

The heavy lifters descended from the *Bonhoeffer* and *Red Hare*, suspended by carbon nanotube cables attached to giant spools anchored within the carriers' hulls. The lifters were specifically designed to clamp onto any of the eight different drop-can types, which they would lift back up to the carriers. Like temporary space elevators or "beanstalks," as many in the Terran Republic referred to them, these lifting platforms were the only viable system for retrieving the heavy vehicles of the Metal Legion.

During peace-time drops, or in non-combat zones, the lifters served double-duty by also deploying the Legion's mechs. But the cables were too valuable and fragile to risk damage from enemy fire, so the braking-thruster-equipped drop-cans had been developed as the lone deployment system for combat insertions.

It would take another day of shuttling cans loaded with mechs before the Terran Armor Corps would be wheels-up from the Brick, but Jenkins received two words from the Finjou long before then.

Those two words were "Thank you."

With the Finjou's gratitude in mind, he helped coordinate the withdrawal of his battered Metalheads.

When it came to the last of the vehicles, Xi's *Elvira* and Jenkins' *Roy*, Jenkins did the right thing and let Xi's mech be the last to go wheels-up.

Even considering his late-hour assist, the Brick had been her command from start to finish. Like every other military tradition, it was important for the commander to be first-in, last-out. And judging by the sentiment throughout the beleaguered brigade, which was one of enthusiastic support for Jenkins' deferential gesture to the talented young woman, he knew he had made the right call.

She had earned her fellow Metalheads' respect the only way that counted: in combat.

The hard way.

21

THE POISONED CARROT

Jenkins hated this part. He truly, madly, deeply hated it, but there was no getting around the bureaucracy.

It was time for the inevitable after-action debriefing, which he assumed would feature another panel of Fleet officers. He very much doubted that this one would feature anyone as friendly as Colonel Jonathan Villa.

It had taken the *Bonhoeffer* twelve days to limp home from the Brick. The proud warship had sustained critical damage to nearly every system during the firefight with the Finjou, and after Jenkins had been debriefed on the naval battle by Colonel Li, he was amazed the aged warship had survived.

The Finjou had punctured the *Bonhoeffer's* hull eighteen times in the firefight. A full third of the *Bonhoeffer's* crew had been lost to explosive decompressions, and another third had sustained serious wounds due to missile strikes impacting directly on the warship's keel.

As hairy as things had been planet-side, things had been much, much worse in orbit.

Coupled with General Akinouye's death, the so-called

"Battle of the Brick" had been far costlier than anyone could have envisioned.

And Jenkins had received ominous word that the casualty list was not yet complete.

As he waited outside the Terran Armor Corps' central planning theater, Jenkins had serious doubts as to whether he could weather the storm he was about to walk into. When those oak and gold-leaf doors opened and he was summoned to provide his formal testimony, he would, for the first time since joining the Metal Legion, be totally isolated.

Somewhat mercifully, his ruminations were cut short when the doors parted. A woman wearing smartly-fitting dress browns with silver lieutenant's bars beckoned from the open door. "The general will see you now, sir."

Jenkins tucked his beret under his arm, fighting down the anxiety he felt as he followed the lieutenant into the theater. It was the same room where Generals Akinouye, Pushkin, and Kavanaugh had briefed him on the Shiva's Wrath op. It seemed like that meeting had taken place mere days ago, but as Jenkins emerged into the theater's lower platform with the iconic Armor Corps emblem proudly emblazoned upon the floor, one look at the far end of the room was all it took to confirm just how much had happened since that day.

A trio of throne-like chairs sat upon the raised command dais on the far end of the room. General Akinouye had previously occupied the central seat, flanked by General Pushkin and Major General Kavanaugh, but now only one of those seats was occupied.

He steeled his resolve as he made his way to the bar set five meters before the command dais. Once he arrived, he braced to attention and snapped a salute. "Lieutenant Colonel Jenkins reporting as ordered, General."

"At ease, Lieutenant Colonel Jenkins," Major General

Kavanaugh gestured invitingly as she leaned back in the central chair.

General Akinouye's chair.

"Although," she continued blithely, "we should probably dispense with the 'lieutenant' bit, don't you think?"

"Ma'am?" Jenkins placed his beret on his head before clasping his hands behind his back and standing at ease.

"Colonel Li's report of Operation Brick Top was absolutely glowing, Colonel." Kavanaugh waved a hand at a number of polymer sheets neatly stacked on one corner of the desk.

General Akinouye's desk.

"Such successes are generally rewarded," the major general continued measuredly. "When you transferred over from Fleet, we withheld what should have been an automatic step up in rank due to the…peculiar circumstances of your transfer." Her lips twisted into an approving smirk. "Out of deference to Fleet, we held off, but deference goes only so far. As the highest-ranking officer in the Terran Armor Corps, it is my privilege and pleasure to bestow upon you the rank of full colonel. The ceremony will be in six days' time," she explained, "where you and a number of your officers will receive the ornaments and implements of your new ranks. Chief among the other promotions will be Captain Xi Bao's ascent to the rank of major. I know it's a little unusual and will cause some consternation among the other branches, especially given her youth and the brevity of her time as Captain, but the Terran Armor Corps has always marched to its own beat when it comes to recognizing talent. Captain Xi Bao is an exemplary officer whose future is brighter than any I have ever seen, and her performance on the Brick was precisely the kind of thing Armor Corps needs in order to resume its place of prominence in the Terran Armed Forces. Don't you agree?"

Jenkins nodded. "Absolutely, ma'am."

"Good," Kavanaugh said approvingly.

"If I may ask, ma'am?" Jenkins gestured to one of the two empty seats. "Where is General Pushkin?"

She smiled, her lips tightening into flat lines designed to mask irritation. "General Pushkin tendered his resignation nine days ago, citing health concerns and a desire to spend time with his family. His departure comes at a most unfortunate time, especially given the death of General Akinouye, but I have nonetheless accepted his resignation. My own promotion will not be official for another three weeks, given the paperwork and oversight requirements, but rest assured that we will reconstitute Armor Corps' leadership with all due haste."

"Who, if I may ask," Jenkins ventured, knowing he was sailing into dangerous waters, "is in line to replace them, General?"

She leaned forward, lacing her fingers and resting her hands on the desk as she peered down at him with an appraising eye. Part inspection, part predatory preamble, the expression on Major General Kavanaugh's face was more than slightly unnerving.

"Colonels Li and Moon are both under consideration," she eventually replied, "although obviously, their elevation will require an even more thorough inquiry than my own, given that they must first be promoted to the necessary stations. And since the *Bonhoeffer* is currently in orbit over Durgan's Folly, where it will remain until it can be inspected and have its condition thoroughly appraised, the matter of their elevation must be postponed for the time being."

"Begging pardon, ma'am," Jenkins said, careful to keep his body language confused and engaged rather than rigid and anxious. "Isn't it against TAF regulations for a single officer, no matter how highly-ranked, to restructure an entire branch's leadership?"

"You are correct, Colonel Jenkins. It's encouraging to see that you're familiar with some of the more arcane bits of the Code," she agreed with a pleasant expression that suggested he was still in the game.

He didn't want to come across as being unfriendly to her hostile takeover of the Metal Legion's leadership, and right now he needed to do everything he could to convince her that he was not a threat.

So far, so good, he thought.

"Which is why," General Kavanaugh continued, "in this interim period during which Armor Corps lacks the necessary framework of leadership to restructure its chain of command, I have called in a few favors to ensure that the process runs as smoothly and effectively as possible."

"Favors, ma'am?" Jenkins quirked a brow in genuine surprise.

"Yes, Colonel," she replied with a smile, although this one was more triumphant than predatory. "Given their recent interactions with TAC, and owing to the fact that Admirals Zhao and Corbyn are old friends of mine, they've both agreed to step in and provide the requisite measure of confirmatory authority that our corps needs in order to keep rolling."

There it was—a ten-megaton bomb that left Jenkins reeling. General Kavanaugh was going to reorganize the Metal Legion under Fleet, just as Admiral Corbyn had hinted might occur during Jenkins' "informal inquiry" and precisely as General Akinouye had steadfastly rejected. Corbyn had spoken of that project's timetable in terms of years, perhaps even a full decade, before such a restructuring could take place, though.

The casual way Major General Kavanaugh flipped the reorganization matter out there, like she was laying down a full house while a flush was still on the board, suggested she was uncertain if he would be sympathetic to her plan.

He had to think fast, or his entire brigade would be in jeopardy.

"Fleet oversight, ma'am?" he reiterated warily. "I thought you were in agreement with General Akinouye that the Legion should retain its independence?"

"In point of fact, I *did* agree with him about that," Kavanaugh replied, projecting an air of somberness that seemed wholly artificial to Jenkins. "But variables have changed, Colonel, as they so often do. And now we must also change if we are to avoid the loss of this precious momentum that you and Dragon Brigade have generated. The Terran Armor Corps has a real future now, Colonel Jenkins, and that future was only made possible by your exemplary contributions. Contributions which were enabled by the valor and ingenuity of the men and women under your command. As Armor Corps' most senior officer, it is my duty to ensure that their talents, and yours, are deployed to maximum effect in furtherance of Terran humanity."

Jenkins could feel the proverbial noose tightening around his neck. General Kavanaugh was more ambitious than he had ever suspected, and she was now making a move which must have been decades in the offing. Even General Akinouye had never confided in Jenkins any real concerns about Kavanaugh's loyalty to the Legion. He had sometimes referred to her as more ambitious than passionate, but her work at his side had been vital in their efforts to keep the Legion's doors open.

And here she was, with the embers of General Akinouye's funeral pyre still warm, moving to tear down everything the man had spent his entire life to build.

The bitch of it was, Lee Jenkins knew the only way through this minefield was straight up the middle—which meant betraying the man whose beloved Corps had become Jenkins' last, best hope for salvation.

"In truth, General Kavanaugh," Jenkins said hesitantly, "I

couldn't agree more. We need to adapt to the times and maximize our assets' effectiveness, which is why, before I went on my fundraising tour, I urged General Akinouye to move toward consolidating the Legion under Fleet's banner."

"Oh?" She cocked an eyebrow, but her expression was otherwise unreadable. "And how did he receive your suggestion?"

Jenkins forced a grimace. "Not well, ma'am. He suggested I was anatomically challenged, specifically pertaining to my cranio-caudal relationship, and went on to detail how an...inventively deployed fifteen-kilo shell would clarify my thinking."

Kavanaugh's eyes narrowed, and for a moment he thought she had seen through him. Then she threw her head back and laughed. "That does sound like Ben," she said agreeably. "His Metal Legion was the only thing he ever truly loved. He probably took your suggestion as a personal threat rather than a tactical appraisal."

"Respectfully, ma'am," Jenkins continued, absolutely hating himself as he did, "his pride got in his way, but worse still, it got in the Legion's way. When I first approached him about my trial program, it was with the declared intention of incorporating armor elements into Fleet operations. I only transferred over to the Legion when it seemed like the program...*my* program," he reiterated with genuine passion, "would get shelved by Fleet brass. I think they saw my proposal as a competing alternative to the Marines, but I never envisioned it that way," he continued, speaking with absolute honesty on this particular point. "I always thought that technologically-updated mechs and power-armored Marines could be deployed in mutually-supportive configurations in a variety of mission profiles, but every time I'd bring it up, either to the Admiralty or to General Akinouye, they reduced it to a conflict over which would be given priority. And Fleet does love their Marines," he added sourly.

She gave a knowing nod. "To be frank, Colonel, I've already encountered precisely the same thing in my preliminary discussions of the matter with Admirals Zhao and Corbyn."

"Rear Admiral Corbyn seemed receptive to the project," Jenkins said with a nod, taking careful aim with another sliver of truth in his high-wire deception, "but he expressed serious concerns about the political landscape and the bureaucratic obstacles to forming a consolidated Combined Arms sub-branch of Fleet. Admiral Zhao, on the other hand..." His words trailed off pointedly.

"Go on, Colonel," Kavanaugh urged. "You can speak frankly. These walls have no ears but our own."

Jenkins believed that. If the Jemmin or their cohorts and sympathizers had gained access to the Armor Corps briefings on either Shiva's Wrath or Operation Brick Top, they would have moved to prevent Jenkins' people from achieving their objectives on those worlds.

So he exhaled shortly before answering with a half-lie. "Admiral Zhao seemed intent not only on uncovering certain classified details discovered on Shiva's Wrath, but during the inquiry, his posture was openly hostile to Armor Corps, ma'am. I think we can work with Rear Admiral Corbyn to mutual gain, but I would advise caution when it comes to Admiral Zhao."

She nodded thoughtfully while tapping her chin with a long, slender finger. "I agree, Colonel," she finally declared, her face twisting into a moue of distaste. "Admiral Zhao has no real love for the Armor Corps, owing in some small part to that business with his son, which between you and me is partly why I was forced to accept him on the temporary advisory board. I must say that I'm impressed with your strategic perspective on these matters. It's clear to me now that I will have to rely on your input in the coming weeks as we lay the groundwork for Armor Corps to merge with Fleet."

"Merge" in this instance was a fluffy word for "bend the knee." For the time being, the Terran Armor Corps retained the privilege of operational security, which extended to blackout classification of certain mission-critical details. General Akinouye's authority had permitted him to conduct off-the-books, covert operations under the auspices of preserving ongoing operational security.

But now, with Admirals Corbyn and Zhao coming into the fold, the books were going to be opened up and information security would be compromised.

If Jenkins was right, the Jemmin would make a serious move against the Terran Republic, and possibly even all of humanity, shortly after the details of Akinouye's operations were revealed.

Jenkins straightened his shoulders, mustering an air of pride as he said, "I'll do my utmost to support your efforts, General. In the interests of Terran security, this merger needs to happen sooner rather than later."

"I wholeheartedly agree." Kavanaugh nodded approvingly, and as far as Jenkins could tell, he had at least convinced her that he was not actively antagonistic to her designs for the Metal Legion. "But we should table the matter of TAC's future. There are several discrepancies in your after-action reports," Kavanaugh explained, producing a data slate and deftly swiping through a number of screens, "which we need to go over."

"Of course, ma'am," he acknowledged, knowing that he was about to betray even more of the people who had put their trust in him.

But he had thought long and hard about this, and despite his moral objections, he had no choice but to play every last card in his hand. The stakes were just too high.

If he was wrong about the Jemmin conspiracy, and Director Durgan had manipulated General Akinouye for some as-yet-unknown reason, careers would end because of the details he let slip. Lives would be ruined, and an interstellar corporation would experience shockwaves that might raze it to the ground. And it would all be because of Lee Jenkins' soon-to-be-made report to Major General Kavanaugh.

But if he and Director Durgan and General Akinouye and the Vorr and the Zeen and even the bizarre entity known as 'Jem' were right about the Jemmin…

Then there was only one possible path to victory, and Jenkins needed to do whatever it took to reach it with enough firepower in hand to do the job.

"Let's start at the beginning, Colonel," Kavanaugh began, and for the next six hours, he gave as many classified details as he thought he could survive, with a single thought ringing in his head as each word passed his lips.

God help me if I'm wrong.

"Let's go back to the Han-built Razorback Mk 2-Vs," Kavanaugh circled back to the issue of the Terra Han mechs for the fourth time. "Were there any technical dissimilarities between them and our Razorbacks?"

"As Mk 2s they had lighter frames than our Mk 1s," Jenkins explained, "owing to the redesigned chassis, which allowed them to shore up the joint armor with ablative mimetics without sacrificing acceleration or top speed. Those modifications, along with the pop-up railguns, were the only notable differences I observed, ma'am."

She flipped through a few pages of information before stopping on another point of obvious interest. "You say here that Lieutenant Podsednik and Chief Styles did not secure the archeological site prior to returning to the surface, is that right?"

"Correct, ma'am," he agreed. "Our orders from General

Akinouye were to preserve the integrity of the site. After the team arrived and found nothing but the attached recording that detailed the lives and deaths of almost five hundred Jemmin from fifteen thousand years ago, they withdrew and we ceded the site to the Finjou in the interests of diplomacy."

"I've had my people thoroughly examine that recording," she said irritably. "So far we haven't found anything actionable. Certainly nothing worth the cost to Armor Corps during Operation Brick Top. There are some interesting technological details in there, but nothing of interest pertaining to the Vorr or Zeen."

"We found nothing useful either, ma'am," Jenkins lied. Kavanaugh knew most of the details from Shiva's Wrath, but Akinouye had not yet let her in on the success of Xi's "diplomatic efforts." At the time, Jenkins had believed the late general had merely been holding his cards close to the chest for reasons pertaining to office politics, but now, standing before Akinouye's usurper, Jenkins knew that Akinouye had never fully trusted the woman. "At this point," Jenkins continued, "my people are inclined to conclude it was a wild goose chase."

"I disagree," Kavanaugh mused, causing a knot to form in Jenkins' throat. A potential moment of truth had just arrived.

"Ma'am?" he asked, careful not to betray his anxiety as he waited for her to arrive at the conclusion that he, Styles, Xi, and Colonel Li had painstakingly crafted during the two weeks as they limped back home from Finjou space.

"I think," she leaned forward, her cold, blue eyes pinning him to the deck, "that the Vorr were trying to stir up animosity between the Finjou and us. I also think that the Vorr were the ones who sold the Solar tech to those rebel colonists using a Finjou intermediary because they have designs on Terran space and want to see us weakened by enemies on multiple fronts. We've pushed back the latest Arh'Kel offensive, in no small part thanks to your work on

Durgan's Folly. I think the Vorr were behind the rock-biters as well."

Jenkins had to force himself to take slow, measured breaths; his heart felt ready to beat all the way through his ribcage and hurl itself onto the deck. She had gone precisely where they wanted her to go, and it was all he could do to keep from breathing the most epic sigh of relief in his entire life.

"With the Arh'Kel threat contained," she continued, apparently more concerned with giving voice to her deftly-manipulated conclusion than with reading Jenkins' anxious body language, "I think they needed to find another way to keep us on our heels. But you, Colonel Jenkins, seem to have thwarted their devious plan not once but *thrice* in as many engagements." She smirked. "I hope for all our sakes that you never find yourself in a dark room with a Vorr."

Jenkins' eyes wanted to bulge out of their sockets at hearing that. He knew it might have been a subtle hint that she had seen through his lie about the meeting with Director Durgan, which in this fable had not included a Vorr. That particular omission had been key to crafting the narrative that had led her to her current position.

He forced himself to project calm as he nodded gravely. "You and me both, General."

"All right," she said, switching the data slate off and setting it aside. "I think that's enough for today. Once again, you've done the Terran Armor Corps proud, Colonel Jenkins. On behalf of its members past and present, I would like to offer my congratulations on a job well done. You and your people have earned a little downtime, so I'm ordering you to return to the *Bonhoeffer* and immediately begin disembarking your crew for some much-needed R&R," she said, standing from the desk.

General Akinouye's desk.

"They'll be glad to hear it, General," Jenkins said graciously as she came to stand before him. She was short of stature, but one look at her made clear that she had *earned* the rank of major general.

"Good work down there." She extended a hand, which Jenkins accepted. "Ben would be proud."

"Thank you, General," he said as she released his grip.

He snapped a salute, which she returned before declaring, "You're dismissed."

He released the salute, turned, and made his way from Armor Corps HQ to the first shuttle he could find back to the New America 2 star system.

He needed to get back to the *Bonhoeffer* while there was still time.

22

SOLIDARITY

"I can't believe we're actually talking about this," Podsednik muttered.

"You can back out if you want, Lieutenant," Jenkins said sympathetically. He knew this was a lot for anyone to process, but they were out of time. Nobody got to have their hand held here. "No one here will look sideways at you if you step out that door. What we're discussing is nothing less than high treason."

"And mutiny," Colonel Li grumped. "Both of which justify summary execution."

"That, too," Jenkins agreed.

"Fuck that." Xi leaned forward intently. "None of us will *ever* have a chance to make this big of an impact again. So what if we're wrong?" She looked around challengingly, fixing Podsy with a fiercely determined look. "I'm not going to begrudge my death if it turns out we had our heads up our asses. But what if we're right?" she pressed. "What if the fate of humanity really *does* rest in our hands? Could you live with yourself if you let the chance to make a difference like that slip through your fingers?" She shook her head adamantly. "I *know* I couldn't. I'm in."

"Me, too," Styles agreed. "I thought I was doing God's work breaking down censor firewalls, but this is the real deal. We're in a position to make a permanent, positive impact on the history of our entire species. I'm not just in, I'm *balls-deep*."

Xi groaned in derision but gave a grudging low-five to Styles after one was offered.

Podsy shook his head skeptically. "Is this possible? I know I'm later to the party on this than the rest of you, but... I mean, come on! Can we *really* be that important?" he asked, fixing each of them with a searching look. "There are over two hundred warships in the Terran Fleet. One point six *billion* humans call the Terran Republic home, forgetting the hundred billion Solarians," he argued to no one in particular. "How can it be *possible* that the six of us are all that stands between life and death for the human race?"

"I appreciate the skepticism, Lieutenant," Jenkins said agreeably. "And I share it, but Xi's right: even if there's only a one percent chance that we're right about this, it would be criminal... No, that's not right," he amended. "It would be *evil* of us to stand down after learning what we know."

"Hear, hear," Colonel Li agreed with conviction

Xi turned to face Podsy, her eyes blazing passionately as she spoke. "We all know this ship was named after a man who protested another holocaust-in-the-making, Podsy. He said, 'Silence in the face of evil is evil itself. God will not hold us guiltless. Not to speak *is* to speak. Not to act *is* to act.' Those were the words of Dietrich Bonhoeffer, who was imprisoned and executed in a Nazi camp for publicly objecting to their evil designs for segments of humanity they deemed inferior. If we don't act in defense of our species, knowing what we know, then we *are* acting in support of agents who have already demonstrated their callous disregard for all of humanity!"

Podsy seemed to have been swayed by Xi's impassioned

speech, and the as-yet silent sixth of their group chose that moment to speak as the ruby-red shaft in Podsy's hands pulsed with a faint inner light.

"The 492 Jem'un who created me," Jem said solemnly, "were unified by nothing so much as their desire to prevent such atrocities. It is that motive which, in a very real sense, drives my existence. The Jem'un were numbered in the trillions prior to the Jemmin holocaust, and the vast majority were eradicated in a span of time no longer than two of your weeks as Jemmin achieved complete control over everything the Jem'un had built. The Jem'un have long since turned to ash, erased from the cosmos by the fires of hatred, but humanity is still alive... although it might not remain so if you hesitate."

"Jem's getting spooky good at English," Styles observed.

"It is a simple language," Jem said dismissively.

Podsy sighed. "Let me be clear: *of course,* I'm in. I just... I don't know, I needed to talk through it a little bit. I'm ready, Colonel," he said decisively. "Let's do this."

Li stood from his chair and made his way to the conference room's hatch. "Now let *me* be clear," the *Bonhoeffer's* CO said gravely, coming to a stop beside the hatch. "Anyone who stays in this room after I close the hatch is signing on for this. There's no backing out, and dissent may be met with a bullet. Your freedom, as well as your right to opt out, are gone until we complete our objective. None of us is free as long as this threat hangs over humanity's head."

Even Jenkins felt a measure of unease at Li's words, but he knew the ship's CO was right.

"Agreed," Jenkins said with a supportive nod. "If we do this, we do it all the way."

"Stop wasting time," Xi quipped, "and shut the fucking hatch. We've got an op to plan."

"Hear, hear," Podsy concurred.

Li nodded approvingly before slamming the hatch shut, locking the team into a twelve-hour planning session that none of them would have thought possible (or even sane) a few weeks earlier.

"You're sure you can do this, Jem?" Jenkins pressed.

"I have analyzed Solar and Terran technology at some length," Jem replied matter-of-factly. "They are in alignment with my predictions. The issue is not the efficacy of my technique, but the range limitations imposed upon us by available hardware. This ship's transceivers are not powerful enough to englobe an entire planet, so my transmission will be unable to overtake the entire system from the single point of the *Dietrich Bonhoeffer*."

Styles whistled appreciatively. "Ok, here's the thing: every living human knows where there's a big enough relay center to upload the signal where it will achieve blanket coverage. But forget about surviving the approach for a second. How are we supposed to gain access to the system even if we *do* manage to reach a direct uplink?"

"This technique is precisely the same one I predicted Jemmin would use to initiate a planetary-scale eradication," Jem explained. "The Vorr corroborated my hypothesis with evidence of a Jemmin takeover of a system similar to the one we intend to infiltrate."

"I love how you gloss over the approach, Chief." Colonel Li cracked a wry grin. "Our objective is the most heavily-fortified human outpost in the entire galaxy. An entire Terran Battle Fleet wouldn't be able to get close enough to chip the paint before it was vaporized."

"Assuming we can get close," Jenkins interrupted, "which I

fully understand is anything but a given, what's to stop Jemmin from reversing Jem's takeover?"

"An appropriate analogy is found in organic immunological function," Jem replied matter-of-factly. "Jemmin uses the hidden mechanism in the quantum processor upon which nearly all human technology is based to infect adjacent systems with override commands that cause catastrophic cascade failures. Think of Jemmin's objective as similar to that of a virus, which seeks to reorganize a cellular interior into a new matrix. I do not intend to infiltrate the system for the purpose of initiating a takeover; my technique is designed to inoculate the system, and every adjacent system, against future takeovers of this type by false-triggering the system in a controlled cascade."

Styles nodded eagerly as Jem spoke, but Jenkins was not yet convinced. "It's like this, Colonel," Styles explained. "Once we false-trip the system, it will reject future Jemmin commands. Or Jem's, for that matter."

"Correct," Jem agreed.

"Won't that cause every piece of attached hardware to fail?" Podsy asked with a concern that Jenkins shared. "We're talking about impacting everything from traffic lights to the electrical grid; fusion reactor containment to weapons control systems. Almost *every* piece of autonomous or cogitative human technology is built on those processors now."

"The simulations we've run show that there *will* be interruptions," Styles said heavily, "but they should be brief and relatively contained."

"Just like an old-school vaccination," Li mused.

"And just like a bad strain of flu," Styles nodded grimly, "the vaccine is less destructive than the disease it prevents."

Xi grunted. "This is sounding eerily similar to what we did on Durgan's Folly."

"I don't think that's a coincidence," Jenkins said pointedly.

Podsy's brow furrowed. "What do you mean, sir?"

"I think part of the reason we were able to trick General Kavanaugh into believing the Vorr are behind all this," Jenkins explained, "is because they probably are."

"What?" Li, Xi, and Styles demanded in unison.

"Hear me out," Jenkins explained. "I don't think the Vorr mean us harm...at least, not in the sense Jemmin does. I *do* think they were behind the implantation of the Arh'Kel on Durgan's Folly. I think they knew precisely when the Jemmin fleet would show up at Shiva's Wrath and orchestrated a withdrawal before we could link up with them. I think *they* provided Solar tech to the rebel colonists on the Brick through a Finjou intermediary. And I *think*," he finished pointedly, "they did all of that to prepare *us* for what we're about to do."

"That's the crinkle of tinfoil if ever I've heard it," Colonel Li observed.

"Think about it," Jenkins urged. "They've been feeding tech and intel to the Durgan group for decades. Why? Is it because Durgan has something valuable to offer? Of course not." He shook his head resolutely. "And the Vorr aren't an aggressive species. They're so anxious about meeting new groups that they literally pop off part of a limb as a token sacrifice rather than risk all-out destruction in the first meeting. This isn't a species that acts rashly or takes unnecessary risks. I'm not saying we should be thankful for the hell they've put in front of us, but I do think that on a pretty high level, they've demonstrated they care about our species' survival."

"They could be manipulating us into delivering Jem into the heart of humanity," Li said, and an ominous silence fell over the room at hearing that. "If Jem's lying, and there's no way we can determine whether it is telling the truth in the amount of time before us," he added pointedly, "we could be doing the very thing we're trying to prevent."

"It's possible," Jenkins agreed, feeling no pleasure at acknowledging that legitimate and terrifying concern. "But frankly, if they're playing some kind of Machiavellian game at *that* level, we were beaten before we even suited up. You can't win a knife fight while you're watching for inbound nukes."

"More is lost to indecision than wrong decision," Xi assented. "Fuck doubt. We've got intel, and we're going to act on it."

"Agreed." Podsy nodded.

"If we all agree to this," Jenkins said pointedly, "our next step is to select a roster. We don't go to them unless we are all one hundred percent on this. I'm already committed after failing to follow General Kavanaugh's order to send Styles and Xi back to HQ, so I say we roll."

"Let's rock *and* roll," Styles said with an eager grin.

"Metal never dies," Xi intoned reverently, snapping the group into perfect unity as she repeated General Akinouye's last words.

"Amen to that," Li said after a respectful silence.

"All right, everyone." Jenkins stood from the chair, prompting the others to do likewise. "Let's do this."

23

VIRTUOUS LEADERSHIP

"Captain Chao," Jenkins greeted the Terra Han Colonial Guardsman at the *Bonhoeffer's* airlock. "I'm glad you were able to make it."

"Colonel Jenkins," Chao acknowledged with a salute, which Jenkins returned before gesturing to the corridor.

"Even with the *Dietrich Bonhoeffer*'s extensive battle damage, these old Behemoth-class assault carriers are impressive," Chao said reverently. "The kinetic impact dampeners we now use throughout the Republic's various fleets were first installed on the *Lao Tzu*, the prototype Behemoth."

"You know your naval history," Jenkins said approvingly.

"Would you expect less of my father's son?" Chao asked, his query as much a challenge as it was rhetorical.

"I appreciate your being direct on that matter," Jenkins said as they arrived at one of the *Bonhoeffer*'s larger briefing rooms. Large enough to fit a company of Jocks, it was standing room only when Jenkins and Chao entered. The room was packed with nearly two full companies of Dragon Brigade's Jocks and Wrenches.

Jenkins had known that these men and women shared a

bond which made impossible the very thought that they might abandon each other. Most of them had been together since Shiva's Wrath, and as Jenkins scanned the room, he knew he had assembled the best possible team for this job.

Operation Antivenom was almost ready to execute, but doing the deed would only be the first step if the efforts of the men and women in this room were to have the maximum impact.

The most valuable lesson of Jenkins' thus-far brief Armor Corps career had been that simply doing good work was rarely, if ever, enough to move the political needle. And where he was taking this group of people, playing politics in the aftermath would be almost as important as achieving the objective.

Which was where Captain Chao came in.

"Captain Chao," Jenkins gestured to the Armored Corps' elite, "these are the finest men and women in the Metal Legion. They're about to undertake a secret mission of vital importance to the Republic, and they need your help."

Chao briefly scanned the room, his razor-sharp eyes flicking from face to face as he took in the assemblage's expressions in a span of just a few seconds. "What can I do, Colonel?"

"Everyone in this room is aware that you're Admiral Zhao's son, and that you aren't on the best terms with your father after transferring from Fleet to Terra Han's Colonial Guard," Jenkins explained, causing Chao's jaw to bunch irritably. "I'm aware it's a sore subject," Jenkins continued, "but I'm also aware that, in spite of significant friction in my past dealings with him, he's one of the finest officers in Fleet history. I need you to deliver a message to him, but only if certain conditions are met."

"Conditions?" Chao asked through briefly-gritted teeth.

"Yes, Captain," Jenkins replied gravely. "I'm not going to beat around the bush here: if a certain theory of mine is correct, then the Republic's wormhole gates are going to go offline sometime in the next few days. If that happens, the men and women in this room," he gestured to the assemblage, "are going to move to secure humanity's interests. We don't expect to come back from this mission, but we *do* expect to achieve our objective."

"Colonel," Chao glanced around the room, a skeptical cast falling over his sharp features, "what kind of intel are you basing this theory on?"

"The same intel that General Akinouye used to keep Operation Brick Top under wraps," Jenkins explained, causing Chao's brow to quirk in surprise. "This isn't *my* theory, Captain. It was General Benjamin Akinouye's. He died before coming into possession of evidence that corroborated the theory, and I'm afraid that Terran Armor Corps' internal security has been dangerously compromised following his death. He didn't trust Major General Kavanaugh with certain operational details and neither did General Pushkin who, as far as we can tell, is under house arrest under the guise of voluntary retirement." He proffered a data slate bearing the last message Jenkins had received from Pushkin. "Generals Akinouye and Pushkin believed the Jemmin have infiltrated the Terran government at the highest levels, and that they will move against humanity in the event their conspiracy is uncovered. Operation Brick Top's primary objective was to retrieve evidence that paints a clear picture of the Jemmin as hostile to humanity and several other Illumination League members."

Chao took the slate and scanned the document several times before realization dawned in his eyes. "Major General Kavanaugh is compromised?"

"Yes, but she's probably not knowingly aiding the enemy," Jenkins replied frankly. "She's dangerously ambitious. My guess is that General Kavanaugh will open Armor Corps' books in order to buy herself political capital, which she'll then use to propel her career as she sells Armor Corps off to Fleet one piece at a time. Nobody here wants that," he said, drawing a chorus of boos and shaking heads supporting his sentiment, "but she's put too many wheels in motion to be stopped by internal dissent, and both Admirals Zhao and Corbyn have already arrived at Armor Corps HQ. She and Rear Admiral Corbyn are close, and both Corbyn and your father have been temporarily assigned to oversee a restructuring of the Metal Legion's leadership in the aftermath of General Akinouye's death. Your father's an honorable man who views the Legion as a rival branch and not a potential subordinate. That's why I trust that he will work to maintain the integrity of Armor Corps rather than tear it down brick by brick. He'll resist immediate declassification, but..."

Chao nodded in understanding as he processed the torrent of information. "Kavanaugh and Corbyn will want to declassify your sensitive intel and will work around my father's objections...which, if your theory holds, will alert the Jemmin to the true nature of your operations."

"That's my guess," Jenkins agreed heavily as he produced a hardened, unmodifiable data storage module containing a full report that included everything they had learned since Durgan's Folly. It also featured the signatures of every man and woman in Dragon Brigade who had signed on for this op, along with full acknowledgments of liability for what were mutinous actions. "Everything is there, Captain, but I cannot stress this enough: those files must be for your father's eyes only. I sincerely hope we're wrong, and that the worst to come of this is a firing squad for the men and women in this room. But if we're right—"

"If you're right," Chao interrupted smartly, plucking the data bar from Jenkins' fingers and tucking it into his uniform's hip pocket, "I need to move ASAP."

"I've arranged for a courier." Jenkins gestured to the door.

Chao stopped at the hatch and his eyes snagging on Colonel Li, who had remained silent throughout the exchange. "Colonel

Li," Chao produced the data module and waved it emphatically, "do you believe in this?"

"I do, Captain Chao," Li replied without hesitation.

Chao nodded in satisfaction before ducking through the hatch. Five minutes later, the courier DC04 pulled away from the *Bonhoeffer's* airlock and initiated a max-burn run to the New America 1 wormhole gate.

Standing in the *Bonhoeffer's* CAC for the next sixteen hours was the most nerve-wracking experience of Jenkins' life. Watching helplessly as the courier drew steadily nearer to the wormhole's event horizon, knowing that humanity would be dealt a grievous blow if the gate went offline before it arrived, was almost too much for him to handle.

DC04 finally slipped through the wormhole, disappearing from sensors and causing both Jenkins and Li to exhale loud sighs of relief. A quick check of his wrist-link showed that Captain Xi should have reached her objective an hour earlier. Aboard DC03, another of Durgan's courier vessels, the talented young captain had gone to secure transit for their admittedly insane operation.

The next leg of this relay was squarely on her shoulders, and Jenkins could not have been more confident that she would come through. The only question now was, would the Jemmin make their move before or after General Kavanaugh sent arrest teams to the *Bonhoeffer* to secure it and its wayward crew?

If the gates didn't go dark before that happened, Jenkins and his people would be helpless to stop the Jemmin.

Silent and motionless, the sleek Terran courier ship *DC03* waited in the cold interplanetary space of the Orca System.

Orca was Vorr territory, and it just so happened that one of the *DC03*'s three occupants was Vorr.

The Vorr's name was Deep Currents of Radiant Warmth, and Xi had conversed extensively with it during the trip to Orca. It had spent most of the past decade locked inside Director Durgan's headquarters, serving as a secret emissary to the business mogul.

"Your species is remarkably fragile, Captain Xi Bao," Deep Currents said, its tentacles weaving back and forth within its transparent, fluid-filled, vaguely egg-shaped enviropod. "Vorr are capable of operating without detriment at pressures over one hundred times human atmospheric norms. We therefore have little need of such crude compensatory systems." The Vorr gestured to Xi's transit couch, which was equal parts torture device and life-saver. "Our fluid-filled compartments are designed to passively support our bodies during acceleration, and without endoskeletons or centralized nervous tissues like yours, we can survive what you call 'gee forces' that would kill humans even with the assistance of such devices."

"Lucky you," Xi quipped.

"Of course," Deep Currents continued thoughtfully, "we Vorr were delayed in our mastery of aerial travel due to our environmental needs, primary among them the need for constant hydration and our relatively narrow thermal tolerances."

"I guess it's kind of hard to design primitive aircraft filled with water." Xi snickered.

"Indeed." Deep Currents' tentacles curled tightly in unison, which Xi had learned was a confirmatory gesture. "Although we did eventually design systems which permitted us to limit the volume of water, that particular innovation required significant advances in nanotechnology. As a result, my people invented graphene before we made our first directly-operated aerial flight."

"Jesus!" Xi recoiled in surprise. "And I thought *we* were backward."

"Your technological development was typical for a terrestrial species," the Vorr assured her. "Until Jemmin intervened, of course."

"Did you know humanity was interfered with when it happened?" Xi asked, suspecting she wasn't going to like the answer however it came. But she was too curious not to ask since she had the exceptionally rare opportunity to do so.

"We suspected that Jemmin was manipulating the sequential induction of younger species into the Illumination League," Deep Currents explained hesitantly. "But we lacked proof. The Finjou were a significantly more obvious case of technological intervention, which was why we conducted remote clandestine surveys of their territory in the hope of uncovering evidence to that effect. What we discovered on the world you call 'the Brick' was more than we could have ever imagined."

"How long did it take for your people to withdraw from the Illumination League after learning the truth about Jemmin?" Xi asked.

"The decision was made in twenty-two of your days," Deep Currents replied matter-of-factly, causing Xi's eyes to bulge in alarm.

"That's just... I... That's insane," she stammered. "How... I mean, you're individuals, right? Surely *some* among you wanted to stay in the League?"

"Our affiliation with the Illumination League was a point of much debate from the beginning," Deep Currents explained. "You must understand, Captain Xi Bao, that our species differs from yours in significant ways. Yours is a hunter-gatherer species, adapted to roam vast territories in search of resources.

The universe has therefore sculpted you into risk-takers and adventurers, investigators and problem-solvers. You are physically weak and fragile compared to many of the organisms you coexist with, but your intellect and ruthlessness make you ideal apex predators. We Vorr were originally a prey species which, through a combination of evolutionary adaptation and fortuitous geological events, narrowly survived environmental changes in our home waters that eliminated all of the species that preyed upon us."

"It wasn't too long ago," Xi smirked, "that human scientists thought the only possible path to higher intelligence was one traveled solely by predators."

"A quaint sentiment." The Vorr's auto-translator issued a light laugh. "And a predictably narrowminded one. Had your species been granted another two or three hundred of your standard years to develop, you would have reached the stars on much firmer philosophical and technological footing than you currently possess. However, it was clear to us from the moment we learned of your species that humanity would play a key role in the affairs of this galaxy."

Xi cocked her head curiously. "What makes you say that?"

"Yours is a remarkably determined and adaptable species, Captain Xi Bao," Deep Currents said approvingly. "While you are physically frail and intellectually limited at least on an individual level, your capacities to individually sub-specialize and collectively coordinate is unlike anything we have observed in the cosmos. The Jem'un were the closest example we Vorr have encountered to humans in terms of individual adaptability."

"I don't know," Xi said skeptically. "The Zeen are awfully adaptable."

The Vorr laughed again, but this time the sound seemed to come at Xi's expense. "The Zeen are the *opposite* of adaptable, Captain Xi Bao. At least thirty-seven distinctive Zeen subspecies comprise what you probably refer to as 'Zeen society,' but none of them is capable of exceeding its base design. To succeed in complex tasks requires enormous coordinative effort between disparate and dissimilar Zeen subspecies. That Zeen succeed at this is a testament not to their adaptability but to their exceptional degree of individual specialization, including the specialization of what we call their 'coordinator caste.' Humans, however, have little difficulty switching roles even in the middle of complex projects. Some of this is due to your lower-than-average intelligence for a starfaring species," it said blithely, causing Xi to go red with irritation as the Vorr continued, "but most is because of your hunter-gatherer roots. We suspect Jemmin recognized the danger you pose to its plans and elevated you earlier than would have otherwise occurred."

"You know," Xi said as respectfully as she could manage, "it's considered impolite in human society to impugn someone's intellect, let alone an entire group of people. Some human societies have actually written laws against it." She did not add, however, that no such laws were found in the Terran Republic. Only in Sol could you find such thought control systems.

"It is therefore fortunate for me," Deep Currents said in an unmistakable mocking drawl, "that we are in Vorr territory, not Terran."

A smile crept across Xi's lips. "You were fucking with me?"

"I would not..."

Vorr trailed off mid-sentence before its auto-translated voice adopted a much more serious tone, and its next three words made Xi briefly go numb from the chin down.

"It has begun."

"Captain," called *DC03's* pilot, Jake Galvis, "I just lost the wormhole's telemetry feed."

Xi's knees suddenly felt weak, but she stood from her couch

and moved to the cockpit. "Go through the realignment protocols," she ordered.

"Running through them now," he said grimly. "But I'm not getting anything. The gate's still there, but the linkage is down." The courier's long-range visual feed focused on the giant ring of the wormhole gate. The circular structure looked precisely as it had a few minutes earlier, but where the dark event horizon should have been, a serene backdrop of stars was now clearly visible. The pilot's eyes widened in horror. "Stars… Stars? I've never seen *stars* on the other side of a gate."

Xi turned to Deep Currents. "How long?"

"The answer to that question is complicated," the Vorr replied. "The Zeen are closely monitoring the situation, but it is possible Jemmin has only shut down the human gates. If that is the case, it could take them several hours to learn about the event. If, however, Jemmin has shut down *all* Nexus-linked gates—"

A brilliant flash of light flooded the cockpit, interrupting Deep Currents mid-sentence and causing Xi to shield her eyes with her hand. Warning alarms went off throughout DC_{03}'s interior as sensor feeds populated with new data, and as Xi lowered her hand, she turned her focus to those feeds.

"It would seem," Deep Currents mused while Xi's eyes went wide at what she saw on the feeds, "that Jemmin deactivated *all* Nexus-linked gates. This should work to our advantage."

She wanted to dispute that statement, but her eyes were glued to the feeds.

"Captain?" The pilot's voice was shaky and faint. "What the hell is that?"

As Xi looked out the viewing portal, her eyes snagged on the spherical object which had not been there a minute earlier. To the naked eye, it almost looked like a grey soccer ball. Covered in hexagonal lines just detailed enough to make out, no natural phenomenon had crafted the sphere's appearance.

Her eyes snapped back down to the sensor feeds and remained fixed on the most alarming factor in the displayed data: its sheer *size*.

Measuring over five hundred kilometers in diameter, the moon-sized structure was equally dazzling and terrifying. But looking at it now, it made perfect sense to Xi's mind that the Zeen would construct such a mobile, self-contained world.

Their homeworld had been destroyed when Jem'un gravity cannon technology destabilized their parent star, incinerating the cradle of Zeen civilization in an unnatural nova. Now that Xi knew it was technically possible to build moon-sized structures like the one looming before her, it was *natural* to her mind that the Zeen would choose to live aboard them instead of being bound to a planet that might get annihilated like their first homeworld had been.

One of the most fundamental facets of intelligence was the ability to learn from past mistakes or catastrophes. The Zeen had done that on the largest scale imaginable.

"That," Xi said after finally coming to terms with the scope of what they were looking at, "is our ride."

The pilot gave her a look that bordered incredulity and horror. "You can't be serious. Do you have any idea how much energy it would take to move that thing around?"

"I don't think that thing moves *through* space," Xi said pointedly.

"A space-folding drive?" Galvis' brow rose incredulously. "Do you have any idea how much power—"

"No," Xi interrupted, "and neither do you, but it's obvious that the Zeen found a hack around Mr. Einstein's seminal work."

"Not the Zeen," Deep Currents chided. "The Jem'un. This

technology is *their* legacy. But Mr. Galvis is correct: the energy consumed by each use of this system is enormous. It has taken the Zeen four thousand of your years to harvest and store sufficient fuel to power this system, and they have graciously agreed to use a considerable fraction of that energy in humanity's defense."

That last bit brought Xi's mind back to the task at hand. She turned to the pilot and urged, "Let's find out where they want us to park."

Galvis shook his head warily before gently firing the courier's engines and flying toward the massive vessel.

Two hours later, the *DCo3* was on final approach to the titanic structure. To call it a ship or a vehicle was inaccurate since it had no external thrust systems. For all intents and purposes, it was an inert moon comprised of nickel and iron. In fact, that appeared to be precisely what it was: an extensively hollowed-out moon.

The *DCo3* drifted silently down a twenty-meter-wide, perfectly cylindrical shaft tunneled twenty degrees off perpendicular from the moon's surface. After half a kilometer's journey down the shaft, the craft emerged into a cavern. A glowing blue hexagon appeared on the far side of the cavern, and Galvis deftly maneuvered the courier ship toward it.

As he brought the sleek courier vessel near to the thirty-meter-wide hexagon, a series of docking arms reached out and clanged against the hull as they grappled with it.

Xi and Galvis had already donned their pressurized suits, and in her gloved hand Xi held the key to making a successful introduction to this world of Zeen.

"We're locked down," Galvis grumbled. "We aren't going anywhere without their permission."

"Come." Deep Currents' egg pod pivoted on its track-mounted base and drove toward the airlock. "They are waiting."

There was so little gravity that Xi felt weightless as she and Galvis made their way to the airlock. The inner door cycled open, and the trio moved into a cramped compartment that began to depressurize as soon as the door shut behind them.

"Why did they jump here?" Galvis asked as the air was bled out of the airlock, causing Xi's suit to expand around her like a human-shaped balloon. "Why not jump directly to the rendezvous?"

"This is the first time Zeen have used the Jem'un FTL system," Deep Currents explained over the local comm link. "They refused to employ it without first making a test passage to confirm their satisfaction with the system. We agreed to provide them with a star system of little tactical value to use as their first destination, so they came here. They are using this system twice in humanity's aid: once to reach the rendezvous system, and again to propel you to your objective," the Vorr said severely as the outer door finally chimed that it was ready to open. "The significant cost of this gesture made by Zeen on your behalf must not be ignored."

"It won't be," Xi promised as Galvis opened the door by inputting his command codes, causing the outer airlock door to open. Beyond that door was a membranous tube, not unlike the soft docking tubes used by Terrans during transfers from one ship to another without the benefit of a hard dock.

And while there were faint suggestions that the tube was at least somewhat organic, it was far less so than Xi had expected after facing Zeen warriors on Shiva's Wrath. Those vehicles had *looked* like living things, because that was precisely what they were. But this docking collar was artificial, and to Xi's surprise,

Deep Currents' egg-shaped pod detached from its lower track-mounted chassis and drifted up with a gentle burst of gas.

Xi and Galvis followed, and soon they were gently floating up the thirty-meter-long tube behind the Vorr pod.

"I thought you'd want to stay with your ship," Xi quipped.

"And miss this?" Galvis scoffed. "You don't get to pilot one of Mr. Durgan's couriers by being weak-kneed, Captain Xi. I'd rather eat a bullet than miss the chance to be part of whatever's about to happen here."

They came to the end of the tube, which gently curved toward a membranous airlock. The first membrane closed like a sphincter as soon as they were through, and they passed a second, then a third, then a fourth, all of which sequentially closed behind them.

The redundant airlock tube opened into a thirty-meter-wide cylindrical chamber, which the Vorr illuminated with her pod's external lights. What Xi saw there in the soft greenish glow was absolutely breathtaking.

And more than a little intimidating.

Lining the entire inner surface of the chamber, which stretched far beyond the meager illumination provided by Deep Currents' pod-lights, were Zeen "insectaurs" precisely like the one she had fought on Shiva's Wrath. They were packed so closely together that they seemed to be touching on all sides, and though they lacked eyes or discernible external sensor organs, she felt the weight of their regard surrounding her as she emerged into the chamber.

And there were *thousands* of them.

She knew that a Terran Marine in power armor would have no trouble taking one of the things out in a heads-up fight. Or two. Or possibly even *five* of them. But there were *thousands* of Zeen insectaurs here.

And this is just the welcoming committee, Xi thought in

awe as she gently bumped into Deep Currents' egg pod. It was only then that she realized the shaft was vertical to the planet's surface, which meant that they were no longer drifting but *falling*.

Fortunately, the Vorr's egg pod had sufficient handholds for both Xi and Galvis to grab, and Deep Currents' thrusters slowed their descent to a manageable degree as the moon's light gravity pulled them toward the shaft's floor.

The airlock above them disappeared into the murky darkness, leaving them surrounded by Zeen insectaurs as they descended.

Fortunately, the shaft was not endless, and at its bottom was a flat circular patch of floor with a single insectaur waiting in the center. During the entire descent, Xi kept one hand firmly on Deep Currents' pod while the other clutched what could very well be humanity's only lifeline.

Beside that insectaur was a chassis not dissimilar to the one Deep Currents had employed aboard the *DCo3*, but this one seemed more refined and robust.

Xi and Galvis let go of the pod three meters above the floor to drop and gently land while Deep Currents' pod slid smoothly into its new receptacle. The Vorr's track-driven undercarriage sprang to life, and as it did so, Xi eyed the Zeen standing before them.

It seemed identical to the rest, but its isolation beneath the tower of its fellows clinging to the shaft above made clear it was indeed different.

Deep Currents' comm came to life with an auto-translated voice like the one Xi remembered from Shiva's Wrath, and she realized the Vorr would act as translator for this exchange.

"You Terran," came the voice, using the same simplistic, broken verbiage as its predecessor.

"Yes," Xi replied, stepping forward, "I'm Terran. You're

Zeen," she continued before gesturing to Deep Currents' pod. "That is Vorr."

"Vorr brave," the Zeen said, repeating the words of the insectaur Xi had communicated with on Shiva's Wrath. "Vorr food. Brave food not symmetrical. Vorr help Zeen. Vorr help Terran. Vorr ask Zeen help Terran. Terran brave?"

"Yes." Xi nodded with conviction. "Terrans *are* brave. And Terrans are not food."

"Terran symmetrical with Jemmin?" Zeen asked.

"No." Xi shook her head firmly. "Terrans are not symmetrical with Jemmin."

"Jemmin infect Terran," the Zeen said, causing Xi's already strained nerves to tighten further. "Jemmin infect everything. Terran Jemmin food. Zeen take Jemmin food. Zeen eat Terran."

"No!" Xi blurted in objection, dearly wishing she had brought a sidearm since it looked like she might be forced to defend herself in yet another "diplomatic" exchange. "We will *never* be food to the Jemmin. We want to *stop* the Jemmin."

"Empty words. Need proof," Zeen challenged. "Bad food still food. Stupid food still food. Obedient food still food. Jemmin need food. Jemmin trick food. Jemmin make food obedient. Terran obedient food."

"You want proof?" Xi snapped, stepping forward and producing the shell-like device given to her by the Zeen she had met on Shiva's Wrath. "This is all the proof I've got, and if it's not enough? *Eat* me!" she snapped, fully aware of the double entendre.

The Zeen stepped forward, extending its delicate pincers to pluck the item from her fingers. It silently took the thing and tucked it into a crease in its torso's armor plates. Xi suspected the device carried some kind of data record that would take the Zeen some time to peruse, but it took it less than three seconds for it to step back and splay its limbs in a gesture identical to the one she had seen back on Shiva's Wrath.

"Terran brave. Terran not food," the Zeen intoned as the mass of insectaurs lining the shaft overhead rippled with movement. "Terran not symmetrical with Jemmin. Vorr help Zeen. Zeen help Vorr. Vorr help Terran. Zeen help Terran. Vorr, Zeen, and Terran symmetrical."

At that last bit, a great, glowing triangle appeared on the floor beneath their feet. Spanning nearly the entire thirty-meter-wide floor of the shaft, one side of the triangle was a faint bluish hue. As Xi looked around, she realized the Vorr's pod-lights were no longer green but had adopted the same blue as that line of the triangle. It seemed the Vorr, a race of ocean-dwellers, would be represented by the color blue.

Another side was a fiery red, and this was the color Xi suddenly saw emanate from the shaft above her. The Zeen insectaurs themselves seemed to glow, and together they created a column of smoldering red that stretched far beyond Xi's sight. The Zeen color was to be red, and it was one humanity had long associated with wrath and vengeance.

The third side was a throbbing pale white, which she assumed represented the relative fragility of humanity. It was perhaps also suggestive of humanity's fading purity in the face of Jemmin interference, but the truth was that Xi had never been good at discerning the messages in metaphors.

But the choice of red, white, and blue had unmistakably been made in deference to Terran culture, which had arisen like a phoenix from the ashes of the so-called American Experiment. On the backs of frontiersmen, entrepreneurs, adventurers, and even criminals like Xi, the Terran Republic had proudly carried the legacy of Earth's Western Civilization to the stars. Even those cultures which did not directly affiliate with America's legacy were nonetheless irrefutably influenced by its rugged individualism and its belief in liberty as the most fundamental human principles.

Like a torch borne from one continent to another, the flames that fueled the Terran Republic's survival in the vast emptiness between the stars had first been lit thousands of years earlier on Earth. Nurtured and protected at every turn, what had begun as mere embers had grown to a bonfire that showed no signs of dying down.

And now those flames were about to return home.

"It is done," Deep Currents declared. "Our species stand together in common cause. First, we safeguard our homes from the Jemmin apocalypse. And then," the Vorr turned toward Xi, who felt a thrill at hearing its next words, "we *end* Jemmin."

EPILOGUE: FLY ME TO THE MOON

It had been twelve hours since the wormholes had gone dark, and Colonel Jenkins was down on the drop-deck helping make repairs to the two companies of mechs still aboard the *Dietrich Bonhoeffer*.

They had no idea how long it would take Xi to bring the Zeen to New America 2, and Jenkins knew he couldn't spend another moment on the bridge listening to Colonel Li deal with the rising level of chaos in the star system. Elements of the 8th Fleet had been stationed at the Nexus-side wormhole gate, including a pair of dreadnoughts, and those ships' commanders were predictably rallying all nearby forces into a defensive posture.

Li had admirably sidestepped the rendezvous orders with half-truths and outright lies regarding the *Bonhoeffer's* condition, but it was only a matter of time before Admiral Wallace, who was in charge of those ships, would decide the good colonel was openly defying orders.

"Hand me that torch, Blinky." Jenkins gestured to a microburner after isolating the offending bit of debris in *Blink Dog*'s front left leg's hull joint.

"Yes, sir," Miles "Blinky" Staubach acknowledged, scrambling to the bench with every ounce of enthusiasm Xi had described in her recommendation that he be given his own mech. He returned with not just the torch but also bearing the magnetic tongs Jenkins would use to remove the misshapen hunk of metal. "Here you go, sir," Blinky said, his eyes fluttering open and shut in classic extra-pyramidal symptoms of someone on heavy doses of anti-seizure medications. His seizure condition was what had caused him to fall into Jenkins' lap. Blinky had applied to dropship pilot's school, but Fleet had medically disqualified him from their program due to his condition.

The real bitch of it was that the meds actually made Blinky *more* stable for neural uplinks, not less. In classic ossified bureaucratic fashion, Terran Fleet had passed Blinky over, and they'd done it because, frankly, he didn't look good enough on a parade line.

"Thanks." Jenkins accepted the torch. He fired it up and began cutting little pieces off the debris so he could maneuver the clamp into place and remove it.

"Colonel..." Staubach began with that hesitant note Jenkins recalled hearing in himself when he was a wide-eyed recruit. Not that Staubach was ever wide-eyed due to his neurological tick, but he seemed every bit as nervous as Jenkins recalled himself being at the onset of his career.

"Yes, Corporal?" Jenkins acknowledged after Blinky faltered.

"I just... I wanted to thank you, sir, for giving me a chance, sir," Staubach stammered, causing Jenkins' lips to curl in a well-hidden smile as he wondered if he had ever sounded *this* uncomfortable.

You bet your ass you did, Lee, he thought as his smile widened.

"I know my condition should have precluded me from

receiving the link implants," Blinky continued, "and I know they're limited. I just wanted to say that I won't let you down, sir."

"Clamp," Jenkins said, finishing with the torch and passing it to the younger man. Staubach gave him the clamp, which he affixed to a corner of the debris before sliding down *Blink Dog*'s leg and putting his boots back on the deck. "Chain." He gestured even as Blinky was running back with the chain they would use to extract the broken piece of gear.

A few minutes' worth of silent teamwork later, the ruined hunk of *Blink Dog*'s armor was out of the way. After two hours of laborious, tedious, but much-appreciated grunt work as far as Jenkins was concerned, the recon mech was ready for Koch's people to do the hard work of replacing its actuators and inspecting the mech's forward frame.

"Good work, Corporal," Jenkins congratulated. "I thought we'd be another hour on that one."

He could see the anxiety on Staubach's face following his non-reply, and Jenkins had difficulty keeping a straight face. It wasn't that Jenkins enjoyed seeing the other man's discomfort, but like all military traditions, projecting stoicism was a key part of setting a winning example for the up-and-comers.

In the face of the other man's earnestness, Jenkins finally relented. "Corporal, when I look at your jacket, I don't see a walking medical disqualification for the TRMC dropship pilot's program. I see one of the most intensely devoted and capable young men the Legion has the privilege of fielding under its banner. I see someone who earned the highest possible marks on every applicable aptitude test, and who impressed the hell out of his CO during his first, second, third, fourth, and fifth tastes of combat against two different enemies back on Shiva's Wrath, *neither* of which the bookies would have given us half a chance to whip. You played key parts in those engagements, and you *earned* this command," he finished firmly, putting a hand on *Blink Dog*'s half-disassembled frame before continuing.

"When I look at you, I don't see someone with a *disability*. I see someone with *extraordinary ability* who Fleet let slip through their fingers because he's got an unsightly tick. And unfortunately for you," Jenkins said with a grin, "I'm going to push you so hard every single day that you think you'll break like a Solarian's fingernail just for rolling out of your bunk in the morning. But if you're somehow still standing after I've punched myself out and thrown everything I've got at you, I'm going to dress you up like a French poodle and parade you in front of those admirals who thought you weren't good enough to pilot one of their dropships. And you're going to do it with your callsign embroidered on your beret. How does that sound, Blinky?"

Staubach's eyes grew moist, and for a long moment he stopped blinking, and his lip began to quiver instead. The young man nodded graciously, smiling as tears ran down his cheeks. "Like a fucking dream, Colonel."

Jenkins clapped the young man on the shoulder. "Good man. Now clean this mess up." He waved a hand at the debris they had spent the last two hours removing from *Blink Dog*'s hull, most of which had been Jenkins' doing. "It's a goddamned pigsty around here."

Blinky wiped the tears from his cheeks and nodded smartly before saluting. "Yes, sir!"

Jenkins returned the salute with a wry grin. "Carry on, Corporal."

Jenkins was just about to move over to *Roy* to see how Chaps' efforts were going, but before he took the first step, his wrist-link chimed.

He accepted the incoming link. "Jenkins here."

"Li here." The *Bonhoeffer's* CO greeted him with a rare,

awestruck note in his voice. "She's back...and you need to see this."

Jenkins made his way to an interface terminal and entered his command authorization, which let him see the ship's direct sensor feeds. His eyebrows rose in surprise at what he saw two light minutes from where the *Bonhoeffer* rested in high orbit over Durgan's Folly.

A moon like no moon any human had ever seen before.

But despite the gravity of the situation, a single thought resonated through Jenkins' mind so clearly, so powerfully, and so perfectly that he couldn't help but throw his head back and laugh.

Heads swiveled in his direction and concerned looks came over the faces of some of the *Bonhoeffer*'s deck crew. He knew he should show some restraint, but it was too rich. This was the kind of thing you only got to laugh about once in your entire life, and he wasn't going to miss it.

"It takes a moon," he shook his head in comical bewilderment, wiping a tear from his eye, "to attack the Moon. How's *that* for symmetrical?" He chortled. "You can't write this crap; it has to actually *happen*."

"Colonel?" Li's voice came over the wrist-link, although it was clear he was only half as concerned as some of the people down on the drop-deck.

"It's nothing, Colonel Li," Jenkins said, regaining control and verifying that Xi's coded authentication had indeed been transmitted from the newly-arrived moon. "Operation Antivenom is a go, Colonel Li."

"Confirmed," Li acknowledged. "We're breaking orbit."

Jenkins swept past the assemblage as the battered *Dietrich Bonhoeffer* gently pulled away from Durgan's Folly. He couldn't help but grin as he looked around, seeing the faces of men and women who would ride with him to change the fate of human history for better or worse. They didn't know if they could succeed. They didn't know if they would survive. But they did know, with every fiber of their being, that they were *ready*.

"We ride for Luna One," Jenkins declared in a voice that echoed through the drop-deck, causing the crew's spines to stiffen and heads to nod in eager anticipation.

They were warriors to the last, and their resolve made him proud to be Terran as he embarked on the most insane mission of his career. It would be one for the history books, one way or the other, and Jenkins was going to lead them into those books the only way he knew how: hard, fast, and straight for the throat.

He nodded approvingly, and his eyes snagged on Blinky's as the young man looked at him with a measure of trust Lee Jenkins would do his utmost to deserve. He took a step toward the young man, who braced to attention and caused the rest of the deck to do likewise in unison. He was more humbled by their support than he could express with words or gestures, so he didn't offer a single one. He stood there looking at each one in turn and feeling their bond tighten with each passing second.

They were ready. *He* was ready. That meant there was just one thing left to do, and that was to sound the charge.

"Let's go save Earth!"

The End

If you like this book, please leave a review. This is a new series, so the only way I can decide whether to commit more time to it is by getting feedback from you, the readers. Your opinion matters to me. Continue or not? I have only so much time to craft new stories. Help me invest that time wisely. Plus, reviews buoy my spirits and stoke the fires of creativity.

Don't stop now! Keep turning the pages as Craig talks about his thoughts on this book and the overall project called Metal Legion.

AUTHOR NOTES - CRAIG MARTELLE

WRITTEN JANUARY 8, 2018

You are still reading! Thank you so much. It doesn't get much better than that.

I've just returned from a long trip over Christmas and New Year's. The winter solstice in Fairbanks, Alaska is harsh. Too much darkness. Too much cold. So we usually take a short trip to Hawaii or somewhere warm. Since my son married into Australia and my grandchildren are Australian, we now to get to go down under, where it's more than warm. It's summer.

We spent a full week in Adelaide, South Australia. We love it there! Plus my son and his family are there so that makes it easy. Family, friends, and a clean and pleasant city. We did more touristy stuff this time and it was great. The Zoo, the Botanical Gardens, and the Adelaide Gaol. They were all righteously fun. So many flying foxes, aka bats hanging in a small area between the zoo and the botanical garden. It was crazy seeing the tree filled with the massive creatures. They were probably the size of a squirrel, maybe a little bigger. Most impressive.

It was a little warmer than last year, but still nice. I got a good suntan, using enough lotion to keep from burning. While in Adelaide, we hosted a luncheon for over thirty Australian authors. I was humbled by the way they came to see Michael Anderle and me. We spent most of the time talking about our stuff, but we tried to get people involved for the last hour and I think that made it a big winner.

Then we traveled to Bali for a three-day author's conference. I was running the show so it was a bit stressful for me as I wanted to roll out the red carpet for everyone and make them feel like it was the best and most personal conference ever. Comments following? How about, "This has changed my life."

Then we came home after about twenty days on the road. I was ready to be home, but there was one minor issue. When we landed in Fairbanks, it was -38F. It was 85 with 95% humidity when we got up that morning.

At least our friend Uncle Alex did a curbside pickup so I only had to shuffle about twenty feet through the cold. It still was a crushing blow. But then we ran back to his house and picked Phyllis up, so all of us came home together. Thank you, Alex!

While I'm thanking the good people who helped me, I'll shout out to Jane Hinchey for being the point man in Adelaide for the luncheon. Jane, Lucie, and Yudhanjaya helped in Bali to make sure that was a great show. Lucie's husband, Paul was a dynamo and helped me in so many ways that I never expected.

For Metal Legion, my insider team, Kelly, Micky, Jim, and John once again made sure this was a great book before we turned it loose with the Just In Time readers. I like delivering ultra-clean books to the team so the last few typos jump out of the page while they are enjoying the story.

Which I hope you did. This is a great story once again that brings some of the formidable capabilities of the Metal Legion to bear on a determined enemy. In the end, we believe in the strength of the human spirit to persevere.

If you liked the book, I'd appreciate it if you dropped a review. Just a few lines to let me know what you thought.

Peace, fellow humans,
Craig

Please join my Newsletter (www.craigmartelle.com – please, please, please sign up!), or you can follow me on Facebook since you'll get the same opportunity to pick up the books for only 99 cents on the first Saturday after they get published.

If you liked this story, you might like some of my other books. You can join my mailing list by dropping by my website **www.craigmartelle.com** or if you have any comments, shoot me a note at craig@craigmartelle.com. I am always happy to hear from people who've read my work. I try to answer every email I receive.

If you liked the story, please write a short review for me on Amazon. I greatly appreciate any kind words, even one or two sentences go a long way. The number of reviews an ebook receives greatly improves how well an ebook does on Amazon.

Amazon – www.amazon.com/author/craigmartelle

BookBub – https://www.bookbub.com/authors/craig-martelle

Facebook – www.facebook.com/authorcraigmartelle

My web page – www.craigmartelle.com

That's it—break's over, back to writing the next book.

CONNECT WITH THE AUTHOR

Craig Martelle Social

Website & Newsletter:
http://www.craigmartelle.com

BookBub:
https://www.bookbub.com/authors/craig-martelle

Facebook:
https://www.facebook.com/AuthorCraigMartelle/

BOOKS BY CRAIG MARTELLE

Craig Martelle's other books (listed by series)

Terry Henry Walton Chronicles (co-written with Michael Anderle) – a post-apocalyptic paranormal adventure

Gateway to the Universe (co-written with Justin Sloan & Michael Anderle) – this book transitions the characters from the Terry Henry Walton Chronicles to The Bad Company

The Bad Company (co-written with Michael Anderle) – a military science fiction space opera

End Times Alaska (also available in audio) – a Permuted Press publication – a post-apocalyptic survivalist adventure

The Free Trader – a Young Adult Science Fiction Action Adventure

Cygnus Space Opera – A Young Adult Space Opera (set in the Free Trader universe)

Darklanding (co-written with Scott Moon) – a Space Western

Rick Banik – Spy & Terrorism Action Adventure

Become a Successful Indie Author – a non-fiction work

Enemy of my Enemy (co-written with Tim Marquitz) – a galactic alien military space opera

Superdreadnought (co-written with Tim Marquitz) – a military space opera

Metal Legion (co-written with Caleb Wachter) - a military space opera

End Days (co-written with E.E. Isherwood) – a post-apocalyptic adventure

Mystically Engineered (co-written with Valerie Emerson) – dragons in space

Monster Case Files (co-written with Kathryn Hearst) – a young-adult cozy mystery series

For a complete list of books from Craig, please see www.craigmartelle.com

OTHER BOOKS FROM LMBPN PUBLISHING

For a complete list of books by LMBPN Publishing, please visit:

https://lmbpn.com/books-by-lmbpn-publishing/

All LMBPN Audiobooks are Available at Audible.com and iTunes

To see all LMBPN audiobooks, including those written by Michael Anderle please visit:

www.lmbpn.com/audible

Manufactured by Amazon.ca
Bolton, ON